SCAN

SCAN

WALTER JURY AND S. E. FINE

G. P. PUTNAM'S SONS
An Imprint of Penguin Group (USA)

G. P. PUTNAM'S SONS
Published by the Penguin Group
Penguin Group (USA) LLC
375 Hudson Street, New York, NY 10014

USA | Canada | UK | Ireland | Australia
New Zealand | India | South Africa | China
penguin.com
A Penguin Random House Company

Library of Congress Cataloging-in-Publication Data
Jury, Walter.
Scan / Walter Jury and S.E. Fine.
pages cm
Summary: "Tate Archer outruns armed government officials as he tries to keep his now dead
father's strange invention out of the wrong hands, alien hands"—Provided by publisher.
[1. Adventure and adventurers—Fiction. 2. Fathers and sons—Fiction. 3. Inventors and
inventions—Fiction. 4. Extraterrestrial beings—Fiction. 5. Science fiction.] I. Fine, Sarah. II. Title.
PZ7.J965Sc 2014 [Fic]—dc23 2013023623

Printed in the United States of America.
ISBN 978-0-399-16065-3
1 3 5 7 9 10 8 6 4 2

Design by Ryan Thomann. Text set in Maxime.

For Mel

ONE

IN MY WORLD, THINGS ARE SIMPLE. AT LEAST, THEY ARE
right now. The hard, pulsing beat of my music is all my head
contains. My muscles are loose. My bare feet are flat on the
hardwood. My ass is on this metal bench, but not for long. Any
second now, they're going to call me.

I am ready.

I raise my head when Chicão taps my shoulder. He motions
for me to pull out my earbuds. I obey, and the sounds of the
tournament fill my ears, shouts and cheers echoing off the
high walls of the massive gymnasium.

"Lightweights just finished, Tate," he says, his Portuguese
accent thicker than usual. "The middleweight semis are starting. You're next." His curly hair is puffed out around his head,
like he's been running his hands through it. My coach is more
nervous than I am, but I don't know why.

I've been kicking ass all day, and I'm about to do it again.

"Good," I say. "It's about time."

I drop my iPod into my bag, stand up and stretch, then straighten my crisp, white *gi* and pull my black belt tight. *Perfeito.*

One more match to win, and I'm in the finals. Ten minutes between here and there. I doubt I'll need that much, though. My goal? Five minutes. If that. I'm going to have this kid slapping his hand on the mat in no time.

I have to. I don't want to see the look on my dad's face if I don't.

This trophy might get him off my back. Maybe he'll let me sleep past four for a few days. Or let me bust my diet up with some fried chicken without freaking out. It might get him to lend me his car so that, for once, I could drive when Christina and I go out. It might even get him to smile at me and tell me I'm good enough to bear the Archer family name. To carry on the Archer *family responsibility,* as he's always saying.

But that might be expecting too much.

Across the mat, watching the first middleweight semifinal match, is my opponent. His lanky arms swing back and forth. Clapping in front. Clapping behind. He jumps up and down on the balls of his long feet. He rolls his head on his neck. His blue *gi* is wrinkled, and dark circles ring his pits. He's obviously been wearing that thing all day—he didn't think to bring a few spares? I wrinkle my nose. Our match *better* end quick or I might die from the stench.

He lifts his eyes to mine. They're wide and brown, with long lashes. Like a cow's. He smooths his hand over his buzzed black hair. His face is so serious. The blades of his cheekbones all severe. Lips flat and tight.

He's scared.

My mouth curls into a predatory smile as the match in front of us ends on points. The ref holds the winner's hand up, and the kid can't hold back his grin. He's going to the finals. I clap a few times, sizing him up. He had a wicked scissor sweep, and I'll have to be ready.

Chicão steps up close and nods toward the cow-eyed guy. "This kid. This one you fight next. He wins by submissions. Every time today."

Impressive. But then again, we're at the semifinals of the Tri-State Brazilian Jiu-Jitsu Championship, so if he's not impressive, he's at the wrong fucking party. *I* trained years to get here. I worked for hours every day. I was taught by the best.

"Not this time," I say.

Chicão crosses his arms over his barrel chest. "Not this time," he agrees, then slaps my back.

Cheers and whistles flow right over me as I cross the boundary and step into the match space, where my focus narrows to the guy in front of me. The crowd, behind the white fence that separates spectators from competitors, is just a chaotic and faceless mass. There are only a few faces I'd care to see anyway, and none of them are here.

The mat ref recites all the rules I've heard a million times before, and then steps back, leaving me with my cow-eyed opponent. He's got an inch or two on me, and it's all in the legs, but my shoulders are wider, and I know exactly how to use it to my advantage. We lean forward for a quick handshake, and then it's game on.

We do our little circling dance for a while, neither of us doing much but waiting for the other to do something stupid. I feint twice, and he falls for it both times before catching himself. And then I get tired of waiting. My world is the size of this mat, and it's time for some empire building. I strike at his wrist and neck, getting handfuls of his sweat-damp sleeve and collar as I jam my foot into his hip. I pull guard, dropping onto my back and bringing him down with me. He's all bent over and off-balance. His fingers scrabble at my leg as he tries to walk himself out, but I've got too good a grip on him.

I wrench his body to the side, and as he falls back, I pin one of his legs between mine and snag his other foot, curling it up like a soft pretzel against his body. The explosion of breath from his lungs as I lock him up tight is the most satisfying thing I've heard all day.

Chicão is yelling instructions from the sidelines, but I tune him out. It's just me and Cow-Eyes, and he's all mine. I jerk his legs skyward and lay him out flat on his back. This dude is one shoulder lock away from crying for his mama. I am thirty seconds from the finals. I scoot around, getting control—

And then I'm out of control. Cow-Eyes grasps the ends of my sleeves and twists my hands inward until I lose my grip on him. I jump to my feet to regain the advantage, but before I can even take a breath, his foot shoots between my legs and he literally kicks my ass. I stumble forward and nearly fall on top of him as Chicão shouts, "*Caramba! Luta direito porra!*"

I squat, trying to keep my balance, but Cow-Eyes doesn't give me the chance. He's like a fucking alligator, the way he writhes around, all sinew and strength. Lying on his back at my feet, he coils an arm around one of my ankles and jams his foot against the other. I can't help the sound that comes from my mouth as he practically has me doing the splits. With no leverage to fight him, I'm pathetically easy to roll over.

I end up on my side, and I grab for his pant leg, his sleeve, *goddamn it*, anything, but he moves too quickly. When his long legs wrap around my waist like an anaconda, I know I'm in trouble. Because he's got one of *my* legs gripped hard against his chest.

A bright white explosion of agony blasts along my right leg as he locks his ankles behind my hip and stretches back, making my joints scream as they bend in ways they were never meant to. Chicão is shrieking now, and it's like his voice is inside my head. *Vai tomar no cú porra meu caralho you are not good enough Tate Archer not even by half.*

I struggle, but it's no use. I grit my teeth as the pain goes on and on, and Chicão's screeching goes on and on, and the shouts of the crowd go on and on, and everyone knows what I have to do, but I won't. I can't. I *won't.*

I do.

Like it has a mind of its own, my hand releases its futile grip on my opponent's sleeve. My palm hovers over the mat for what seems like a million years but is only half a second. The space between here and there. The distance between hope and despair, between victory and defeat.

And then it falls. Slaps the mat. Cow-Eyes releases me. The pain in my leg subsides. The pain everywhere else is just beginning.

It's over.

Cow-Eyes leans over me. He puts out his hand. I blink up at him and see my father's face. I let him help me up, and I see by the twist of his lips how little he thinks of me. I can't really blame him at the moment.

The realization that I've lost rings in my head. It swirls in golden coronas around the fluorescent lights above me. It seeps up from the mat and eats away at the soles of my feet. The ref has my wrist now, holding it down while he lifts Cow-Eyes's high, and I let him drag me around like a zombie, facing each direction so we can pronounce my suckage to all four corners of the room. To all the faceless people. And to one person who isn't here.

Especially to him.

When the ref is finally finished with the whole parade of shame, I walk back to the bench, my *gi* all bunched up and hanging open, my belt wrapped tight against my naked skin. I look like what I am. A loser. I dive for my iPod as Chicão says, "*Puta que pariu,* Tate, you lost focus. You left yourself wide open."

I open my mouth to argue, but all that comes out is "*Me perdoe.* Sorry. I'm sorry."

He shakes his head and pulls his keys from his pocket. "Grab your bag. I'll get the car."

"No," I say. "I'm not done yet." Cow-Eyes is over in the corner, talking to his coach, wearing a satisfied smile. "I need to watch the finals. I need to figure out what happened."

"*Cacete,*" he mutters. "You don't know what happened? Spider guard sweep. Leg lock. Game over."

"Have I ever told you what an awesome coach you are?" I laugh without smiling. "I'm not kidding. I'm staying to watch. Go home. I'll call Christina and she'll come get me." My heart lifts just thinking of her. I need to see her face. Watch her smile. Hear her tell me I'm all right. And she will, too. She always does. Not sure it'll help this time, but it's worth a try.

He stares at me for a few seconds, and I wonder if he thinks

7

I'm about to run off and get crazy. My dad made it clear to both of us how important this tournament was, so who knows? Maybe poor Chicão thinks I'm suicidal. And hell, maybe I am. I barely know right now, because I'm a giant fucking bruise on the inside, and I can't face my father like this.

"I'm fine," I say. "I—I can't let this happen again. It was my fault. I was stupid."

He shrugs, because you just can't argue with that kind of truth.

Once he's gone, I put my music back on so I don't have to listen to the *thunk* and scrape of feet on the mat, the echoing shrieks and claps of the crowd, the throbbing pulse of my defeat. I turn up the music so loud that I'm sure I kill a few brain cells, which is exactly my intention. I want to liquefy the memory of what happened and let it ooze out my ears.

I watch the semis for the next three weight classes. I watch the men's black belt matches. I watch Cow-Eyes win his final match the exact same way he did mine. He moves fast and decisively into that spider guard, locking up his opponent's arms and kicking him off-balance in three different ways before finally rolling him over.

As the finals go on, I text Christina and ask her to come get me. It's at least an hour from New York City, so I've got to give her time. Within a minute, I have her response.

On my way, baby.

After letting myself stare at those words for a long minute,

I drop the phone back into my bag. No more watching. I need to move. I need to fix this. A bitter taste fills my mouth. *Fix this. Ha.* If only it were that easy. But I have to do *something* or I really might go crazy.

I head over to a side mat set away from the competition, where a couple of the other losers are nursing their wounds. One of the middle-heavies looks game, so we spar. And when he gets tired, I spar with a guy who I swear is twice my weight. And when he gets tired, I spar with a lightweight, who I nearly hurl across the mat before I adjust to his little body. Over and over, I practice where it went wrong for me. I practice the spider guard, recalling exactly where Cow-Eyes put his hands, how he twisted me up. I practice escaping from it, too.

This will not happen again.

It should never have happened in the first place.

When the final shout goes up from the crowd, I realize I probably have only about five minutes before Christina arrives. I scoot to the locker room and wash myself down, wishing I could wipe away defeat this easily. But no. It clings to me like athlete's foot.

I towel off, throw on sweats and a T-shirt, and then I'm out front, looking for her. Her little red car is my life raft, and when I see it in the long line of traffic, I don't wait. I jog over.

She sees me coming and pops her trunk, then pushes the passenger door open. I can hear her girly pop music playing inside, and it makes me smile even though it's not my thing at all. If that music had a flavor, it would be cherry lollipops, and for that alone, I love it. Because, I remember as she leans over and kisses me, welcoming me home, that's the way she tastes.

"How'd it go?" she asks, turning down her music. She sweeps her wavy, dark blond hair over her shoulder.

I sigh, sagging in the bucket seat. She's put it all the way back for me so my legs aren't crowded. I take her hand, running my thumb along her soft skin. "Can we just go home? It's been a long day."

She watches me for a moment, and I let her. I don't mind. I want her eyes permanently glued to me. She reaches up and slides her fingers through my hair, and I close my eyes and breathe, exhaling the weight of the day.

"Stupid stuff?" she asks.

"Yeah," I say, leaning into her touch. "Stick to stupid stuff."

Her hand disappears, and the car moves forward. "Lisa decided to give her dog dreadlocks," she says. "I helped her, even though I'm pretty sure it's animal cruelty."

"What the hell? Doesn't she have a poodle?"

"Uh-huh. But her dad told her he was tired of paying for the grooming."

I open my eyes, and my gaze slides from painted toenails to smooth, shapely legs to *oh, man, I so wish we were not in a moving vehicle right now.* "Huh."

She chatters on for a few minutes about how the dreadlock experiment went awry and they all ended up at the groomers anyway, begging for a pair of shears and a doggie Xanax. I let her voice wash over me, slosh between my ears, soothing the raw places. As powerful as it is, though, it can't quite chase away the dread that's creeping along the inside of my skull and spreading its jagged wings inside my mind.

She glances at me out of the corner of her eye as she pulls onto the highway. "You are definitely not listening to my stupid stuff, Tate Archer."

"Get me outta Jersey and I'll listen to your stupid stuff all day, baby." I give her my best smile, which doesn't fool her.

Her slender fingers flutter down to my thigh, and she squeezes gently, right over the spot that was, a few hours ago, on fire with pain and imminent defeat. "It was just a tournament, Tate," she says quietly. "A bunch of brackets and referees and scoreboards. It wasn't *real life*. You know that, right?"

I cross my arms over my chest, thankful for the anchor of her small hand on my leg, because it's the only thing that's keeping me from leaping from the moving car *right now*. "Yeah. Right. Just a tournament. Try explaining that to my father."

TWO

FIVE BLOCKS . . . THREE BLOCKS . . . ONE BLOCK . . .
My stomach churns as Christina whips her car into a parking space the size of a tin can. Right in front of my building.

She doesn't rush me, even though I know she has to get home. Her phone's been buzzing. Her parents are going out tonight and apparently the sitter fell through, so they need Christina to watch her little sister, Livia. But Christina twists her key from the ignition and sits back. Her hand slides up my arm, and the tips of her fingers brush my neck and give me chills. The good kind. And I need to feel something good right now. I need it so badly.

In a few minutes, I have to face him. He's in there, waiting for me. He had to work this morning, but he told me he'd make it home by late afternoon so we could celebrate when I brought my trophy home. He pointed to the spot in his display case where it would go. To the place he'd cleared between a heavy crystalline pyramid-and-ball thing he got from the men's black belt competition at Tri-State a few years ago, and another obelisk-shaped one he got from a national team competition. Sure, he's already put a few of my medals and little trophies in there, but this would have been the first big one, the first one that *belonged* in there, in the center of the whole damn case. It would have meant I was ready to compete on a national level, that I was worthy. I'd stared at that empty spot, my heart hammering, already filling it with my plans for domination.

Now I stare at my empty hands.

Christina fills them with her own. "I could come in if you want. You know, cut the tension a little?" She grins, her blue eyes glittering with fun. And more than a little hope. I've never introduced her to my dad, and I know she wonders why.

My fingers close around hers and I squeeze gently. The expression on her face is making my chest ache. "Nah, it's fine. I know you have to go."

I don't have the heart to tell her that, though he couldn't even pick her out of a crowd, my dad despises the very idea of her. He hates anything that *distracts* me, and according to him, that's all Christina is, which is grade-A bullshit. I've told him so. Over and over again. Now I avoid the topic. Which means keeping her away from him, because I can't stand the idea of him putting her down in some subtle I'm-the-smartest-man-on-Earth kind of way. He's not nearly as subtle as he thinks, and Christina's perceptive and would pick up on it.

Just like she's picked up on it now. Her face falls for an instant, enough to make that ache in my chest turn sharp, but then she forces the corners of her mouth up again. She's going to let me get away with it, even though she deserves better from me and we both know it. I am simultaneously filled with gratitude and dripping with guilt. She leans forward and kisses my cheek, leaving a little smudge of cherry lip gloss on my skin, a tiny treasure I'll carry with me through whatever's coming next.

"Call if you want to talk, all right?" she says. "I'll be playing Barbies for the next three hours and could probably use the break."

"I'd gladly switch places with you." I tug on her hand, unable to let her go, wishing I could spend the whole evening in this enclosed space with her. Her kiss is sweet. Her hands on my neck are so warm. She smiles against my lips and puts her hand on my chest. I'm sure she can feel my heart pounding.

"Now you're just avoiding going inside," she accuses, but there's no bite in it.

I close my eyes and inhale her scent, cherries and almonds. "I wouldn't be so sure about that." She's completely right.

She touches my nose with hers. "See you tomorrow?"

"Absolutely."

And then I open the door and unfold myself onto the

sidewalk. Rooted to the spot, my duffel hanging from my fist, I watch her pull away from the curb and slip into traffic. I don't take my eyes off her car until the taillights disappear around a corner, and then I know my time is up.

I walk through the lobby and take the stairs, because taking the elevator is pointless. We live on the bottom three floors and the front door is just one flight up. I stand outside for a few moments, knowing I'm being a flat-out pussy.

And of course, he doesn't wait for me to be ready to face him. He doesn't like waiting. He opens the door.

Tall and lean, an unreadable expression on his smooth-shaven face, my father rakes his slate-gray gaze from my toes to my shoulders. It takes less than a second for him to collect, weigh, parse, and analyze my failure. Without meeting my eyes, he says, "I waited to warm up dinner. I expected you an hour ago."

I follow him into the living room and drop my bag on the couch. Johnny Knoxville, our irritable cat, the only thing my mom left behind when she gave up on us four years ago, gives me a surly meow and jumps off his favorite cushion. He prowls over to my dad and rubs against his legs, leaving black fur on Dad's crisp khaki pants.

"I wasn't sure you were home," I lie. "I know you're going to Chicago for that board meeting."

The corner of Dad's mouth twitches up. "Which I leave for *tomorrow*, as you know."

I look away from his cool, assessing stare, his black-brown

hair cut military and neat, his perfect posture. "I'm not that hungry anyway."

It's like he doesn't even hear me. He goes into the kitchen and pulls our prepared meals from the fridge. I recognize from the label on the box what I'm getting tonight. Meal Number Fourteen. Two cups of pasta, two slices of wheat bread, large spinach salad with two ounces of sunflower seeds and one ounce of low-fat dressing, eight ounces skinless grilled chicken breast, eight ounces 2 percent milk. All measured out carefully, down to the milligram. Tailored to my unique nutritional needs, as determined by Frederick Archer, aka the guy who runs my life, aka my dad.

He pokes a fork through the plastic film over the pasta compartment and pops the dish into the microwave. "Did you supplement with the protein gel after your last match?" he asks, his voice completely controlled, as usual.

"Yeah, of course." My supplements are still in my bag . . . unconsumed. I was too busy drowning in defeat to remember.

He raises his head and gives me a penetrating, you're-full-of-shit glare. But all he says is "You never eat enough on competition days, and you need to replenish. You probably have at least three hundred seventy grams of carbohydrate left to consume today. And protein. At least fifty—"

"I can't eat all that tonight. Seriously, I just want to—"

"Tate." His voice skewers me. "You're going to be hurting

tomorrow. And if you're careless like this, you're going to lose muscle mass."

I walk to the table and sit down. He turns his back and returns his attention to our food, knowing the argument is over. He's got broad shoulders and a V-shaped torso, ripped and lean under that custom-made oxford shirt of his. I'm built like that, too, lucky me, but I haven't filled out yet. I'm nearly as tall as he is now, thanks to what felt like a thousand years of piercing growing pains, but I'm still all lank and no bulk. I've fought and scraped for every gram of muscle mass I've got, and I have no intention of losing it. Which he knows.

He takes the time to put our food on actual plates instead of leaving it in the plastic compartment trays we usually eat from. I get up and grab us some forks and knives, because I can't stand to watch him anymore and I need to do something or else I'm going to bolt. When I return to the table, he's already sitting down, cloth napkin in his lap, four ounces of red wine in a glass next to his plate, long fingers drumming drumming drumming. I think that might be the only bad habit he's got, if you don't count busting my balls on a regular basis, that is.

I lower myself onto the chair, noticing for the first time the searing pain in my right leg, a gift from Cow-Eyes and an excellent reminder of how pathetic I am. I grit my teeth and keep my expression bland, but my father's gaze misses nothing.

"You were hurt today." He never wastes time asking questions he already knows the answer to.

Which saves me the trouble of answering him. I shove a forkful of pasta into my mouth and chew.

"You didn't get it wrapped after the match."

Chew chew chew swallow. Bite of spinach salad, bitter on my tongue. Chew.

His jaw tightens. He takes a sip of his wine. My eyes stray to the trophy case across the room. The display lights are on, spotlighting an empty space that isn't really empty. It's filled to bursting with my failure.

I tear my eyes away from it. Bite of bread, nutty sweet. Chew.

He smooths his napkin over his lap. "And Chicão didn't bring you home."

I raise my gaze from my plate. "He called you."

"No, I called him."

I exhale heavily through my nose. Here. We. Go. "Checking up on me."

"Is it so far-fetched that I'd want to know how my son did in such an important competition?"

"No more far-fetched than the idea that you might call your actual son to find out." I feel a strange sensation between my fingers and realize I've crushed my bread to gooey dough in my fist.

He nods, pressing his lips together. "Logical enough. I

thought it might be better if I got the information in advance from a third party."

I drop my mutilated bread onto my plate. "Because you thought I'd lie?"

"Because I thought it would be easier on you."

"Does it look easy?" My heart is thudding against my ribs, and my stomach is tight.

He sighs. "Actually, it looks unnecessarily difficult. Chicão told me about the semifinals. He said you could have beaten the guy."

Yes. Yes, I could have. "That's crazy. That *guy* won the whole freaking tournament. By submissions. It's not like—"

"The only real failure in life is not to be true to the best one knows," he says calmly.

My laughter has a sour taste. I hate this game. "You're quoting Buddha? Come on, Dad, you can do better than that. How about a little Sun Tzu? Nothing like *The Art of War* over dinner."

"It might have helped if you'd considered Sun Tzu's teachings *before* your match. Sounds like your opponent did. 'Pretend inferiority and encourage your enemy's arrogance.' *Ni ting shuo guo ma?*"

Great. Now he's questioning my intelligence in sarcastic Chinese. My eyes are burning. I want to punch something. Mostly because he's so fucking composed, and I'm on the jagged edge, hanging by my fingertips. Oh, and also because he's right. Again. And I'm wrong. Again. Again. A-fucking-gain.

"*Shi ma? Ni zhen hui taiju ren,*" I snap as I shove away from the table. "So sorry I didn't bring you a shiny prize for your shiny case. Sorry I'm not perfect like you are."

He winces, and it kind of freezes me up for a second, like— did I just affect him? But then it's gone, and his expression is smooth again. "I don't need you to be perfect," he says. "I need you to be *your* best. If you can look me in the eye and tell me you did your best today, this conversation can be over."

He waits. And I sit in my chair, arms folded across my chest, my leg throbbing in earnest now, my eyes glued on my still-full plate. Unable to say anything, because I've got my words bottled up so tight that I'll explode like a grenade if I open my mouth.

He takes a few bites of food, chews each one forty times before swallowing. Then he says, "You'll train an extra hour each day for the next few weeks. Chicão has cleared his schedule. In addition to your morning workouts, you'll have a sparring session with him after school, before you meet with your language tutors."

Holy hell, he's just pulled my pin. I shoot to my feet. "I can't! I already made plans with Christina to help her with her chem—"

"No," he barks, his eyes sparking with fury at the mention of her name. "This is much more important."

"*She* is important," I shout. "I promised her, and I'm not going to let her down."

Now he's on his feet. There might be a few silver hairs at his temples, but he's nowhere near past his prime. He could probably kick my ass without breaking a sweat. It would almost be a relief if he tried, because I *want* to hit him right now.

"Nothing is more important than your training," he says in a low voice. "You—*we*—have a responsibility, and the stakes are far higher than you can—"

"Screw my responsibility! I don't even know what that is!" Rage fizzes and pops through my veins, the heat of it coursing along my limbs. "You're always talking about it, and you don't even realize how stupid you sound."

I puff my chest out and lower my voice an octave. "Bearing the name of Archer is a great responsibility, Tate, one you must prepare for by subsisting on a diet of grilled chicken and pasta and by turning your brain inside out on a daily basis."

My father pinches the bridge of his nose. "Tate, stop."

But I can't. I'm on a roll. "You're already a junior in high school, and you speak only eleven languages? Not good enough. I speak twenty-three for some incomprehensible reason. And forget about your girlfriend. Sure, she's the best thing that ever happened to you, but it's probably wise to think of her as a living, breathing waste of time." I wag my finger at him. "But don't worry. You can work out your frustration on the mat with a sweaty Portuguese man who wears too much

Old Spice. You'll never be as perfect as I am, but maybe I can turn you into a cheap imitation."

He crosses his arms over his chest. "Tate, calm down."

I'm right in his space now, which is tempting fate, but I'm too far gone to care. "And I'll never actually tell you *why* I put you through this, Tate," I say from between clenched teeth. "It's part of the fun. I'll give you a bunch of bullshit about family responsibility, sure, but it's really because I'm a scientist, and I care about you exactly as much as I care about all my other experiments."

My breath is sawing in and out of me. I'm close enough to him to see the tiny scar at the corner of his chin and the flash of fire in his eyes as he stares steadily at me. He doesn't move, though. Doesn't flinch or back up or shove me away. He just stands there. And when he speaks, his voice is rock solid and dead calm. "I'll tell you everything when you're ready, son. Unfortunately, today you have proven that you are *far* from ready."

His blunt words are sharp as knives, and they deflate me, leaving me sagging. Another Sun Tzu quote comes to me, and like always, it's too late to do me any good. *To subdue the enemy without fighting is the height of skill.*

No one's more skillful than Frederick Archer.

I nod, buckling under the weight of defeat, which is heavy enough to make me slow but not enough to let me sink through the floor. "Thanks, Dad. Enjoy your dinner," I mumble.

I turn on my heel and slowly walk to my room, thankful he can't see the grimace on my face as I force myself not to limp.

THREE

I OPEN MY DOOR IN THE MORNING AND FIND MY BREAK-
fast on a tray. Meal Number Six. Two cups iron-fortified cereal, banana, eight ounces milk, eight ounces orange juice, blue vitamin pill. Also, a note from my dad saying he'll be back from Chicago late tonight and a reminder that Chicão's coming this afternoon to give me my first extra training session. Nothing about yesterday at all.

Nothing except the bottle of Advil he left sitting in the middle of the kitchen table, next to a glass of water.

It might be Sunday, and I might have been through hell yesterday, but that's no excuse to slack off. I walk my aching leg to our workout room and don't come out until I've punished myself adequately. It takes about five miles on the treadmill and an hour with the weights, thinking all the while about the *family responsibility* and what the hell he could possibly be talking about, coming up with absolutely nothing except a headache the size of Manhattan. Then the cleaning lady shows up to do her thing, filling the apartment with the scent of 2-butoxyethanol and sodium petroleum sulfonate—Windex and Pine-Sol—and making my already-pounding head feel like it's going to detonate.

Ah, but just before it does . . . Christina shows up at my door, wearing a short skirt and carrying a box of doughnuts.

No one can tell me I don't have the best girlfriend in the world.

"Hello." I pull the door wide to let her step into the entryway, unable to wipe the huge smile from my face.

She flips open the box and raises an eyebrow. "I thought you might be in need of a sugar high."

I'm still grinning as I snag a glazed monstrosity from the box and take a huge bite. My dad would have a stroke if he could see me now. "You have no idea," I say with a full mouth.

Once we've each polished off a pastry, I take her down to my father's lab, partly because it's the only way to escape the cleaning lady, and partly because I enjoy the fact that he has no idea I can get in here. And also because alone time with my girlfriend is a rare gift, and I have no intention of wasting it.

"Just out of curiosity, how did you figure out how to get in here?" she asks as we approach the door. "I thought your dad was super-secretive about this place."

I wave the fingertips of my right hand at her. "That's what this is for."

She squints at the almost-transparent film over my index finger, a thin strip of plastic I fetched from my room on our way down here. "And that is . . ."

"His fingerprint." I slide my finger into an opening in the control panel next to the door, then use my other hand to punch in my dad's code, which took me six solid months of hacking to figure out. "It's his fault, really. He's the one who started teaching me chemistry when I was still in kindergarten."

"Is that why you're so good at it?" she asks, lifting my hand to the light. She's a senior, and though she breezes through every other subject, I'm tutoring her in chemistry.

"I guess. It's not that hard."

Christina rolls her eyes as I carefully slip the transparent tape off my finger and place it in a little plastic case I pull from my pocket.

"Really," I say. "Take this here, for instance." I wave the plastic case at her before putting it away again. "When you touch something, your skin leaves behind all sorts of stuff—amino acids, isoagglutinogen, potassium, and a bunch of other compounds. You can't see any of it, of course, and it can be wiped away easily. But it's there and available if you know how to find and use it. All it took to gather the fingerprint was a lightbulb, some foil, a bit of superglue, this strip of tape, and some vodka."

She gives me this raised-eyebrow look. "Vodka?"

I shrug. "Okay, maybe vodka was just the beverage of choice for the evening."

She slaps my arm because she knows I'm full of shit—vodka's one thing we definitely don't keep in the house. "Aren't you afraid he'll catch you?"

I tug her through the door and pull her close, sliding my fingers through one of her dark blond curls, tracing its path around her collarbone. "My father *will* catch me someday, and then we'll have it out. In the meantime, it's a great place to explore."

In more ways than one. I lower my head and touch my mouth to hers.

Kissing Christina is like instant anesthetic. Her lips taste like powdered sugar, and her hands are liquid soft as they skim up my arms, raising goose bumps. The air in my father's lab is temperature controlled, kept right at a chilly sixty degrees no matter what time of year.

I don't really feel the cold, though, because I'm on fire right now.

I nudge Christina back up against one of the lab tables, and she lets out this breathy sigh and gets up on her tiptoes. Her arms are around my neck and her body is pressed against mine. I can feel every curve. The warm tip of her tongue slides along my lips, and as I open my mouth and let her in, something inside me roars. My hands find her waist and lift her up so she's sitting on the table. I pull her hips toward me, so I can stand between her legs, so I can get a little closer and feel her—

Her hand on my chest, giving me the gentlest of pushes.

It's the only signal I need. Even though it's like pulling

the brakes on a speeding train, I manage to reverse course and lean back, giving her some space. Her other hand, which until this moment was tangled in my hair, slides down to my cheek. Her own cheeks are flushed this incredible shade of lush pink. Her eyes are on my shoulder. "Um," she whispers, "if we could just . . ."

She wriggles her hips and wrenches the hem of her skirt down to midthigh, and I feel like a total douchebag. I didn't mean to push it that far. I know she isn't ready for that. We've been friends for nearly three years, but we haven't been *together* for that long. That's not how it feels to me, though. I've been gone for this girl for so long that I can barely remember a time when she wasn't the first thing I thought about in the morning . . . and yeah, the object of my fantasies, too. But as much as I want to touch her, I'm not about to screw this up. She means too much to me.

"Yeah, of course." I step back and turn away, staring at one of my father's many flat-screen computer panels. This one wasn't here the last time I sneaked in. The display is black, with three numbers in the center of the screen:

2,943,288,494

4,122,239,001

14 (?)

As I watch, measuring my breaths by the seconds, willing myself to calm down, the bottom number with the question mark next to it stays the same, but the top two numbers change, faltering down by two, up by one, down by three, up by five. The first number is shrinking steadily, but the second one is growing in a jumpy pattern.

That's exactly how the awkwardness between me and Christina feels right now.

She's silent, which makes my heart start to pound for a different reason altogether. My eyes and brain move a hundred miles an hour, trying to find a way to surf the tsunami of weirdness that's hit us. Feeling jittery, I reach over and tap the screen with the numbers, and it flashes and evaporates like it was a screensaver. For a split second, the display is filled with an incredibly complex blueprint of some type, but it's immediately replaced by a lurid red screen requesting a password. I back toward Christina quickly. "What's that?" she asks.

"No clue." It was dumb of me to touch it like that—in this lab, there's no telling what could happen, and I'm usually more cautious. But I'm not ready to leave yet, so I direct Christina toward the things I've already figured out. "Want to learn a few different ways to kill someone?" I offer.

Her laughter is high and shaky. "What?"

"We could play with some of my dad's toys." I gesture at the rack of slick black weaponry that takes up the far wall. My dad used to work for this company called Black Box Enterprises, a private weapons manufacturer. He quit right around the time my mom left us, but he still does jobs for Black Box as an independent contractor, and for some reason he attends all their board meetings. That's where he is right now, in fact. I look over my shoulder at Christina.

She hooks a finger through one of my belt loops and tugs me backward. Her arms slide around my middle, and her expression glows with mischief. "This sounds like an *excellent* plan."

She hops off the lab table and approaches what looks like a towel rack, over which hang several silver sacks woven from delicate steel thread. Thin wires coil from the bottom of each of them and connect to a black panel beneath the rack.

"I'm not sure how you'd kill someone with these," she comments dryly, pointing to the sacks. "Though they are kind of pretty."

"Oh, those won't kill you." I know because I was stupid enough to play with one once. Obviously, I survived, though at the time I wished I hadn't. "You can put one of these babies over someone's head and turn it on . . ." I flip a switch on the black panel, and the bags start to pulse with muted light. "It's much brighter if you're looking at the inside of the bag—or if your head is in one. The strobes from the fiber optics inside flash at the same frequency as human brain waves. It's called the Bucha effect. Recipe for a seizure." I would know. It took me a day to sleep it off.

She takes a step back and runs into me. "I think I'm scared of your dad . . . but also in awe."

Which is kind of how I feel, and somehow, it makes me angrier at him.

I lean over and snag a smooth black disk from a shelf full of similar devices. I leave my own grimy fingerprints all over it but don't even care.

"This one is actually pretty cool," I say, pressing a tab at its edge. A screen appears across its surface—a map of the world, along with tiny command buttons.

"Is that a GPS?" Christina leans close. Her hair smells like almonds, and I breathe deeply.

"I'm pretty sure it can do a lot more than that." I push one of the buttons and a prompt comes up:

Ramses Satellite IV-467 password:

Christina's eyes go wide. "Do you know the password?"

I chuckle. "I might." I do. It's my mother's middle name. I have no desire to crash a billion-dollar satellite today, though. I may be angry at my dad, but I'm not *that* angry. I turn the satellite-controller thingy off and set it back on the shelf.

Christina's eyes dart along the wire racks and lab tables in the center of the long, hangarlike room, which hold an array of objects of various shapes and sizes, all black and slick and enticing. "So not all of these are weapons?"

"Nah. Only that wall over there and the stuff on this table." I gesture at the seizure bags, which are hanging right next to a set of innocent-looking vibracoustic stimulation probes that I'm fairly sure could stop a guy's heart.

She smiles, no doubt feeling safer now that I've directed her toward things that are less likely to kill her—or me—on contact.

"Hmm. Let's see," she says as she moves toward the largest table in the room. Her fingers tap lightly along its surface as she approaches a device I've never seen before, one that's sitting out in the open like my dad forgot to put it away. It's just over a foot long, and about two inches wide. Like everything else my dad makes, it's smooth and black, except for a port next to the power switch, kind of like a USB but not quite the right shape. Christina picks up the device and arches an eyebrow. "This has potential."

"Be careful," I say. "I have no idea what that does."

"It looks like a security wand. Like at the airport?" She presses a button on the handle, and a strip of yellow light gleams from its center. Her lips curve into a suggestive smile. "I think I need to check you for contraband, Mr. Archer."

Her hips swaying, she slinks over to me and stands close enough to touch, close enough for me to smell the cinnamon and powdered-sugar scent of her breath, close enough for me to curl my fingers over the edge of the table behind me and hold on tight. She slowly extends the wand and waves it over my arm, sending blue light reflecting back at us. "Ooh, I like that. What a pretty color," she says in a voice that raises my temperature a few degrees.

She runs it up over my shoulder and around my neck, and then slowly, slowly, skims it down over my chest, that blue glow reflecting brightly in her eyes. Her gaze is fixed on mine, and that wand is sinking lower, and all I can do is hope the thing doesn't detect blood flow or something, because I could be in trouble if she keeps this up.

And then, just as the light reflects bright blue and blinding off the metal button of my jeans, Christina laughs and looks down at her feet. Johnny Knoxville is winding his wiry body around her ankles. I glance toward the lab's door and realize I left it hanging open. Johnny meows, all high pitched and innocent, and I feel a rush of gratitude because I think he's saved me.

"Hey, Johnny," Christina coos. "Are you feeling left out? Should I scan you, too?" She bends over and runs the wand over his back, sending plain yellow light bouncing along his sleek black fur and the gray tiles beneath his paws. He startles when he sees it and takes off.

"Sorry!" she calls, then looks up at me. "I didn't mean to scare him."

"Meh. He's a total neurotic grump. Hard not to be when you live with my dad."

She spends a few moments looking for him under the lab tables, and before she straightens, she glances up at me and gives me a look that shoots fire through my veins. "Should I scan myself, do you think?"

I . . . can't speak. I just watch without breathing as she skims the thing up her bare legs from ankle to knee, wishing I'd had enough working brain cells to grab the scanner from her and do the job myself.

She takes her eyes off me and looks down at her legs. "Hey," she says, frowning. "The light is red."

She swings it in my direction. Blue. And back over her belly. Red. "What does this thing detect?"

"Red hotness," I say, because . . . damn. I'm still staring at her legs.

She barely smiles at my lame joke. Instead, she turns the scanner off and sets it back where she found it. I slide my arm around her waist. "Okay, fine. The most obvious explanation is that I'm a guy. And you are most definitely *not* a guy. See? Blue for guys. Red for girls." Even as I say it, I know there's more to it than that, but it's the only explanation that occurs to me at the moment.

"Yeah. Hey. I'm getting kind of cold." She points to the goose bumps along the usually smooth skin of her arm. "Do you think the cleaning lady's done up there yet?"

I pry Johnny out from under my dad's desk and drop him in the hallway, then take her hand and lead her out the door. Just before I hit the button to slide it shut behind us, I look back at the screen I touched when we first came in. The screensaver is back on, the two huge numbers on top doing their little jittery dance, the final row still reading: 14 (?). It's a mystery, a puzzle to solve. Then my eyes land on the scanner, and I smile. Two more puzzles to solve. The words of Sun Tzu come to me again, and for once the timing is perfect:

Opportunities multiply as they are seized.

FOUR

AH, MONDAYS. MY ALARM GOES OFF AT FOUR, AND IF I don't get my ass out of bed, I know my dad's going to be in here at 4:01 a.m. with a glass of cold water to dump over my head. My sleep-weary carcass is in the workout room by 4:05 a.m., and my dad's already there. Judging from the sweat drenching the front of his T-shirt, he's been here for at least half an hour.

"How was the board meeting?" I ask, just to be civil. I was in bed before he got home last night.

"A bunch of wealthy people who think they should get whatever they want whenever they want, whether it's good for them or not," he says between sharp breaths.

He returns his attention to the panel of his stair stepper, and I leave him to it. Surely if he'd noticed evidence of my little break-in yesterday, he would have said something. I think I'm in the clear.

After my workout, I take a shower and then head to my room for a few hours of studying. Not for school. School is child's play compared with what my dad has me doing. This morning, it's finite element analysis and differential equations, and then modeling and dimensional analysis of biological systems. After that, I spend a bit of time on tactics and strategy, basic history of war stuff, followed by a half hour of drilling on the latest language I'm learning—Arabic. I swear my dad is training me to be a Navy SEAL or something. Maybe the family responsibility is to take over a small country somewhere.

I emerge into the kitchen to find my dad sitting at the table with his best friend, George. *Dr.* George Fisher, to be precise, who works for Black Box Enterprises.

". . . that way I can be sure Brayton is being honest about his plans," my dad is saying.

George nods. "He's eager to negotiate. He's sending a vehicle for you at noon."

"Driver?"

"Peter McClaren. Angus's oldest nephew? A good kid. He just graduated from Yale, and Brayton hired him a few weeks ago." George flashes an easy smile, maybe to counter the stern frown on my dad's face. Things are always more relaxed when George is around. I can't say the same thing for Brayton, though. He's George's boss, and he used to be my dad's—until my dad quit. I've met Brayton only once—when he showed up at our door a few years ago, right after Dad resigned from

Black Box, demanding to speak with my father immediately. I lurked in the kitchen as they argued in the living room, but they started speaking some language I don't know yet. I didn't catch a word after my father shouted, "How dare you come to my home." One thing I knew, though: Brayton was pissed about something, and he didn't leave any happier than he'd arrived. I walked away with the distinct impression that he needed surgery to remove the stick from his ass.

"Hey," George calls when he sees me, inclining his head of silver curls in my direction. "Look at this guy! I swear, I think you've grown two inches since I saw you last week."

"Hey, George." I sit down in front of Meal Number Eighteen, which is steaming and fresh from the microwave. Ten-egg-white omelet. Four ounces chopped lean ham. One ounce cheddar cheese. Three ounces red pepper. Whole wheat English muffin. I am also lucky enough to get two tablespoons of apricot jam and eight ounces each of milk and juice. Plus my blue vitamin pill. And my dad has tucked a protein gel supplement next to my tray.

Dad points to the supplement. "You forgot after your workout again."

I rip the tab off the little metallic envelope and suck it down. Lime flavor. As the slimy gunk slides over my tongue, I flip on the little flat-screen on the wall behind my dad, focusing on the recap of the Yankees game while he and George chat about the latest world population reports from the United

Nations and the CIA. Baseball is much more interesting, until I hear my dad say, ". . . want you to see the anomaly. There are fourteen that don't match."

"You have a theory as to why," says George, watching him closely.

Dad nods solemnly. "But I think the other numbers are accurate—and changing much faster than my previous estimates suggested."

I mute the television, thinking of the screen in my dad's lab that displayed those three numbers. "Planning to end the problem of overpopulation with some of your weapons of mass destruction?"

I say it as a joke, one of the many digs I toss at him over the course of a day. But George's eyes go wide, and my dad sits back like I've landed a solid gut punch. His shock tells me it was a seriously low blow, but the feeling of power is irresistible. "Oh, sorry. Did that hit too close to home?"

"Not at all. And once again I am reminded that my business will be none of yours, at least until you learn to think before you speak." My father's voice is a weapon unto itself. "I apologize for Tate's lack of tact," he says to George.

Heat slowly creeps from my chest to my neck as George waves him off, and I let out a long, controlled breath. I'm not going to let it get to me this morning. "Maybe if you told me more about it," I say quietly, "I wouldn't say so many stupid things."

My dad slowly puts down his fork and wipes his mouth with his napkin. His slow, precise movements are a total danger sign, and I'm not the only one who notices. Always the peacemaker, George chuckles and leans back, clutching his thermos of coffee. We don't have any in the house, so he always has to bring his own. He takes a sip while giving my father an amused look. "Come on, Fred. You can't blame him for being curious about your work. Where do you think he got that particular trait from, anyway?"

Dad sits up very straight in his chair. His dark hair is neatly combed. His shirt is neatly pressed. He stares across the table at me. I am neither neatly combed nor pressed.

Nor do I care.

"'Learning without thought is labor lost, but thought without learning is perilous,'" he begins, and I groan.

"Forget it," I say, plowing the last few bites of my breakfast into my mouth as quickly as I can, anything to get me away from this lecture, one I've heard a thousand times. It usually ends with how I'm *not ready* to know what he knows, so I should get back to my studies and shut up. "I'm sure you're right. I'm sure I'm wrong. Happy?"

I say most of this with my mouth full, and a few flecks of egg white hit my tray while I talk, which draws a narrow-eyed look of disgust from him. It feels like pure win, seeing his face twist up like that because of me. "Nice seeing you, George. I've got to get to school."

I turn away from my dad before his expression can shift back into that neutral, impenetrable mask he usually wears. I swing my pack onto my shoulder and smile. I've pissed him off, and I want to carry that thrill with me a little bit longer.

Shouldn't be too hard. I've got his magical scanner doohickey tucked safely in my bag.

I whistle as I walk out the door.

My good mood sticks with me through the morning. My first two classes—Ancient History and Economics—are utterly snooze-worthy, but I can't blame the teachers. It's my dad's fault—he made me learn that stuff a few years ago. But my next class is Advanced Chemistry, and I'm in there with a bunch of seniors . . . including Christina. So it's great on a few levels. First, because even though I pretend to despise the class just to piss off my dad, it's actually really cool. And second, because I get to stare at my girlfriend for an entire hour.

I have to enjoy it now, because she's graduating in a few weeks.

When the bell rings and we all jump from our seats to get to our next classes, Christina turns to me with a tight, anxious expression. "I'm so glad you're going to help me study for this final," she says quietly as she slips her book into her backpack. "I'd like to escape this place with my GPA intact."

My heart clenches like a fist in my chest as she runs her hand down my arm and heads for the door. I completely forgot. Chicão. The extra training sessions. I should stop her. I should explain what's happened, that it's already set up. But the look on her face was so grateful just now, like she thinks I'm her hero, and I can't let that go quite yet. I'll tell her at lunch. Maybe I can figure out a way to weasel out of training with Chicão before then. Maybe this is fixable.

My fourth-period class, Game Theory, had serious potential for awesome, which was why I signed up for it in the first place instead of going for an easy free period. But . . . Mr. Lamb is the teacher. And there is just something about the guy that I cannot like.

Maybe it's the way he always seems more interested in my dad than in me.

There are few things I hate more than that.

Sure enough, as soon as I take my seat in the front row and pull out my notebook, Mr. Lamb is standing in front of my desk. He's weirdly tall, with a hooked nose and thinning hair. Like some sort of human-vulture hybrid. "How was your weekend, Tate?"

He's got a stain on the front of his dark tan pants, right next to his fly. I raise my head to see him grinning down at me. There's a full millimeter of space between his two front teeth, and I find myself wanting to mash them together. "Uneventful, Mr. Lamb."

He pushes his glasses up with a grimy fingernail as his smile twists from friendly to skeptical. "No way. I know you had that tournament! Will mentioned it last week. Did your dad go with you?"

I'll have to thank Will for that when I see him at lunch. Maybe with a wristlock or a palm strike. I love the guy. He's been my best friend since we were in kindergarten. But he never knows when to keep his mouth shut.

"No, my dad was working." I look over at the clock, willing the bell to ring and save me from the slow agony of small talk.

And because it is my lucky day, it does exactly that, right as Mr. Lamb is opening his mouth to ask another question. He pauses, his lips reshaping around his next words. "Tate, can you go up and write the equations for weak and strict dominance on the whiteboard?"

Yes, yes, I can. I'd love to, actually. Mr. Lamb is a sycophantic tool, but he knows his game theory—probably because it's not about actual fun. It's about mathematical equations that model real-life conflict and cooperation, but that's fine with me. I lose myself in iterated elimination of dominated strategies for the next forty minutes. I reach a Nash equilibrium just as my stomach growls, breaking my concentration.

As soon as the bell rings for lunch, the memory of what I have to tell Christina hits me in the center of the chest like one of Chicão's wicked elbow strikes. I'm a dead man walking as I trudge toward the cafeteria. In fact, I don't even see her as she comes out of the bathroom with her best friend, Lisa, and a bunch of her soccer teammates, not until she threads her arm through mine and squeezes. It's like a little miracle, this touch, like a jolt of pure euphoria straight through my nervous system. She looks up at me with a sweet smile on her face, and I immediately decide I can't have this conversation with her until later. We're with our friends, after all, and lunch is like this oasis for all of us in the desert wasteland of school. Thirty minutes of laughing and flirting, half an hour of escape.

Lisa and the others spend a few minutes buying tickets for prom while Christina and I scoot through the lunch line before it gets jammed up. I bought our tickets last Friday, the moment she said she'd go with me.

We claim our usual long table. Even though we're the first ones there, we scoot so close that her chest brushes my arm when she turns to me and asks, "How's your day been so far?"

I grin. "Nothing compared with right now."

I'm leaning forward to sneak a lightning-fast kiss when someone taps my arm. The kid pulls his hand back quickly, like it took all his courage to reach out and get my attention. He looks ten years old. Freshman, for sure. He's got a moon-shaped face and a stubby, almost upturned nose, and is looking at me like I'm a rock star.

"Hey," I say.

"Um, hi," he replies, turning to look over his shoulder at a group of similarly shrimpy kids, half who are staring at me the same way he is . . . and half who are staring at Christina in an entirely *different* kind of way.

"Can I help you, bud?" I ask, wanting badly to turn back to Christina and finish what I started before our other friends get here.

"Are you the guy who made those firecrackers out of Red Bull and chopsticks?" he blurts.

It was just a little prank, a concoction I whipped up to celebrate the first day of my junior year by creating a few lasting memories—and a lot of chaos. Now it's been elevated to the status of legend and I'm being credited with creating explosives out of completely *un*-explosive materials, which is pretty cool, but not something I can brag about publicly. "Dude. I will neither confirm nor deny involvement in that incident." I wink at him.

His face lights up like a sodium nitrate flame, and his voice squeaks as he says, "I heard you're, like, some kind of modern-day MacGyver. You did the thing with the jet-propelled silly string in Ms. Ganswick's office, too, didn't you?"

Yeah, I did. Mix acrylic resin with sorbitan trifoliate and a shitload of propellant like dichlorodifluoromethane—all conveniently heisted from my dad's lab—and you have an excellent way to exact revenge on a teacher who gives you a C just because she doesn't like your views on nuclear energy or whatnot.

Christina nudges my arm. She told me this story would get around, and she was right.

"I have no idea what you're talking about," I say, but I can't keep from smiling. That was one badass prank, if I do say so myself.

Apparently Moonface thinks so, too. "Can you teach me?"

I get this question at least once every few weeks. Usually from geeky little freshmen like him. "I'm sorry," I say, keeping my voice regretful, which is hard now that Christina's hand is squeezing my thigh under the table. "I'm all booked up at the moment."

The eager spark in his eyes dies, and as he turns away, I can't stop myself from grabbing his arm and whispering, "Powdered sugar and stump remover. Mix and light. Have fun."

He skitters off to share his new and forbidden knowledge with his friends. They are about to get themselves in untold amounts of trouble—I've given them a harmless little recipe for a quick and dirty smoke bomb.

Just as I'm slipping my arm around Christina, Will sits down across from us, behind a tray piled high with french fries smothered in ketchup. His eyes meet mine, and his look is all expectation. A fraction of a second later, I notice his new hairdo. His pecan-brown scalp is smooth and shining, save for the two-inch-wide runway of short black hair right down the center.

"Holy shit. You got the Mohawk." I reach over to pat the top of his head. "Your mom must have had a seizure when she saw it."

He laughs, running his hand over the thing. "She might have said a few choice words. Especially when I told her I did it for a girl."

I squint at him. "You did?"

"Nah, man," he says, looking at me like I've lost my mind. Then he glances at the table next to ours—which is full of freshmen and sophomore girls—and raises and lowers his eyebrows a few times. "But I would, for the right one!"

Christina snorts, but a bunch of the girls giggle. Several of them look like they might want to *be* that girl. Even though he's an asshat half the time, *everybody* likes Will.

He lifts his chin in my direction and waves a red-tipped fry at me. "Has your dad calmed down about Saturday or is he still busting on you?"

"There's never a time when he's *not* busting on me. But that's okay. We always play this game. Check out my latest move."

I pull the scanner from my backpack and feel a surge of satisfaction as Will's face breaks into a huge smile. That feeling subsides quickly as Christina's face does the opposite.

"I can't believe you brought it to school," she says, shifting away from me. "Won't your dad be pissed?"

I roll my eyes. "I'm past caring what he thinks."

"What is that thing?" Will asks.

"Some type of scanner," Christina says. "It shows the different genders . . . or so Tate thinks."

As soon as Christina says it, I understand how ridiculous that sounds. My father never develops something that simple. Ever.

Will drops his fry. "A boy-girl thing? Oh, gimme that."

His hand shoots across the table and his fingers close around the handle, hitting the switch that turns the scanner on. As he snatches it from me, it flashes red in front of Christina's frowning face.

"Hey," he says. "Red for girl, huh?"

She crosses her arms over her chest. "Nothing gets past you, does it?"

Will gives her a little bow and waves the wand at me, sending blue light reflecting back at him. "Ah, I get it. Blue for boy."

He slides it over his head.

And it reflects red.

"Uh-oh," he says, getting up from the table. "Either I've misplaced my boobs or you're wrong about this scanner, T-boy."

Which I already knew. "I've always thought you were a little girl," I say, rising from the table, too, intending to grab the scanner back. For all I know, the thing's a weapon. I was an idiot to bring it to school.

Will's eyes light with the challenge, and he takes off, using the benefit of years of soccer training to weave in and out of the human traffic now clogging the cafeteria as B-lunch gets into full swing. I'm right behind him, doing some weaving of my own and already wishing I'd taken another few Advil before leaving for school.

Will circles by the lunch line, running the scanner along the bodies of most of the cheerleading squad, all but two of whom reflect cherry red. At the end of the line, back by the lunch trays, Miranda Hopkins bends over to pick up the cell phone she's just dropped. Will is behind her in a second, sliding the scanner up her legs—and then up her skirt. The light blue material can't hide the red light from the scanner as he runs it over her ass. She shrieks and then starts to laugh when she sees the hilariously worshipful look on his face as they both straighten up.

He flips the scanner into the air and catches it, sending my heart into my throat in the moments before he gets a firm grip on it again. I jog a few tables closer, but then Miranda's boyfriend, a thug named Kyle Greer who happens to be captain of the wrestling team, shoves Will to the side with a murderous expression on his face. Will stumbles, his arms flailing in this overly dramatic way—right in front of Kyle's face. The scanner reflects red off him, too.

As Will sprints away from the couple, he shoots me a smart-ass look. The boy-girl thing is shot completely—Kyle Greer has more testosterone than the rest of the senior class guys combined.

Will runs back along the line, holding the scanner over his head now, and it flashes blue off the gray-haired lunch lady standing by the taco salad. She gives him a baleful look that says she's counting the seconds until she can retire to Florida and never have to look at another teenager again.

My now-former best friend continues his campaign of chaos for a few more minutes before I finally corner him by the salad bar.

"Time for a new theory, T," he says.

"No shit. Now hand it over before you get us both suspended." I give him a look that says I'm perfectly willing to hurt him if that's what it takes. He rolls his eyes and gives me the scanner. Nearly all of B-lunch is staring at me as I stalk back to my table, but I'm staring right back. Will just scanned nearly all the few hundred people in this lunchroom.

Besides me, the lunch lady, and a handful of others, everybody scanned red. And it's clearly not boy-girl or black-white or young-old or anything like that. Maybe it's a biological marker? A genetic thing? Probably even that is too simple. My dad's inventions are ruthlessly complicated. Sometimes it takes me days of dismantling them and running through his encrypted computer files to unlock their secrets. But as I look at Christina and wonder what makes her—and almost everyone else—different from me, I know I won't stop until I figure it out.

As soon as I get through this day—preferably without drawing any more attention to myself . . . and the scanner.

FIVE

I'M IN THE PROCESS OF MOOCHING A FRY FROM WILL when I hear a voice that makes me cringe inside.

"That's a cool-looking toy." Mr. Lamb and his stained pants are right next to our table, shattering my hope of keeping a low profile. He must have lunch duty today. "Looks like a security wand."

My eyes dart up to Will's as he sits down, and I see an apology there. Christina's fingers find mine, and I hold on tight. She could totally take an I-told-you-so attitude about this, but instead, she's right here with me.

Mr. Lamb looks at us expectantly. "Where did you get this?"

"It's the new wand controller for my gaming system," I say. "I brought it in to show my friends."

Will gives me an almost imperceptible nod. He'll go down for this with me if he has to. I just pray he doesn't say anything wild or give too much away.

One of Mr. Lamb's eyebrows rises, bringing it close to his receding blond hairline. Game on. "Really? I've never seen one like this." Before I can stop him, he picks up the scanner and examines it. "I'm not that into video games, though, believe it or not." He reveals that gap between his teeth again.

"Really, Mr. Lamb?" Will asks with overly innocent, wide eyes. "I had you pegged as a total ninja gamer."

Mr. Lamb's smile turns indulgent. "Well, maybe I've played a few games. Enough to know this must be brand new!"

He brandishes the scanner like a light saber. Christina bows her head and her shoulders shake with silent laughter, because he looks like a grade-A tool. I wish I found it as funny, but right now all I want him to do is put my dad's invention down and get the hell away.

"So what system is this thing for?" Mr. Lamb asks. "It doesn't look like Nintendo or any of the others."

"It's a limited edition PlayStation accessory," Christina says. "For a new game."

Mr. Lamb's eyes glint with something I can't read as he looks down at her. "Is there some kind of real-life tie-in, then, Ms. Scolina? I mean, this reacts to its environment even when it's not connected to a system."

He switches it on and waves it over my head, sending blue light cascading over the table. And then over his own chest.

Red.

My brain is whirling. "It's just your standard console-based MMORPG, Mr. Lamb." I wave my hand at the scanner, resisting my impulse to snatch it from him and run. "You . . . upload results to the system and . . . rack up points for your character . . ."

Shit. I should have let Christina run with this one—she was doing just fine, and I sound like a fucking idiot.

"These things are going to be everywhere by summer," says Will, so loudly that kids at the table behind him all turn to look.

I want to shove my gym socks down his throat to shut him up. Will has a gift for taking things a step too far.

"Yeah? This is the next big thing?" Mr. Lamb gives my best friend a fake wide-eyed look that's strikingly similar to the one Will gave him a second ago. I'm pretty sure he knows we're full of shit, but he's trying to be clever about it. "What's this game called? Maybe I should check it out."

"Wand of the Cyclops," Christina says solemnly, with only the slightest tremor in her bottom lip.

Mr. Lamb waves the scanner in front of Christina's face, making her blink as the bright light shines in her eyes. He purses his lips and nods. "I'll definitely be looking it up. While I have you here, give me some pointers." He tilts his head in my direction. "Is it a dominant strategy game? I've read that a lot of these MMORPGs are your standard rock-paper-scissors design, like every class of character is strictly weaker than at least one other class, and stronger than at least one other."

Ah, Christ, now he's asking me to apply game theory to a video game that *doesn't freaking exist.* Pure hatred for this man flows through my veins, nearly—but not quite—overwhelming the panic. Because the longer we sit here talking to him, the more we risk defeat.

As in, he might confiscate the scanner, and then I. Am. Doomed.

"It's more of a dynamic Bayesian signaling game at its heart," I babble.

Mr. Lamb's mud-colored gaze bores into mine. Then he hands the scanner back to me. "Hmm. Fascinating. You should do your semester project on this game, Tate. You have an excellent grasp of the concepts." He gives me his gap-toothed smile. "You can bring the wand back and give the class a demonstration!"

"Um." I swallow hard and clutch the scanner, trying to find the escape hatch in this conversation. "I was actually thinking of doing my project on game theory applications to violent conflicts—"

Mr. Lamb frowns, and Christina leans close to me, lending me her warmth as shards of ice fill my stomach. I quickly say, "But I'll think about it."

His thin lips curl into a nasty smirk. "I'll leave you to your lunch."

He walks away, and I expect him to go ruin someone else's meal, but he strides out of the cafeteria, heading toward the mathematics and science wing. Will and I look at each other for a long second. "I'm sorry, man," he says, once again rubbing his hand over his head.

"Don't worry about it. I'm the jackass who brought it to school." I pull my pack into my lap and am sliding the scanner into it when the voice of Mr. Feinstein, our principal, blats over the intercom.

"Tate Archer, please come to the central administrative office."

At least a hundred pairs of eyes are on me. I'm sure they all think I'm about to get busted for having contraband in school, and I'm not sure they're wrong.

I push the scanner into Christina's lap. "Keep this for me? I don't think I should stroll into the office with it."

She tugs her own backpack up from the floor and puts the scanner inside. "No problem. Stay out of trouble?"

I think it might be too late for that. "I'll do my best."

I push myself up from the cafeteria bench, sling my pack over my shoulder, and walk away from her, wondering if my luck has just run out.

I walk down the hall at a decent clip. Ten minutes left in my lunch period. Maybe this isn't about the scanner or any of the pranks I've pulled; maybe it's some administrative glitch or a problem with my records. Maybe I won't even be late to my next class.

By the time I get to central administration, which is a grand name for the suite of cramped rooms filled with overworked, grumpy secretaries, I've almost convinced myself this is nothing.

My dad dashes that hope when he steps out of the guidance counselor's office and motions for me to follow him. His slate-gray gaze is flinty. His usually neat hair is disheveled, like it's either really windy outside or he's been running his hands through it, which I can't even picture. He stalks out of the office and leads me into a little alcove by the front exit. Just when I think he's going to keep walking right out of the school, he whirls around and grabs my upper arms.

"You broke into my lab," he says in a low voice.

His face is too close to mine, and I try to lean back, but he's not letting me go anywhere. Resignation fills me up. Lying is pointless right now. "Yeah, I did."

His expression twists. He looks like he didn't want to believe it, like my admission has physically hurt him. "How did you get in there?"

"Superglue method. After that it was just a matter of making the impression compound. Remember when you taught me that?"

"You were eight," he says, looking at me like I'm a stranger to him.

"I paid attention."

He shakes his head, and his bruising grasp on me tightens. I want to struggle, to shove him away, but now the bell is ringing, and my classmates are filling the halls. The last thing I need is for my dad to put me in a leg lock in front of the whole school.

"Give me your backpack," he says, already reaching for it.

I let him yank it off my arm. He rips it open and paws through it, his movements quick and impatient. His fist clenches over the strap. "Where is it, Tate?"

Oh, crap. Here we go. "Where is what?"

He steps close to me. "You know very well what I'm looking for. The scanner. It's not a toy, Tate. I need it back. Now."

It was a huge mistake for me to pawn that thing off on Christina. I almost hope she's given it to Will, but I know that won't happen. I entrusted it to her, and she would take that seriously. I tell myself I'm going to stay silent to keep her out of this mess, but the look on Dad's face is so foreign and frightening that it doesn't take long to jar my tongue loose. "I left it with some friends back in the cafeteria."

I don't miss the flash of intense disappointment and boiling rage in Dad's eyes before he looks away. He tosses my backpack toward the door of the guidance office as he pushes me down the hall. "Take me there. Go."

The wail of sirens reaches me from somewhere out in the city. My dad startles, his fingers practically cutting off the circulation in my arm. His eyes go wide, and he curses under his breath.

"What's going on?" I ask, lengthening my stride to keep

him from dragging me along. We turn the corner to the hall where the cafeteria lies.

He doesn't answer my question. His grip on my arm tightens again as the sirens sound off louder and closer.

My heart has picked up a heavy, hard rhythm. My blood is pounding in my ears. In all the years I've known him, my dad has operated at exactly three speeds. Mildly amused. Harshly disapproving. And utterly composed and calm, which is his default. He wears his cool like a bulletproof vest, like a full body tattoo. I thought it could never dent, never shatter, no matter how hard he got pushed, and Lord knows I've pushed him.

But right now, he looks nakedly freaked.

He steps close to the wall and pulls me along with him. Kids are heading to fifth period, streaming from the cavernous cafeteria through the three wide doors along the corridor. I spot Will's Mohawked head bobbing through the crowd. When he sees me, he does a double take, then gives me a nervous grin. One that says he hasn't missed the scary look on my dad's face—and that he's going to try to save me.

He saunters toward us. "Hey, Mr. Archer! What's up?"

"Is he the one you gave it to?" Dad asks, barely opening his mouth.

I give Will a hopeful once-over, but he's empty-handed. "No," I say quietly.

My dad doesn't even look at Will as he muscles past him. "Get to class."

Will flattens himself against the wall to keep from getting run over. All I can do is shoot him an apologetic shrug as I'm towed along.

This is much worse than I expected, and as we dart through the nearest entrance to the cafeteria, I know it's about to descend straight into unforgettably horrible. When she sees me coming, Christina stands up, holding her backpack against her chest. She must have been waiting for me, hoping I'd return before she had to go to class, and I wish she hadn't. Her eyes are round with alarm when she spots us, and I almost steer my dad away from her. I want to protect her from this moment, from my own father.

She unzips her pack and pulls the scanner out. She wants to protect me, too. She holds it out to my dad, whose attention is drawn to it—and her—immediately. He strides toward her, not even flinching as at least four of my classmates go ricocheting off him like bumper cars. We're battling the tide because everyone's trying to get to the exits, but none of them are a match for Frederick Archer's wide shoulders and brutal, single-minded purpose.

I try to get ahead of him, to get between them, but he shoves me away as he releases my arm. He rips the scanner from Christina's grasp so abruptly that she stumbles forward. Her face crumples as her hip hits the side of our table. I swing around, seeing red, ready to have it out with him right here.

He can yell at me all he wants. Hell, he can kick my ass from here to Jersey.

But I won't let him hurt Christina.

I open my mouth, explosive words cocked and ready to launch. My dad's not looking at me, though. He's not looking at Christina anymore, either. His eyes are on the far entrance to the cafeteria, over by the math and science wing and the back parking lot.

Three of New York's finest are standing in the archway, next to a guy in a black suit and tie. He's got the most sharply angled face I've ever seen, and his hair is buzzed military-style. His fierce gaze rakes the cafeteria with systematic precision as the C-lunch crowd pours past him, eager to begin their thirty-minute escape from the drudgery of the day. Buzz Cut's dark eyes sweep over them and narrow when they focus on someone standing to my left.

My father.

I glance at my dad and see the answering recognition in his face—undisguised hatred mixed with raw fear. It's such a foreign expression that I can't process it. All I want to do is get away from him.

"No," he growls, taking a step back. His fingers close over my shoulder. "Tate, I know you're angry with me. But we can fight later."

I wrench myself away from him. "Get off me."

He's acting so weird. Not one minute ago, he pretty much assaulted Christina for doing no more than trying to hand him the scanner *I* stuck her with. And now he looks so desperate that all I want is for him to go—without me. "Why don't you just—"

"*Tate.*" Dad grabs my arm again. "It's very important that we run. Now."

Just then, Mr. Lamb turns the corner and says something to the officers and Buzz Cut. My Game Theory teacher looks at us with a familiar smirk that tells me he's probably the one who called Buzz Cut in the first place. He points to me, like he's painting an invisible bull's-eye on my chest. And then he points at Christina, who shrinks back and turns to me with a look so frightened, it sends a frigid wave of guilt crashing over me. He obviously thinks she's wrapped up in this, too.

The officers and Buzz Cut move into the crowd, flowing along with it, coming straight for us.

My dad tries to tug me backward, but I don't budge. I can't take my eyes off one of the cops, who has his hand on the butt of his gun and his gaze locked on Christina. I don't know what Mr. Lamb told these guys. I don't have any idea what the fuck's going on. But I do know that if we leave Christina here, she could be in serious trouble.

"I'm not going anywhere unless we can bring her, too," I say, shaking off my father's grasp and reaching for Christina's hand.

Her fingers are icy cold as she laces them with mine. She hesitates as she looks back at the cops, who are still about eight tables away, advancing on us slowly, fanning out across the cafeteria. When she sees the way that one cop is homing in on her like prey, a shiver courses through her body, sending her terror jittering up my arm.

My dad glares at her. For a moment, I'm certain he's going to refuse, but then he looks at my face, and surrender softens his expression before it hardens once again. "Fine. Let's go."

I hesitate, still fighting all my instincts. You're not supposed to run from the cops if you've done nothing wrong.

"*Tate, wir müssen fliehen. Jetzt. Jetzt!*" my father barks, snapping me out of my trance.

We have to escape. Now. Clipped German words, tinged with pure desperation.

When he sees the understanding in my expression, he pivots on his heel and runs for the exit that will lead us back to the central office and the front of the school. An oblivious student with her head down walks into his path and he crashes into her, sending food, plates, cups, and plastic cutlery flying everywhere. He staggers but is moving forward again in an instant, hurdling over the stunned girl with spaghetti in her hair. I catch Christina around the waist to keep her from falling as her feet slide through salad dressing and pasta sauce. We scoot through the mess and pelt after my father, only to run into him as he comes to a full stop.

Two more cops are blocking our escape route.

I don't hesitate. I yank Christina toward the lunch line.

"There's a back door through the kitchen," I whisper to my father as I pull her past him. The two sets of cops are closing in, so I let go of Christina and make like I'm going to run for the middle exit, and they all move to head me off, which takes them farther away from the kitchen.

All the students are frozen now, their gazes darting between us and the cops, dumbfounded expressions on every face. I reverse direction and plow through them easily. Christina's right behind me as I jump up on the table that holds the stacks of trays and plates, which slide and crash to the floor as we scramble over them. I vault over the glass hood that protects the food and land in a crouch next to a startled cafeteria worker. I help Christina over the hood and push her toward the door to the kitchen. My father leaps over the hood a second later and heads straight for the door, salad dressing dripping down his face from the earlier collision.

As I follow him, my gaze gets snagged for a split second on that gray-haired lunch lady, one of the few people in the cafeteria to send off blue light under the scanner's glare. She stares up at me like she thinks I'm a terrorist. I wonder what we have in common, and if that blue light is the reason five cops and scary Buzz Cut man are now leaping onto the tray table so they can get to us.

I tear my eyes from the lunch lady's, zip past her into the kitchen, and slam the door behind us. Then I lock it. I don't want to think about what will happen if Buzz Cut catches us.

SIX

THE KITCHEN STAFF, THEIR PLASTIC HATS AND APRONS streaked with moisture in the sweltering room, all look up as we come through. Their expressions range from alarmed to disapproving, like they're mad we've invaded their turf.

"Get down," I shout, my voice cracking with my own terror. If I don't take action, one of them is going to open the door for the cops. "They have guns! They came in dressed as police, but they're taking hostages!"

A few of the lunch ladies shriek and flatten themselves against the metal shelving, sending cans of industrial-grade pasta sauce flying to the tiled floor. Several other workers crouch behind vats of spaghetti. One swarthy guy waves a giant slotted spoon in the air, like he's going to take on the invaders single-handedly. I put my head down and focus on getting to the exit, taking a tiny detour to grab a two-gallon plastic container from one of the shelves.

My dad is almost to the back door, his cell phone at his ear, his words staccato and commanding, talking so fast, I can't catch any of it. Christina is close behind him, pale as a ghost. I look over my shoulder to see all the kitchen workers staring at the door to the cafeteria. The cops are pounding on it, shouting, "Police! Open the door!" over and over again. But I've created just enough uncertainty to hold them in place for a few seconds.

I squat low by the heavy metal door to the outside, feeling the breeze at my back as Christina holds it open for me. I wrench the cap off the container in my hands. A few seconds later, I've laid a little vegetable-oil welcome mat for anyone who chases us out this way. Again, it will gain us only a few seconds, but I'm thinking we need every advantage we can get.

Christina takes off, and I weave through a set of Dumpsters and recycling containers, hot on her heels. She's fast as hell and agile, too, and she streaks into the open and sprints behind my father, who's several strides ahead of us, cell phone in one hand and the scanner in the other. He runs straight up the sidewalk. A few faces are pressed against the classroom windows, no doubt happy for the distraction. A black SUV skids around the corner, from the street at the front of the school, and accelerates toward us. For a second I think we've got another enemy, but my dad waves his arms at the vehicle.

He brought a getaway car?

His powerful strides don't slow as he looks over his shoulder, as if to gauge our distance from him. As soon as I see the expression on his face, I know the cops are closing in. I don't even turn around to look. Instead, I kick it into overdrive and close the distance between me and Christina. We're a few car lengths from the SUV, and whoever's inside has thrown the passenger-side door open. We're going to make it.

My father doesn't dive through the open door like I expect him to, though. He turns back and runs toward me as Christina sprints past him and ducks into the SUV. Before I have a chance to wonder why, I hear a series of echoing cracks and the windshield of the car next to me shatters. A voice back by the Dumpsters yells something, but I can't make it out. My dad is right behind me a second later, shielding me with his body. The police are firing at us like we're terrorists or criminals, like we're a threat, and I have no idea why. They're not supposed to shoot at unarmed civilians, right? Especially right next to a school?

My brain is a soupy fog of questions and fear as we stumble the last few feet toward the SUV while the world explodes around us. My dad flinches and falls against my back with his full weight, nearly knocking me over. The groan that rolls from his throat is pure, animal pain. He reaches around me and presses the scanner into my chest. "Take this," he says, sinking to one knee.

I turn toward him, the scanner dangling from my fist. The back of my father's pressed white shirt is blossoming with red.

The driver of the SUV, a muscular young guy with a baseball cap pulled low, opens his driver's-side door and stands up on the step, aiming a handgun at the cops. "Get him in the car! It's bulletproof!" he roars at us just before he sends a barrage of bullets toward our pursuers.

I am vaguely aware of the shouts of the cops as they dive for cover, giving us a moment to get to safety. But I can't get myself to move, can't feel my aching leg, can't see that SUV, the only way we're going to get out of this alive. I'm too busy staring at my dad, my limitless, perfect, invulnerable dad, who's clutching at his back with scrabbling fingers. He spits blood onto the sidewalk at my feet. My stomach heaves.

Christina, her pale face set with determination, jumps from the vehicle and tugs the scanner from my grasp. She gets on my dad's other side and helps me drag him to the back door of the SUV. My dad's driver is still shooting, adding another clip whenever he runs out of bullets. He's the reason we're not perforated right now.

I jump into the backseat after Christina, hook my arms under my dad's, and heft him onto the seat.

"Hey!" I yell at the driver. "We're in! Let's go!"

As the guy takes several more shots, I lean around my dad and reach for the passenger-door handle. A bullet buries itself in the panel a scant inch above my hand. I flinch, then slam the door shut. A flash in the rearview mirror has me whipping around to see a few cops racing toward us. They're coming at us from both sides.

"Get us out of here!" I shout as our driver starts to slide into the SUV.

He never makes it. He jerks and falls to the side, his blood splattering on the windshield. I press my face against the window and see him splayed out on the asphalt. He's been shot right in the center of his forehead.

Christina's blue eyes lock with mine, and there's this moment of absolute stillness. Probably only a fraction of a second, but it feels like an eternity. Her shocked expression mirrors my own. I want to reach for her, but I can't move. I want to save her, but I'm powerless. An hour ago, we were joking in the lunchroom, and now we're surrounded by blood and death. And it's all my fault. I did this to us, brought this down on our heads. My bleeding father is next to me, slumped against the seat, and our driver is dead, all because I was stupid enough to bring that damn scanner to school. I know that's why they're after us, and none of it would have happened if it hadn't been for me.

I don't know what Christina reads in my face, but her eyes flare with something white hot and knife sharp.

My girlfriend throws herself over the front seat and slams the driver's-side door shut. With no hesitation at all, she gets behind the wheel and hits the gas. A crashing *thunk* lurches the SUV just as we start to move forward again. One of the cops is clinging to the back, his feet on the bumper. Christina hunches over the steering wheel and peers through the blood-spattered windshield, swerving back and forth as we streak past the other cops, who are shooting at our tires now, like they don't even care that their buddy is hanging on to the back and could get hit with a stray bullet. We're moving so fast that we somehow make it past them, and as we do, I get one last look at Buzz Cut, whose face is rigid as he waves his arms and shouts at the cops, probably telling them to chase after us. But with one heavy, sudden pull of the wheel, Christina muscles the SUV around a sharp corner. The cop on the back yelps as he's thrown onto the road. He lands in this broken sprawl right next to the wheel of a school bus. I'm not sure if he's dead or alive—and not sure which one I'd prefer, a thought so filled with *wrong* that it turns my stomach.

We speed down a side street. Christina, her breaths coming from her in high-pitched bursts, threads her way through the busy roads like a NASCAR driver before she hits the West Side Highway. It has to be taking everything she has to hold it together, but she's doing it. For me. For us.

I peer out the rear window. No one seems to be chasing us, as far as I can tell.

But we didn't get away cleanly.

My father moans and raises his head. My chest caves in as I see the slick, black-red mess that's dripping onto the seats.

I peel my shirt off, bunch it up, and press it against his

back. He clenches his teeth and arches, but I don't let up. He's bleeding too much. Too much. No one should bleed this much.

"Dad, this is bad," I say, wishing my voice wasn't cracking. "We need to get you to a hospital."

He looks at me, his mouth halfway open, gulping air like he's drowning. He shakes his head. "Too dangerous. Keep driving," he calls to Christina, whose blond head is still low over the wheel. Her gaze is glued to the road. But her shoulders are shaking, and I know she's crying now.

"Listen to me, Tate," my father says sharply, dragging my attention back to him. He sounds like himself, and it fills me with hope. "The scanner. It's important. It's—" He hisses and clutches at his side. Blood leaks around his fingers and turns my insides to acid and ice. I can't tell if that's the exit wound or he's been shot twice, but neither seems good.

He blows a halting breath through gray-pink lips. "I wanted to tell you this only when you were ready. I wanted to wait until then . . . but—" He looks me in the eye and chuckles. He actually chuckles. "I've waited so long to say this that I don't even know how to do it."

"Just tell me," I say, all air and no command, all little boy and no man. I'm buried in this, like I'm in a grave and they're shoveling dirt over my head. I can't breathe.

"I protected you from this for too long." He presses his lips together and watches me for a few seconds. Then he says, "We're not alone here."

"What are you talking about?" I'm trying to translate, because I know this is huge, but I don't speak this particular language.

"We're not alone on this planet. We haven't been for a very long time."

I stare at him, my mouth opening and closing a few times around a word I can't seem to say out loud. Is he talking about . . . ?

"An alien race," my dad says. "We call them the H2."

The laugh comes burbling out of me before I can stop it. "The Archer family responsibility . . . is aliens," I say stupidly.

He exhales a shaky sigh. "The H2 invaded about four hundred years ago. They look human, so they were able to blend in and breed with the population. But their elite—their leadership—they infiltrated governments all over the world."

I watch his face for any signal that he's making a joke, but it's not there. "Infiltrated?"

"They hold positions of influence in every country. Some of the major corporations—but not all."

"How many humans are left?"

He sucks a gurgling breath through his teeth. "A third of the population and falling fast." That's why he and George were talking about world population stuff at breakfast. And that's what those numbers on the screen in his lab were showing, too, I'll bet. I—

Dad abruptly tries to push himself upright, but his trembling hand slips in the blood pooling beneath him, and he falls back to the seat. He closes his mouth and grits his teeth, but I hear the wrenching moan he keeps locked in his throat. When he catches his breath, he says, "Very few know the truth. It's a secret the H2 are determined to keep. And it's nearly impossible to tell human from H2."

This can't be true. It doesn't make sense. I can't accept it. All my arguments tumble around in my head and come shooting from my mouth unformed. "But then—how could they—we're not—this isn't—"

"Some of us have guarded this truth throughout the generations, even though the H2 Core have suppressed or discredited any attempts to reveal it."

His eyes meet mine, and suddenly I know exactly what he's telling me. It hits me like a subway train, knocking the breath out of me. "This is why, isn't it?" I ask airlessly, hoping he'll understand what I mean.

This is why I've spent years learning history. Math. Science. Self-defense. This is why I get up at four every morning. Why he pushes me every day to go beyond what I think I should have to do. Beyond what I think I can achieve. It's not because he wants me to be perfect.

It's because he wants me to be strong.

He nods. "The Archers have fought to protect the evidence of what happened, the true historic record—and our species— for nearly four hundred years. But it's more . . . more than that."

Drops hit my forearms, and I look around in confusion.

It's not raining. We're inside a car. And then I feel the tears streaking down my face. I don't know when I stopped laughing and started crying, and I'm not sure it matters. I reach for my father's hand, and he lets me take it. For the first time since God-knows-when, I'm his boy and he's my dad, and I wonder how we lost this. I squeeze his fingers, and he winces, but he doesn't complain.

All these years I've resented him. Defied him. Snuck around behind his back. Even hated him. And he's borne it all, patiently, impassively. Like a wall of stone I've been beating my head against, never straying from his purpose—to prepare me for this moment.

And I'm not ready. I'm just me. I'm not him.

"I don't know what I'm supposed to do," I whisper. "I don't—"

"The scanner." He coughs wetly, spraying tiny droplets of saliva and blood over the front of his shirt. "When the H2 first arrived, they crashed . . . One of our ancestors found something . . . and kept it secret . . ." He pauses for a moment, maybe trying to gather energy to speak, or maybe trying to decide what's most important to say. "The scanner is made from H2 technology and must be kept safe. If it's used the wrong way, so many would die . . ."

My fists clench with a diffuse sort of rage as the warm stickiness of my father's blood, now having seeped all the way through my shirt, trickles between my fingers. "Why don't we fight them? How can they be allowed to take over like this?"

My father's lips twitch. "It's not about that. An interspecies conflict would lead to devastating casualties. The scanner should stop that, not cause it."

An alien race has invaded the earth, is living among us, and is apparently running the show. And I've just done exactly what my father was trying to avoid—I've exposed his invention to the public.

Deep inside me, fault lines crack and shift, tearing chasms of fear and regret right through my heart. My fist shoots out, punching the seat over and over, causing Christina to flinch and cry out, but I can't hold myself back.

"This is my fault!" I howl. God, I want to jump out of the car and smash myself on the asphalt. I want to shatter on impact, break into nothing. I am a fucking waste of space.

My father's hand closes over my arm, but his grip is weak and falls away instantly, leaving a streak of red along my skin.

"Tate. *Tate.* Calm down, son. Listen to me," he says softly.

I have no idea how many times he has to say it before he reaches me, before his voice halts the cataclysm inside me, if only for a moment. "I kept this secret from you for too long," he says when my arm falls limp into my lap and I sag against the seat next to him. "This is *my* fault. If I had taken the time to think about it, to think about *who you are,* I would have realized you're just like me. You could never sit back and take things. You fight. You fight *so* hard, son. And because I kept you in the dark, you fought *me.* I thought . . . I had more time."

I bow my head, averting my eyes from my father's broken body. He thinks I'm like him. And I realize: I want to be. I want to earn the words he just said. I want them to be the truth. I glance at his face. I want him to keep looking at me like he is right now, and I want to feel worthy of that.

He touches my fingers with his, and I sit up, breathing again, ready to do whatever he says. "That man, back at the school. The one in the suit."

"The guy with the buzz cut?" I ask, recalling the way my father looked at him—both hatred and fear at once.

Dad nods. "His name is Race Lavin."

"And he's H2."

"More than that. He works for the Core, their central leadership. He's very dangerous."

"Aren't they all dangerous?"

"Not all H2 are the same. Most don't know they even *are* H2. Those in power want to keep it that way. If they knew what this technology was—and it seems like Race suspects it— they would suppress it or use it as a tool to oppress humans. But it's crucial that it be used in the right way . . ."

I curse, but it's more like a whimper, slipping from my mouth and fluttering weightlessly in the air. My dad's face is so pale, grayish white, and he's fighting to keep breathing. In the back of my mind, a terrifying realization shears loose, a glacier sliding along the inside of my skull, slow and frigid. I push back against it with everything I have, trying to slow it down before it crushes me.

"Lavin is an enforcer," my father is saying. "And he'll do anything to maintain H2 domination."

As he talks about Race, my father's eyes flash with rage. If I didn't know better, I'd say my dad has some history with this guy.

"I wish I could protect you now, Tate." His voice breaks. Not from pain. From fear. For me. I can tell by the look in his eyes. "They'll come after the scanner with everything they have. But you also have to be careful with the fifty . . ."

His eyes flutter shut. "The fifty what? Dad," I say softly when he doesn't answer. "Hey. Stay with me. Please." I need to keep this connection with him, but it's like a snowflake on my skin, melting fast.

His eyes open halfway. He looks so tired, but I can tell he's trying to be strong, to smile at me and reassure me, to be my father, if only for a few more moments. He looks at the device on the floor at his feet, the invention I treated like my personal toy. "The scanner reflects blue off humans," he says wearily. "And red off H2. But it also—" He coughs, his whole body shuddering.

I remember the cafeteria. A sea of red dotted with blue. When he said we were outnumbered by the H2, he wasn't exaggerating. "What am I supposed to do with it?" I whisper.

His eyes meet mine, and they're so desperate, shouting a million instructions, begging me to understand. "This technology is the key to our survival, and when the time comes, when you . . . it's Josephus . . ." He trails off, and something inside him seems to let go, subtly uncoiling, silently giving up the fight. His gaze goes unfocused, the sharp intelligence and ruthless determination evaporating, fading away forever.

Lost, broken, slabs of me falling away, I raise my head and look at Christina.

Whose skin flashed red under the light of the scanner.

From her posture, trembling and tight, I can tell she's heard everything my father said.

And she doesn't say a word. She just keeps driving.

SEVEN

I AM SITTING NEXT TO MY DEAD FATHER IN THE BACK-
seat of a blood-smeared, bullet-pocked SUV driven by my girlfriend. Who is an alien.

I can't summon any intelligent thoughts into my head,
because the complete batshit craziness of this situation is
wrapped around me like a hungry anaconda. *H2? Josephus? I
have to be careful with the fifty . . . somethings? What the hell does
that even mean?* I can't breathe; my chest is tight with grief. I
can't stop shivering; my teeth are chattering with the rhythm of
a jackhammer. I can't look anywhere but the horizon, the road
fading to a pinpoint in the distance, because I don't want to see
him, don't want to look at his ruined body and be reminded
again that he'd be alive if it weren't for me.

Almost exactly twenty-four hours ago, I was in my dad's
lab, kissing Christina. Running my hands over her curves. My

whole universe was just her and me. My only care was making the space between us disappear. And now . . . there are a lot of things I'd like to make disappear, but the space between us isn't one of them.

I have no idea how long it takes me to notice the buzzing coming from my dad's pocket. It stops, then starts again. Stops, then starts again. Someone wants to reach him very badly. I flex my numbed fingers and steady my hand so I can reach into his pocket and pull the phone out. The screen reads *Alexander*. It's Brayton, George's boss at Black Box, the guy they were talking about going to meet today. I push the button and mutely hold it to my ear. I can't quite get my tongue to work.

"Fred! What the hell happened? What's your status? You're going north—where are you headed?"

I look at the SUV's dash, remembering what George told my dad this morning: *He's sending a vehicle for you at noon.* This thing obviously belongs to Black Box, and it must have some kind of GPS tracking device in it.

Brayton is still talking, firing words faster than I can process them. Then I realize he's just saying the same.thing, over and over again, loud enough that Christina must hear him all the way in the front seat, because she flinches every time he says *Fred*.

"He's dead," I whisper.

"Who is this?" Brayton asks, his voice flat—but full of threat.

"It's Tate."

He exhales right into the phone, filling my ear with static. "Tate. All right, son, where's your father?"

I can't believe he's going to make me say it again. Every word cuts deeper than the last. "He was shot. He's dead."

There's a sound like he's covered the phone, and I hear his muffled voice saying something to someone in the background. Then he's back. "My God, Tate, I'm so sorry. I knew they got Peter, but I thought the rest of you got away."

Peter McClaren. The guy who graduated from Yale and started working for Black Box a few weeks ago. The guy who saved our lives at the cost of his own. Was he human, like me? Like my dad? Does his family know they've lost him yet? I . . . Brayton's voice is a constant drone in my ear. "Tate. Tate? Where are you headed?"

"I don't know," I mumble. "We're just driving."

"We?"

Christina's shoulders are trembling again, and I blink and look away. "I'm with a friend."

"And do you have your father's invention with you?"

It's on the floor of the backseat, next to my father's neatly polished shoe. Droplets of his blood decorate the toe. "Yeah. Wait—how do you know about that?"

"It's something he made for Black Box, and it needs to be secured. We want to get you as far away from the city as we can. Can you make it to Princeton? We have a safe house there. Can you meet us?"

Safe. That sounds good. "I'll meet you at the stadium." Like I'm watching myself from the outside, I wonder why that's the first place to come to mind. Then I remember that, as a Princeton alum, my dad took me to their games once or twice every year.

Those are some of the very few happy memories I have with him.

I rub at the ache in my chest and open my mouth to say we should meet somewhere else, but before I get a word out, Brayton says, "Sounds good—I'll pick you up. I can be there by two thirty. They seem to be keeping the whole incident at your school quiet, but keep your head down and be careful."

I look at the phone and can't believe it's not even one o'clock yet. This day has lasted a lifetime already. "Okay." It comes out quiet and strained, but he seems to hear me, because he hangs up.

My hand drops into my lap, and I stare at the phone, its smooth screen smudged with my fingerprints. I hit the CON-TACTS button and scroll through, staring at a bunch of names I don't recognize. And then I come to one I do.

Mitra Archer.

My mother.

Who happens to be a professor of biochemistry at Princeton.

I hit SEND before I know what I'm doing. But as it starts to ring, I realize how much I need to hear her voice, how she is the only one who can make me feel safe. I know she left us, but I'm still so raw from what's happened that I just need a parent.

And my mom's the only one I have left. "Pick up," I whisper. "Please pick up."

She doesn't. Her cool, confident voice tells me she's not available, that I should leave a message. But I can't. What the hell am I supposed to say? So I hang up, and then waste several minutes composing and erasing a text that in the end reads *Coming to Princeton. Please call me as soon as you get this.*

It isn't until I send it that I realize she'll think it's from my dad. I lower my forehead to my knees and suck wind, trying to get my heart to slow down, trying to navigate the nuclear wasteland between my ears. This whole situation is so massively fucked, which makes it doubly important that I get ahold of myself. I need to think. I need to figure this out.

"Which stadium?" asks Christina.

"What?"

It comes out of me sounding hard-edged, irritable. I hear her exhale a long breath before she speaks again. "You said you were going to a stadium," she says, a bit louder. "Which one?"

"Princeton," I say.

"Then I have to take the bridge to the turnpike, and we have to get gas while we're still in New York." The vehicle slows. "Is there . . . is there anything you can cover him with?"

Oh. God.

In full-on zombie mode, I look into the back and see there's a tarp over some computer equipment. I yank it up and hold my breath as I cover my dad's face and body with the tarp and ease him onto the floor of the SUV. I use my ruined, soaked shirt to mop up what I can of the blood on the seat.

Christina exits the highway and pulls into a gas station near the George Washington Bridge. I scoot low, because I'm half naked back here, and we're already likely to catch someone's attention; the vehicle might be bulletproof, but there are pock-marks in the windows and probably all over the metal.

"I think the glass is tinted," she says when she sees me duck. She stops next to a pump. Her voice cracks as she says, "I don't think people will notice the blood on my shirt because it's black . . ." She squares her shoulders. "I'll be right back."

She gets out and unscrews the cap for the gas tank. Her face is pale, her expression solemn. I watch the pink tip of her tongue slide over her bottom lip, this tiny mannerism I know so well, one that usually drives me wild. But now it leaves me cold. She's wearing this beautiful disguise, this skin I long to touch. All this time, it's fooled me. I wonder what she's like on the inside, what makes her different from me. I know her blood runs red; I had to watch her limp off the soccer field earlier this season, her knee raw and dripping after she col-lided with another player's cleats. I know her heart beats; in my luckiest moment I've had my ear pressed to her chest as her fingers stroked through my hair. I know she breathes and sleeps. Hell, I know she pees, because she always needs to go at the most inconvenient moments, like right when we're arriv-ing at the theater, ten minutes late for the movie.

Despite all of those things that make her normal, that make her like me, I know what my father said. This girl, this gorgeous girl who is right now tucking her hair behind the delicate shell of her ear, who is slipping on sunglasses to cover her tear-stained face, is an alien.

Just like the ones who shot my dad.

Just like most of the people in the *world*, apparently. I look down at my dad's legs, which are dead weight on top of my own feet. He wouldn't have lied. He wouldn't have screwed with me. He knew what was happening. He knew we were in danger. He was telling me the truth. He was trying to tell me everything, but ran out of time.

When I raise my head, Christina is gone.

It's like an electric jolt to my system, sending prickling shocks from my brain to my limbs. I look in all directions and process only the random stuff, the trucker with bloodshot eyes and sweaty hat-hair at pump number three, the hot pink sandals of the little girl holding her mother's hand as they walk into the convenience store, the bumper sticker that reads *Nobody Likes Your Celtic Arm Tattoo* on the back of a banged-up Honda.

The dread knots inside me as I swivel my head, looking for Christina. Just as I'm panicking, she walks out of the store, still wearing her sunglasses, clothed in a new Yankees sweatshirt and clutching a plastic bag. But instead of returning to the SUV, she heads over to a college-aged guy at one of the pumps a few rows down and strikes up a conversation with him. A minute later, he hands her his cell phone. With one glance over her shoulder at our car, she starts to dial.

And I start to sweat.

She wouldn't, would she? Call the authorities? Turn me in?

Why *wouldn't* she? Dad said most of the H2 don't know they're not human, but who's to say she hasn't known all along? What if that's the reason she's with me in the first place? Lamb was obviously some kind of plant—what if she is, too? She knows I'm in possession of something the H2 want, and that we're on our way to meet one of my dad's colleagues. This is her chance to call us in. She'd probably be rewarded for her loyalty to them.

Right as she hangs up, hands the guy back his cell, and comes back to the SUV, another Tate interrupts my mental meltdown, the me from this morning, from a few hours ago. This is *Christina*. I *know* her. I—

She unhooks the pump, then opens the door and pokes her head inside. Without taking off her shades, she holds the bag out to me. "I got you a shirt."

I stare at her for a moment, and all I can think is that I need to see her eyes. I'd know the truth if I could only see her eyes. But then I shake myself into action, take the bag, and peek inside. It's a dark green Jets T-shirt. I hate the Jets, but hey, what the fuck does it matter right now? I pull it out and tug it on.

Christina climbs up into the driver's seat and turns around. "Are . . . you going to come sit in the front seat?"

I guess I should. Yes, I definitely should. I should stop wondering if she's just called Race Lavin down on my head, and I should sit in the front with her.

I climb over the seat and strap myself in while she puts the SUV in motion. As we pull out of the gas station, I swear that every single freaking person turns their head to watch. The fat trucker. The little girl. The Honda driver. All of them. Everyone. I wonder how many of them are human. I could grab the scanner from the backseat and find out, but I don't think I want to know.

I squeeze my eyes shut and rub my hands over them.

Christina gets back on the highway, heading over the bridge and onto the southbound Jersey turnpike. Her slender fingers are gripping the steering wheel so hard that it looks like her bones are going to come popping through her skin. I stare at them flexing, turning white, so human. So *human*.

But she's not.

"I'm sorry about your dad," she says.

I grit my teeth and turn toward the window. The scenery is a hazy gray-green sea beyond the glass, and the view doesn't sharpen up until I blink a few times. "What an original sentiment," I snap. "It took you this long to think of it?"

"I can't believe you said that." Her voice is thick, like she's going to cry.

I exhale a sharp breath through my nose. "Why? What are you sorry for? You still have your parents. They're happily married aliens without a care in the world."

She taps the brakes to avoid colliding with a car transporter in front of us. "Tate, I know you've been through a lot, but—"

"I've *been through a lot*? Are you taking your lines from Generic Condolences 101? Do you have the brochure in your pocket? Christina, you're one of them. I would think you'd be happy he's dead."

"What?" Her voice is all trembly and high-pitched. "I didn't even know I was 'one of them' until about half an hour ago!"

"Well, congratulations, you're on the winning side." Somewhere, deep in the convoluted folds of my mind, there's a small voice that's shouting for me to shut up, but this feels too savagely good. I've got a target now, a place to aim all my rage, all my grief.

Christina's quiet for a moment, but a pink flush is slowly spreading across her cheeks. When she speaks again, it's almost a growl. "You're being an asshole. Of course I'm not happy your dad's dead. That's the stupidest thing I've ever heard."

"Try looking at it from a *human* perspective," I snarl.

She swerves into the middle lane and accelerates. "Oh my God, Tate! You're the one who snuck into your father's lab. You're the one who stole that freaking scanner. And you're the one who brought it to school!"

I punch the plastic window frame. "So it's my fault he's dead? That's what you're saying? That a bunch of trigger-happy aliens had nothing to do with it?"

"I'm saying *I'm* not your enemy!" she shrieks.

"You're one of them!" I shout. I'm gone. Totally gone. My head is one giant pulse, throbbing, beating red and raw. "You called them just now, didn't you? You told them where we were going and who we were meeting! That's what you were doing, wasn't it?"

"That's what you think of me?" Christina veers back into the slow lane and shoots down an exit ramp. "I was calling my freaking *parents,* you jerk! Did you think they'd be cool with me disappearing from school?"

Even in all my craziness, I know she's driving too fast. The metal poles of street lamps are flitting by in a steel blur, along with signs telling me we're in Secaucus. She skids off the exit ramp and careens onto a city street, and for a second I actually think we're going to roll over.

Tears are streaming down her face now. "I need to go home! I was an idiot to come with you!" she cries. She wipes her cheeks with the back of her hand and sniffles, but she barely slows down, even when she takes the sharp left into the tiny lot of a sparsely wooded playground, cutting right in front of a city bus.

We skid to a stop next to a sign indicating there's a train station up the road. She rips the keys from the ignition and flings them at me. They hit my chest and fall to the floor.

"I'll find my own way home." She throws the door open, then loops her arm through her backpack and takes off. I sit there, watching her pistoning strides, trying to catch my breath. The red is fading fast from my vision, and that voice in my head is louder now.

It's telling me what a douchebag I am.

As the curtain of sanity descends, too little too late as always, I see it all. I dragged her into this. She has done nothing but help me, stick by me, believe in me. If she'd been in on it, if she'd known who was after me, she could have refused to come. She could have left me then and there. But she didn't. Instead, she risked her life. She threw herself into the driver's seat—when its last occupant had just had his brains blown out.

"Goddamn it," I grind out, and then I'm out of the car and running after her. "Christina!"

She doesn't slow at all. I stumble over a crumbled patch of sidewalk, and by the time I've caught my balance, she's made it across this huge intersection. And of course, the light has just changed.

I'll never reach her on foot. I run back to the SUV and scrabble for the keys. This isn't the safest area, and she's all alone. And once again, it's my fault.

I pull out of the parking lot and head down the road, my thoughts landing strike after strike on the inside of my skull. *Idiot. Idiot. Find her. Find her.* The light at the intersection turns green as I get to it, finally a lucky break, and I don't even slow down as—

Everything around me explodes.

EIGHT

I AM DIMLY AWARE OF MY WORLD TILTING, OF IMPACT that drives the air from my lungs, of glass flying, of pain. All the other sounds fade away except this awful *skid-scrape-rend-shriek* . . . silence.

I am lying on my side, my head resting against the deflating curtain airbag, the only thing between me and the asphalt. I look out at the wheels of cars and the feet running toward what used to be the bloody windshield but is now a clear view as far as my eye can see. Which is not very far.

"Tate!"

"Christina?" I try to say, but I choke on something and start to cough. Blood. It's dripping from my nose, my mouth. I gag and spit, trying to get the metal taste off my tongue.

Then her face is right there, where the windshield used to be. "Oh God," she whispers.

"You came back," I mumble. My hands are tingling. So are my legs. I look down at myself. They're still attached to me, and I seem to be in control of them. Kind of.

Her face crumples as she watches me, and she draws in a shaky breath. "Can you unbuckle your seat belt?"

"No problem." I sound like I'm drunk. It feels that way, too, only without the happy buzz.

With fingers that feel as thick as sausages, I fumble with my seat belt and finally get it undone. Christina reaches for me. She strokes my face, then hooks her fingers in my armpit and pulls while I push. I slowly slide-crawl-flounder over glass and gravel, and then I'm resting with my back against the hood of the SUV, which is lying on its side at the edge of an intersection, half on the sidewalk, its ass-end out in the road.

Christina uses her sleeve to wipe the blood from my face. "Where are you hurt?" she asks.

"Nowhere." All of me is cold, but nothing hurts, not really.

"You've got a cut over your eye, and your nose is bleeding."

With a feather-light touch, her fingers flutter along my nose. I wince as sensation returns and she draws back quickly. I run my own fingers over the mess, less gentle, and nothing seems broken or out of place. My fingers are slick with blood, and I wipe them on my shirt.

Someone yells something about an ambulance. Christina squeezes my hand and stands up to peer over the hood, then takes a quick step back. She drops down on her stomach, and then all I can see is her sneakers protruding out of the shattered windshield. She scoots out of the wreckage a second later and crawls over to me. "Can you stand up?" she asks quietly.

A guy with a scraggly blond ponytail brandishes his cell phone as he leans around Christina. "Hey, dude, you all right? We called an ambulance for you and the other driver. They're on their way."

There's something in the stormy blue of Christina's eyes, something she's trying to tell me. But my head is so foggy, and all around me there's noise, and I can't quite make sense of it. A siren. A cry. A shout. A honking horn. Skidding tires on asphalt.

Christina takes my face in her hands, forcing me to look at her. "Get. Up. I think they're coming."

I blink, focusing on her mouth, translating the words. "The ambulance?"

She shakes her head, and then scoots next to me and gets her shoulders under my arm. She wraps her arm around my waist. "I'm sorry. I know you're hurting. But they're going to catch us if you don't get up. Please, baby. Get up."

"The scanner—"

"I got it."

"And my dad," I say stupidly as she struggles beneath my weight.

"When the ambulance comes, they'll take care of him," she says. Her grip on me tightens, her fingers pressing against my ribs and digging into my forearm. "He'd want you to get to safety, Tate. You know that."

I can't find the words to argue. She helps me to my feet and holds me tight as I get my balance. She leads me around the back of the wreckage and onto the sidewalk. Sirens shriek nearby, and three cruisers stutter-stop their way into the intersection, blocking traffic from all sides. A hundred yards or so away, I see the flashing lights of what is probably an ambulance.

In the middle of the intersection, a crowd is gathered around a blue sedan with its front end smashed in. The windshield has a circular spiderweb fracture in it. Where the driver's head hit.

"Guy ran the red light," the blond guy says, shaking his head. "I saw the whole thing. He didn't even slow down."

Christina's lips are against my ear. "Look up the road. That way."

She angles her head. I squint and see three black SUVs in the stopped line of traffic, a block away. The passenger door of the one at the front opens. A man gets out and shades his face with his hand as he peers in our direction. It's Race Lavin.

"How did they find us?" Christina asks, all breath and no noise. And then she looks at me. "I didn't do this, Tate. I swear."

I think she's sincere, though I'm not exactly at my most perceptive. But as Christina guides me toward the rear of the SUV, my gaze snags on its bumper. No bigger than a mouse, clinging to the rear panel, glinting dully in the light. "Could be a tracking device," I say. "Remember the cop who jumped onto the back?"

Christina's fingers brush over it as she leads me away. "That must be it."

Race waves his arms and points to us, and the doors of the black SUVs all open at the same time.

My thoughts snap back into focus as a jolt of adrenaline roars through me. "Come on!" I tug Christina's hand and stagger away from the wreckage of the SUV as the thing starts to smoke and spark. A woman standing on the curb screeches something about fire, and everyone scatters as ominous popping sounds come from under the hood. We're caught up in the crowd, letting them carry us away from the intersection— and the people chasing us. Christina drags me all the way to the front of the throng of panicked people, who are thinking more about their own safety than the fact that we're about to leave the scene of an accident.

"The train station," she pants as we break away and veer down a side street. Her eyes are fixed on the blue-and-white sign up ahead that tells us it's close.

And we run. I don't do anything but dog her steps as she leads the way, her steady, freakishly fast strides giving me my rhythm. She looks over her shoulder a few times, her hair whipping around her face, but keeps sprinting as her pack bumps up and down on her shoulders. I don't even bother trying to check behind us—I'm so off-balance right now that if I try, I'll go flying.

A few blocks later, she swings herself over a fence separating the warehouse district from the train station area, and I follow, losing my footing and ending in a sprawl on the asphalt. She cries out and turns, but I'm already using the fence to pull myself to my feet. It gives me the chance to see if we're being pursued, but there's no one there. I know they're coming, but maybe we've lost them. Maybe we'll catch a break.

But I'm not taking anything for granted. Not anymore.

I spin around and kick myself off the fence.

"Don't slow down for me again," I snap, wiping the blood and sweat from my face.

She takes off, straight for the enormous commuter parking lot. She ducks low and weaves through the parked cars, then reaches back and pushes me down between two massive SUVs.

"How do I look?" she asks, breathing hard.

I blink. "What?"

"How. Do. I. Look," she says more slowly, like she's afraid I might have brain damage.

So I focus on her face, which is glowing with exertion. "Awesome, all things considered."

She tucks her hair behind her ears, pulls a tube of lip gloss from her pocket, and dabs it on as I watch in bemused silence. "I'll be right back." She skims her way around the SUV and out of sight. A second later, I hear her voice, her laughter high and crystalline. Then a guy. He's laughing, too. I peek around the rear bumper of the SUV to see her standing a few rows away, hip cocked, head tilted, smile blinding, taking something from a middle-aged guy in a business suit. He's holding on to the handle of his little rolling suitcase and shaking his head. He's wearing this shit-eating grin that makes my stomach turn.

I whip behind the SUV as she turns and looks in my direction.

A few seconds later, she's back. "That guy let me off easy," she whispers. She hands me a purple-striped button-up shirt and a baseball cap, keeping a second shirt for herself. "Let's go."

She sprints into the open with her shoulders drawn up to her ears, like she thinks someone's going to start shooting at her any moment. I'm not convinced she's wrong. We race under the overpass for the turnpike, and then through the automatic doors of the New Jersey Transit station.

"Should I ask what just happened?" I ask between breaths.

She rolls her eyes and holds up her wallet. "Ten bucks."

"For all this?" I gesture at the shirt she's holding.

"I might also have given him some digits."

"You gave a complete stranger your phone number." Considering she's saved my life at least twice in the last few hours, I should really try *not* to sound like an untrusting—or jealous— ass right now, but seriously. Today has worn me kind of thin.

She looks at me like I really am brain damaged. "Of course not. I gave him yours."

She winks at me and scoots into the ladies' bathroom.

I go into the men's and peel off my ruined Jets T-shirt. I rinse off in the sink, splashing the frigid water into my face and letting it bring me back to my senses. The cut over my eye isn't too bad, and my nose has stopped bleeding. With a dull ache in my heart, I clean my father's blood off my chest and arms. I'm drying myself off when a toilet flushes and a bald guy comes out of a stall with an iPad tucked under his arm. His eyes meet mine in the mirror as he washes his hands. He shakes them off and then reaches into his pocket, pulls out a business card and a few bills, and slaps them onto the metal shelf below the mirror. I brace myself, because I'm certain this guy is about to ask me for a blow job or something like that, but he just says, "I hope things get better for you, man," and walks out.

I lean forward. He's given me the phone number for some local detox facility.

If only my life were that simple right now.

I put on the baseball cap, button up my nifty purple-striped shirt, and head back out into the station. Christina's waiting for me. She's used a tissue-thin scarf to put her hair up in this crazy knot on top of her head, and she's donned one of the suit-wearing guy's shirts, too. This one is pink with blue stripes. Christina has it unbuttoned halfway, with the tails tied up in a knot and a thin strip of her belly showing. "I'm disguised as Miranda Hopkins, head cheerleader," she says, putting a finger to her lips. "Shh."

"I'd never blow your cover. Come on."

With our eyes darting back and forth, looking for any sign of Lavin or his agents, we get ourselves a train schedule. "We have to get to Princeton," I tell her. "Northeast Corridor Line."

She leans against me, her head bowed over the map, and then she looks up at the clock on the wall. "There's one leaving in ten minutes."

Our eyes meet. "We need to be on it." I pull out my wallet and look inside at my debit card. "If I use this, they could track us." I hand her the two tens the guy in the bathroom gave me.

"It should be enough," she says, and taps me on the arm with her little change purse. "I cashed my babysitting check this morning. It's how I bought the gas, too."

"I'm seriously going to owe you when we get out of this."

She gives me a somber look. "Yeah."

I stand close behind her while we wait in line at a little kiosk to buy our tickets. Christina looks relaxed, but I can feel the tension vibrating from her body. She's like a wire stretched tight, ready to snap. She pays for our tickets, with only the slightest tremble in her hands as she slips the bills into the machine. "I don't have much left after this."

"We'll figure it out," I say. We ride up the main escalator with our heads down. Our train is waiting on track five. Christina beelines for it, but a familiar figure below us catches my eye.

Mr. Lamb is standing at the base of the escalator. His back is to me. His hands are on his hips. His bald spot shines under the lights. He's turning in place, staring at the people around him.

Looking for me.

I skip back from the top of the escalator as his gaze slides upward, my heart jacked into a painful fist behind my ribs, and jog toward the tracks. Christina's already on board. We've barely made it, but all I can think is how badly I need this thing to move, to carry us far away from this place. We stand in the junction between cars, pressed together, holding our breaths, her looking out one set of windows and me looking out the other. I don't want to tell her Lamb is here. I don't want her to be more scared than she already is.

Finally, after a million years, the train lurches forward. I slide my arm around Christina's waist and hold her steady, and she lets me. From our concealed position, I watch the platform start to recede. As we accelerate, Lavin himself steps onto the platform, his head low, his eyes on the windows of the last cars as the train pulls away. His jaw is ridged with tension and his lips are a tight, flat line.

I keep my eyes on him until we burst into the bright sunlight and speed away.

NINE

WE DID IT. WE MANAGED NOT TO GET SHOT AT AGAIN,
and we're on our way to Princeton, off to meet Brayton and
figure out what the hell is going on. The relief nearly knocks
me over, or maybe that's the exhaustion combined with the
aftermath of being in a serious car accident. Either way, it feels
pretty good for a second or two . . . until Christina untangles
her arms from my waist and heads for a seat, her shoulders
slumped, and I realize something.

We're not okay.

I follow her, reviewing everything she's done over the past
thirty minutes. Pulling me out of a car wreck, leading me to
the New Jersey Transit station, using her charm to get us some
new clothes, being everything I needed to get me out of there,
to keep me safe. But now that I am safe, now that some of

the urgency is gone, she's pulling away. Probably remembering why she ran from me in the first place.

I drop into the seat next to hers. She unties the knot in the pink shirt and buttons it the rest of the way down. It swallows her. She pulls the scarf from its tangled coil on her head and lets her hair fall over her shoulders. Then she tucks it behind her ears and stares out the window, her backpack in her lap.

"Hey," I say softly.

She keeps staring out the window.

"I'm an asshole," I say. I brush my fingers along her arm to let her know I'm there, but that I'm not going to push her. She doesn't pull back, but she doesn't come my way, either. Something is broken between us, and I don't know how to fix it, or if it can be fixed at all. I cross my arms over my chest and face front.

I can't believe this is happening. Any of it. I close my eyes and let the throbbing ache in my head crush my thoughts. All of them are too explosive and ugly to examine right now anyway.

About twenty minutes before we arrive at the Princeton station, I drag myself into planning mode and pull out my dad's phone. My own phone was in the pack he tossed away in those final minutes before everything turned to shit. Not that I would use it anyway—I'm certain it can be tracked. My dad's phone is a different story. It's one of his own design, and nothing he made could be tracked at all. I know because I've tried.

I send Brayton a text telling him we're going to be late. He responds instantly.

R U still in Secaucus?

I forgot about the GPS tracker on the Black Box SUV.

Left the SUV and took the train. Can be at stadium by 4.

Smart. See you then.

Smart. I'm not so sure. How have I lived my whole life without knowing our little family responsibility? Sure, Dad was secretive, but I've been in his lab. Hell, I've gone through his encrypted files, those that I could crack, that is. I've figured out his weapons while managing not to die in the process. I did all that without him knowing about it, a major accomplishment. So how did I miss any hint that the world is run by aliens? Is that why he created all those weapons in the first place? He said he didn't want his inventions used in an interspecies conflict against the H2, so what did he want to use them for?

I shift restlessly as my father's voice streams through my head like a loop track. *When the time comes . . . it's Josephus.* Who the hell is Josephus? Should I be trying to find him instead of meeting Brayton? My dad didn't seem to fully trust Brayton, and I'm not sure I do, either. But then again, I don't know a single fucking thing about Josephus, either. Dad was trying to explain everything right before he died, about Josephus, fifty things I should be careful with, and the scanner. He said that device showed blue for human and red for H2. But there was more, and he never got to say it, never even got to finish his sentence. That missing bit of information could make all the difference, and I haven't the first clue how to figure out what he was talking about. Hopefully Brayton will have some answers for me.

The questions continue to whirl through my head until Christina pokes my arm to let me know we've pulled into the station. She lets me hold her hand as we get off the train, but I can tell she's doing it for security and not because she wants to be close to me. She looks up at me, a tiny worry line between her eyes. "Where to?"

"The stadium. But I need to pick up a few things first."

I keep my head down as we walk out of the little train station and into the sunny-white almost-summer day. We follow the signs for the stadium, even though I don't need them. I know my way. I've made this trip before when I've come to visit my mom. It doesn't happen very often, maybe a few times a year in the last four years. Every time, my dad would send me off with something like

Tell your mother I hope her grant gets funded.

Tell her congratulations for getting tenure.

Tell her I wish her well.

Like he'd greet a colleague. An acquaintance. Not someone he'd woken up next to for fifteen years, not someone he'd loved.

Still, he couldn't fool me. My dad's ace at hiding his feelings, if he has any at all, but when he talks about my mother, I see the sadness in his eyes.

No, wait. I *saw* the sadness in his eyes.

It hits me that I'm going to have to tell my mother he's dead. It makes me want to curl in on myself and die right there. Because I've seen it in her, too, the sadness, and I don't know why they didn't stick together. They were good together, or so I thought. I was shocked when she left us. Not that my dad was a picnic, but he was at his softest when he was with her. I sometimes wondered if he'd have been kinder to me if I looked more like her—olive skin, light brown eyes, rounded features. Mom is Iranian, which makes me half, but I look more like my dad, with gray eyes and skin more likely to burn than tan. And maybe the reason she and I have this kind of push-pull relationship is because I'm so like him, Archer through and through. I spent a whole year wondering if I was the reason they didn't stay together. If I was the deal breaker, if maybe she couldn't watch us butt heads anymore, so she just let him have me and split.

The pain in her expression when I finally broke down and asked was overwhelming.

So no, it wasn't me. But I have no idea what the hell it was. And I have to admit, it's pissed me off more than a little. Once I quit blaming myself, I started blaming her for leaving me with him, for not fighting for me.

I wonder if she knows why he treated me like a science experiment, like a recruit instead of a son. I wonder if she knows about the H2 and about Race Lavin in particular. I wonder if I should stay away from her, if I shouldn't bring her into this at all.

But I need her. I know she cares about me, at least a little, and I don't know that about Brayton. That—and the very real possibility that Race and Lamb could turn up at any moment—is why we're stopping at this grocery store on the way to the stadium. I will not take anything for granted.

"I've got thirteen dollars left, and some change at the bottom of my bag. You hungry?" Christina asks as we walk through the door of the grocery.

"No." I'm numb, actually, like the inside of me is just a gaping, empty hole. I hope the feeling, or lack thereof, lasts me through this day. "But I could go for some juice."

I grab a cart and walk straight for the bottled-juice aisle. Christina watches me pick up the bottles, squeeze them, turn them over, and put them back. "Should I even ask?"

"I need the right thickness."

She snorts. "I've got a bad feeling about this."

I decide on the Gatorade. It's a nice, thick plastic bottle with a wide mouth. The right size, too. I put three of them in the cart.

"You must be really thirsty."

She follows me to the utility aisle. I get some aluminum foil, two bottles of lighter fluid, and some toilet bowl cleaner, reading each label before I drop them into my basket, the words of Sun Tzu echoing deep in my memory: *A victorious warrior wins first and then goes to war, while a defeated warrior goes to war first and then seeks to win.*

Christina steps up close to me. "What are you doing?"

"I want to be prepared for anything," I say. "Can you go grab me a wand lighter?"

She pales a little but heads down the aisle. I pick up a few other random items, like a bag of hamburger buns, some chips, and a bag of oranges, because it's best for everyone if the checkout person assumes we're planning a barbecue. Also, really, I don't know where our next meal is coming from, so it doesn't hurt to have some supplies.

Christina drops the lighter in the cart and looks over my haul. "Tate, I don't know if we have enough for this . . ."

She's right. This is more than thirteen dollars' worth, and we can't use a traceable debit card. "Do you think you could maybe . . . distract the cashier?"

Christina raises her eyebrows. "I've never . . ." She sighs. "All right," she says in a small voice.

As I walk down the aisle, my eyes land on the display of pool and beach toys, tempting items in preparation for Memorial Day weekend.

On impulse, I grab a compact little Super Soaker water blaster and drop it into the cart. I instantly feel more secure, because these things have been my trusty companions on many an adventure into chaos. Christina lets out a short huff of laughter when she sees the water blaster. "You were so obnoxious with that thing at the beach last summer."

Indeed I was, and with good reason. "Have I ever told you how excellent you look in a wet T-shirt?"

"I'd like to stay dry today, thanks." Her smile fades instantly. Like a drop of water on a hot stove, our moment of connection fizzles to nothing.

While we walk around the store, I do some calculations and transfer a few items to the bottom rack of the cart, leaving about twelve dollars' worth of stuff in the top.

I strategically select the checkout lane, and Christina gets in front of me and chats up the heavyset, acne-ravaged cashier, flashing her adorable smile and probably making the guy feel like he's hit the lottery. I back off and skirt around the lane to meet her at the exit, but stay close in case she runs into trouble.

It doesn't happen, though. The cashier has such a hard-on for her that he barely makes her pay for the stuff in the top, and he's so focused on her ass as she walks away that he doesn't notice the items on the bottom rack. I don't know whether I want to thank him or punch him.

Once she comes out with the bags, I slide the strap of her pack off her shoulder.

She lets me take it, and I unzip it so we can load the groceries in. I pause when I see the scanner. "Thanks for getting this after the accident. I was so out of it."

She nods. "I knew you wouldn't want to leave it behind. Your dad didn't want them to have it." She raises her eyes to mine and sticks her chin out, and I can almost read her thoughts: *I'm* not *one of them.*

So badly, I want to drop the backpack and hash this out with her. I need to know if she's really on my side or if she wants to bail right now. If she does, I'll let her. At the same time, I don't want to ask, because I'm not ready to let her go, for a thousand reasons. And . . . we don't have time for that now, because it's after three, and we need to get to the stadium before Brayton does.

Just in case.

TEN

AS CHRISTINA JAMS OUR PURCHASES INTO HER BACK-
pack, I take one of the Gatorade bottles and chug it. But
instead of tossing it into the recycling bin, I slide it into the
pack. "You should have something to drink," I say.

She gives me an odd look, then drinks about a quarter of
one of the bottles and hands it back to me. I dump the rest of
it out into the grass, then do the same with the third bottle. I
cram the empty bottles into the pack and put my arms through
the straps. "The stadium is a three-mile hike from here. Are
you up to it?"

She rolls her eyes. "Don't treat me like a girl, Tate Archer."

We start off down the road, past the congested tangle of
Princeton Junction to the wooded road that leads to Princeton
proper. As we walk along the shoulder, passed by joggers and
bikers, the wind cooling our brows and blowing Christina's

hair around her face, she takes my hand. I force myself not to squeeze her fingers too hard, not to hold on as tightly as I want to right now.

"So," she says, "I know we're going to meet someone who knows your father. I assume they know about the scanner?"

"His name's Brayton. My dad worked with him. And actually, I'm not sure if he knows about the scanner. Not exactly." This has been chewing away at the back of my mind since my brief conversation with him. He didn't ask about the scanner. He asked about *the invention*. I pull my dad's cell out of my pocket and scroll through his contacts again. No Josephus. Not even a Joseph. But there is one that might be able to give me answers. I can't believe I didn't try him before, but I was so messed up, I wasn't thinking straight.

George's number goes straight to voicemail. I wonder if he knows my dad is dead, if Brayton told him. I wonder if he's going to be at the stadium, too. That would make things so much better. I send him a text:

It's Tate. Call me when you get this?

As soon as I hit SEND, the phone beeps.

When are you getting in?

It's not George—it's my mom. I picture her, black hair pulled away from her face in the ever-present ponytail, her amber-brown eyes sharp and intense as she taps away at the screen of the phone. She feels so close, just on the other side of this electronic thread of connection, but I don't know how to reach out to her. Because as soon as I do, I'm going to have to tell her my dad's dead. And I don't want to, because that will make it real, will make it impossible to deny or forget. I can't bear to deal with her grief on top of my own right now, so I text back:

Meeting associates at stadium at 4. Will contact you after.

I silence the phone and stuff it into my pocket.

I glance over at Christina to see her watching me. "My mom," I explain.

"Does she know . . . about all of this?" Christina makes this circling gesture with her hand, encompassing the whole world, the craziness of everything.

I shrug. "We'll find out later. I'm going to have to talk to her soon, but I want to get this over with first. I need to know what Brayton wants, and if he can really keep us safe."

Not for the first time today, I wonder if it was the smartest thing to bring Christina along. Obviously, it's better for me, because if it weren't for her, I'd probably be on a morgue slab right now. But she . . . she'd be finished with her school day, and the biggest thing she'd have to worry about would be understanding exothermic reactions in time for the chemistry final on Friday.

"It's beautiful here," she says, looking out on the river as we hike over the bridge. The sun is slanting along the water, yellow beams on navy blue, glinting off the crew boats skimming along the surface of the river. And for a second, I pretend.

I imagine we're hiking through Central Park on a Saturday afternoon, walking over the Bow Bridge, headed into the rolling side trails near Belvedere Tower, paths that offer many a spot to sneak off and get close. In this moment, I forget that my girlfriend's a member of an alien race that's infiltrated all the governments in the world. She's just Christina, and being with her makes everything all right. But my little fantasy lasts only until the first university buildings come into sight, and it evaporates in the heat of my tension.

We walk through town, looking like a pair of Princeton students with really weird taste in clothing. Christina's hand is sweating in mine, and I squeeze it tight. "We're going to approach from the side, all right?"

She gives me a look. "You don't trust this guy."

"No, I don't *know* if I can trust him. Yet. And until I know I can, you're staying out of sight."

She pulls up short. "Okay, and while I'm hiding out, you're going to . . . ?"

"Talk."

She tugs her hand away from mine. "Is it that you don't want me to hear your conversation?" she says, all choked off.

She wouldn't even be asking me this if I hadn't basically accused her of being a traitor. "No. That's not it at all. It's just . . . I don't know him that well."

She stays quiet as we cross to the athletic fields, but it's a loaded silence, one that weighs heavy on me. I can't deal with it right now, because I need to stay focused. Brayton could be my greatest ally, the guy who saves the day, the guy who explains everything. I hope he is. But in case he's not . . .

We cross the Streicker Bridge leading to Powers Field, home of the Princeton Tigers. There's a meet going on at the adjoining track field, the one at the south end of the empty stadium. I'm guessing Brayton, when he gets here, will be at the north entrance, because he's arriving by car and because it's deserted right now. We're coming from the west, and the sun is warm on my back as we near the massive concrete structure with big rectangular openings every fifteen feet or so, allowing access to the shaded area beneath the stadium.

When we're close to the north entrance, maybe a dozen yards away, I pull Christina between two enormous columns and tug the backpack off my shoulders. I lean around and peer up a wide set of concrete steps to where the two metal Princeton tiger sculptures stand looking out on the road. No one there. Not yet.

I kneel and pull the aluminum foil from the backpack, along with the empty Gatorade bottles. Christina squats next to me while I start tearing strips off the foil and wadding them into balls the size of large marbles. I drop about a dozen into one of the bottles, then set it aside and do it again with another bottle. Christina does the same with the third bottle. "I know you have something planned, but I'm scared to ask what."

"Remember how I said I'd help you study for chemistry?"

She stares at the bottles, the blue and red dregs of Gatorade, and the little foil balls, and then she glances back at me. "Yeah?"

"Well, think of this as a real-world demonstration of exothermic reactions."

She gives me a blank look. I pull the toilet bowl cleaner out of the pack. "Listen, I'm just going to talk to these guys. But in case everything heads south, I need you to do exactly as I say."

She bites her lip, and a thrill of fear shimmies up my spine. I'm absolutely counting on her to have my back, but if she doesn't . . . My eyes linger on her face, and when she notices my scrutiny, her expression goes smooth again. "I'll try," she says.

I spend a few minutes explaining my plan to her, making sure she knows how to do everything without getting hurt. As I finish, I glance at the time. Brayton should be arriving soon. I stand up and tug her to her feet, then make the most of my leverage and pull her into my arms.

"I trust you," I say quietly, and then I lower my head and kiss her. At first, I'm not sure I mean it—I just need her to be on my side right now. But the moment I taste her, I know it will never be enough for me, will never last as long as I want it to. Christina locks her arms around my neck and gives me the feel of her lips, her tongue, her body. With every shared breath, I try to tell her I'm sorry for all my cruel words, for everything that's happened. I have no idea how to read the warmth of her hands or the soft, vulnerable sound that comes from her throat. I hope it means she hears me. Whatever the translation, it makes me desperate for her, desperate to take anything she'll offer me right now, because I have no idea what's about to happen next.

When I finally tear myself away, we're both flushed. "I trust you," I say again, and I hand her the backpack—and the scanner. She takes it from me and nods, her breaths still ragged.

I leave her there with our pathetic arsenal and head to the front of the stadium to stand at the top of the steps, between the two enormous tiger sculptures. In front of me is Ivy Lane, where I expect Brayton to arrive. Behind me, at the base of these steps, is a smaller access road that rings the stadium, and beyond that is the building itself, where Christina hides in the shadows below the sight line of the street.

The sun is still high over me, warming my face and neck, drying the cold sweat that's beading on my skin. My heart is thumping away, rattling against my rib cage. I feel so exposed, naked almost, like I'm asking to be a target. Every time someone walks by, my muscles wind up tight until they pass. I wait and wait, my thoughts crawling like hard-shelled beetles along the inside of my skull, tap-tapping me from sane to wildly anxious in a matter of minutes. I am so tempted to look over my shoulder, to see if Christina's still there, if she's watching me, or if she's run off. Standing here with only these tigers to keep me company, it's nearly impossible to keep my mind steady.

Two gray sedans roll slowly along Ivy Lane and pull into

spots on the street. I squint at them as the sunlight bounces off the windows. But as soon as Brayton's white-blond head appears, everything in me coils tight again. He's here, and it's time. He and four other guys, all wearing casual clothes, golf shirts, blazers, and khakis, climb out of the cars and come toward me. I can tell by the bulges at their waists and ankles that they're armed, but that's not necessarily cause for alarm. My father never left the house without a few concealed weapons. What bothers me more than the weapons are their sunglasses, preventing me from seeing their eyes, but Brayton takes his shades off as he approaches me. His ice-blue eyes are watery, shiny. He holds out his arms. "Tate," he says quietly. "I'm so sorry."

I cross mine over my chest. "Thanks, Mr. Alexander."

His arms fall to his sides when he sees I'm not going to engage in a session of man-hugging. "Call me Brayton. Your dad and I were good friends, and I hope you and I are going to be friends, too." He ducks his head, trying to see under the lowered bill of my hat. "Jesus, Tate. What the hell happened to you? Are you all right?" He steps forward, the rounded, softish contours of his face folding in on themselves as his expression creases with concern.

I shove my hands into my pockets. "We had an accident in Secaucus. It's just a bloody nose, really. But there were . . . Someone was chasing us."

All the golf-shirt guys tense up, as does Brayton. "Race Lavin," he growls.

"He's the one who killed my dad," I say. I actually have no idea who fired the shots that hit Dad. I can't even remember if Race had a gun in his hands, but he's the one I hold responsible for my father's death.

Brayton's nostrils flare as he sucks a slow breath. I think he's clenching his teeth, but it's hard to tell because the flesh on his face is so thick. "He must have known how important your father's invention is since he came to get it himself. But how did he know where it was?"

"I think my Game Theory teacher is working for him."

He draws back. "What? They had an agent at your *school*?"

"They have agents everywhere, don't they? How do I know you're not one of them?" Is that why my dad didn't trust him?

Brayton's eyes widen for a moment, and then he laughs. "Your father didn't tell you anything about our families, did he?"

No, but my father didn't tell me anything about *anything*, so this does not surprise me. "Enlighten me," I say.

Brayton runs his hand over the top of his hair, then carefully smooths and tucks the stray sprigs back into place. It's a fastidious, precise little movement, and I'll bet he does it about a hundred times a day, one of those personal tics that gets programmed straight into our cerebellums. "We're related, Tate. Third cousins, I believe, on your dad's side. Most members of The Fifty are, however distantly."

"The Fifty?" Oh . . . *But you also have to be careful with the fifty . . .*

116

Brayton smiles. "I guess he hadn't told you yet. The Archers are one of the few families on the planet with a purely human line that can be traced back to before the H2 invasion. The Alexanders, too. We take care of each other, help each other. I'm going to look out for you like I would my own son. The first thing we need to do is get your dad's invention back underground. It's obvious Race wants it—which means it must be strategically important to the H2 somehow."

"I figured that out when he shot up my school."

Brayton purses his lips and nods. "Very few people know the truth, Tate. Most H2 think they're human. They have no idea they're part of a hybrid species. No idea they're contributing to the slow extinction of the human race, gradually breeding us out of existence." His eyes meet mine. "And every time someone's tried to go public to explain it, the H2 in power manage to silence them. This invention has the potential to blow the secret wide open in a way that even Race Lavin can't control. That's why it's so dangerous. Where is it now?"

There is something about the way he's looking at me, something glacial and calculating, and it runs down my back like a trickle of icy water. "I don't have it here."

He takes a quick step toward me, and I descend one of the steps to maintain the distance between us. The golf-shirt gang's hands all jerk toward their waistlines.

"Wait," Brayton says. "Tate, think about this. It's critical that this thing doesn't fall into the wrong hands. And I have the resources to keep it safe. If you just give it to me, I—"

"You don't care about my dad at all," I say quietly.

"What? Son, we're—"

"Don't call me that. You haven't once asked where he is, what happened to his body."

Brayton's fingers are twitching. "Maybe because I knew Fred, and I know what he cared about. He cared about his work. And he cared about *you*. That's what he'd want me to take care of right now."

I relax a little. He's right, and I'm a mess, and really, I want to hand everything over to a grown-up right now because I can't manage it anyway. "Look, I put it in a safe place. Once we're at the safe house, I'll get it for you."

Brayton's cheeks tremble, like a little earthquake is going on inside of him. "It's portable, isn't it? Does your friend have it? Is he here?"

"My dad didn't even tell you whether it's portable or not? Are you sure he wanted you to have it?"

He comes down one of the steps, and I backtrack again toward the stadium. He frowns. "We were going to negotiate this afternoon. Why don't you give it to me now? You don't even know the kind of danger you're in, do you?"

The laughter razors out of me, cutting me up on the inside. "Are you serious? Did you really just ask me that?" After I held my father's hand while he died? My fists clench.

"You're a kid. You have no idea how much of his life your father invested in this technology. He told me all about it, Tate." Right as I'm about to call bullshit, he continues: "The Archers discovered pieces of wreckage after witnessing an H2 ship crash into the Irish Sea four hundred years ago. They had no idea what it was, but they knew it was proof that the H2 weren't from this planet. They kept it secret for generations— most members of The Fifty still don't know of its existence. Your father only told a few of us after he figured out what the H2 technology could do." His mouth twitches. "Or, at least, what *this* part could do and how to use it."

"And how would *you* use it?" Brayton's part of The Fifty, and my dad told me to be careful with them. But if Brayton's telling the truth, my dad was part of it, too. I have no idea who to trust, but Brayton isn't winning my confidence. He obviously knows a lot about my dad's work, but he's not exactly acting like my friend. While we've been talking, he's been herding me down the steps, below the sight line of Ivy Lane. The golf-shirt gang has spread out in a line in front of me. I back off the steps entirely, onto the narrow access road and into the shadow of the enormous building.

Brayton shakes his head, and there's a weird kind of grin on his face. No humor in it at all. "You are so very much like your father, you know that?"

"Thank you." I almost give in to the urge to look behind me, but I don't.

"Your bloodline has extended for centuries. Don't do anything to jeopardize that, Tate. Your father wouldn't want you to endanger yourself."

"My father wanted me to keep his work out of the hands of people who would use it the wrong way." I'm not convinced this thing doesn't do more than differentiate H2 from human. Dad was trying to tell me as much in those final few moments. But also: I can't help but think of those numbers in his lab. The ones that indicated each group's population count with the exception, apparently, of fourteen anomalies that my father was working on resolving. Even if telling H2 from human was all the technology did . . . if someone had the power to differentiate the species on a worldwide scale, they could selectively target one or the other. Maybe even develop weaponry that affects only one group—*that's* the kind of thing the CEO of Black Box might be interested in.

"Use it the wrong way? That's pretty paranoid," Brayton says in an amused voice. "This technology could help us do great things. Build great things. And Black Box has the resources to make it happen." He leans forward eagerly. "You could benefit from it, too, Tate. Your father's estate would definitely own the majority share."

He must think I've *very* naïve, or maybe just greedy. "Build great things . . . like weapons, perhaps? That's what Black Box does, right?"

The eager expression turns rigid. "It could also be used to save an entire species, Tate."

What has the power to save also has the power to destroy. My father taught me that.

"Why is it so important to be able to tell the difference between H2 and human? I can actually understand why Race Lavin doesn't want it in the open—he doesn't want people to freak out when they realize their kids' teachers and their neighbors and maybe even their senators are aliens or whatever. And maybe he even wants to use it to track down humans and kill us one by one. But you're human, right? What do *you* want it for? And with all due respect, please don't give me more *do great things* bullshit."

And that's it. Like a thread snapping, Brayton's face changes. The thick flesh of his cheeks goes from pasty to mottled in less than a second. His eyes go from cold to blazing. "Stop messing around and give me the invention!" he shouts.

The golf-shirt gang all pull their weapons at once, but they're keeping the muzzles low and not aiming directly at me. Yet.

I raise my hands in the air.

The explosion, when it comes, is deafening.

ELEVEN

IT ISN'T GUNFIRE.

The golf-shirt gang doesn't know that, though, and they all throw themselves behind the metal tigers as the second explosion goes off. I take my chance and spin around, relief singing in my veins. Christina didn't bail. And she followed my instructions perfectly.

The telltale click freezes me in place before I can reach the safety of the concrete pillars just beyond the narrow access road. "Nice trick," snaps Brayton from behind me. "Very cute."

I slowly turn around. He's got his gun leveled at my chest. His hands are steady.

"Tell your friend to come out. Now. Your stupid prank is going to bring the authorities down on us, and I think you understand that they will not exactly be interested in protecting your rights. Or mine. We're on the same side, Tate," he hisses.

"Which explains why you're pointing a gun at me."

"I'm going to shoot him if you don't come out," he calls.

Before I can shout for her to keep out of sight, Christina steps from behind one of the pillars, right into the line of fire. She's holding something behind her back, and her eyes are wide. "I have it right here," she says in a high, clear voice. "Don't hurt him."

Brayton puts his hand out. "Give it here, then."

"Catch."

Christina throws the Gatorade bottle high in the air. It's swelling like a balloon under the pressure of the chemical reaction going on inside it and is the size of a soccer ball as it arcs up over us. Brayton follows it with his eyes, squinting as he loses it in the slanting rays of the late-afternoon sun. I duck low and dive for Christina, slamming us both against the nearest pillar and holding her head against my chest.

Just as the bottle explodes directly over Brayton's head.

With my ears ringing, I tug Christina behind the column as Brayton screams and the golf-shirt gang opens fire. She whimpers and presses herself to the concrete. Her muscles are locked, cemented in place by all that fear. She's like a deer in headlights. And I can't blame her. This is the second time today she's been shot at, and at some point, it got to be too much.

I'm trying to decide if I'm going to drag her, calculating the odds of us getting perforated in the half second it would take us to sprint from this column to the next, when I hear the screeching of tires. I peek around the concrete pillar to see a black minivan grind to a halt on the access road, between us and the golf-shirt gang. The passenger door slides open, and so does my mouth.

It's my mom.

"Get in!" she yells as Brayton's men start shooting again.

I half carry Christina to the car as several bullets hit the driver's side. But they don't go through. Not through the glass, not through the metal.

It's bulletproof.

"Shut the door, Tate. And put on your seat belt," my mother says calmly.

I do what she says, and I fasten Christina's seat belt as well, because she's staring with wide eyes at Brayton, who levels his gun and fires—straight at her face, even though I know he can't see it through the dark tint on the windows. The bullet hits the glass with a loud *thwack,* and she cries out, a sound of pure terror.

Someday, I will pay him back for that.

Two of the golf-shirt gang land on the hood. My mother guns the engine and we shoot forward, but they hang on. I see a flash of red in the rearview and look behind us. "Mom, the cops . . ."

"Sit tight."

She flips up a small plastic tab on the dash and jabs her finger at the button hidden beneath it. The result is immediate.

The two golf-shirted thugs clap their hands over their ears, and my mother yanks the wheel left, then right, throwing them both off. I stare at them as we shoot by, at the blood spurting from between their fingers.

"Something your father installed for me a few years ago," she says. "High-powered sound waves to disrupt equilibrium and destroy the eardrum. They won't be able to chase us."

I stare out the back window and see the cops slowing to a halt next to the tiger statues, where Brayton and a few of his minions are strewn across the steps and lawn. My mom accelerates smoothly and then whips us around a corner. Her eyes flick to the rearview mirror. "Are you all right?"

She's not looking at me. She's looking at Christina.

"Yes," says Christina, her voice small. Her arms are wrapped around her middle in a way that makes me ache.

My mom turns onto yet another tree-lined road, a two-lane affair dotted with signs indicating we're near a state park. This is not the way to her house. "Tate, please fill me in. Where's your father?"

I can't tell her this now. I stare out the window. "Where are we going?"

"A safe house."

"For Black Box?"

She laughs, dark and low. "That wouldn't be very smart right now, would it? Your father and I keep a few safe places, just for us."

"How did you know to come?"

She arches a sculpted eyebrow. "Your father doesn't meet with *associates* at *stadiums*. How did you get hold of his phone? Have you been fighting with him again? And while you're at it, please tell me why Brayton Alexander was shooting at you. That is a major violation—" She presses her lips shut.

I set my elbows on my knees and hang my head. "Brayton was after one of Dad's inventions."

She's silent for several long seconds. "Does your father know you've stolen his scanner?" she finally asks.

My mouth drops open. "How do *you* know that?"

"Just tell me."

I glance down to the backpack sitting between me and Christina, and I fight the urge to throw the scanner out the window and watch it shatter into a million pieces on the asphalt. I would, too, if it wasn't the thing he died trying to save, the thing he said was the key to our survival. And Brayton probably wasn't spouting *only* bullshit—I can believe this technology could be used to do great things. Without my dad, who can I trust to help me figure that out? I stare at the back of my mother's head. She's almost a stranger to me. But obviously my dad still trusted her enough to tell her about the scanner.

And now I have to tell her about *him*. There's no use putting it off anymore.

"He's dead, Mom," I say, my voice cracking. While I explain

how it happened, my mom's expression doesn't change. She doesn't ask questions. She barely says anything at all.

She finally turns onto a gravel road. The woods are so dense here that the trees block out the sun, and there's no hint of human habitation. After a few miles, she veers down a steeply sloped drive that makes me feel like we're diving into the trees, drowning in the leaves.

The cabin is in a little clearing, but before we reach it, my mother rolls down the window and places her hand on the trunk of a spindly, smooth-barked tree growing right next to the road. A flap pops open beneath her palm, revealing a small keypad, and she punches in a code.

$C_{21}H_{22}N_2O_2$

Of course, it's not a loved one's middle name or maiden name or birthday or whatever.

It's the chemical formula for strychnine.

I'm kind of glad Christina isn't great at chemistry, because I'm not sure I want her to know this about my mother, that she's the type of woman who chooses her passwords by lethality rather than sentimentality.

My mother pulls the minivan forward. I'm not sure what punching in that code did for us, but if my father had anything to do with it, the security around this cabin is probably thorough, effective, and utterly deadly.

She hits a button on the visor as we approach, and the door of a ramshackle shed next to the cabin slides open, revealing a bright, modern interior. We get out and follow her through the back of the shed, along a narrow, steel-reinforced hallway, and into the cabin. Christina looks like she's about to collapse, and when my mother pulls out a chair for her at the kitchen table, she practically falls into it.

My mom holds out her hand to me. "Let me see it," she says, motioning at the backpack on my shoulder.

I hand it to her, and she unzips it, pulls out the scanner, and turns it on. With no hesitation, she waves it in Christina's direction. Christina winces as the red light reflects off her face, and then she shrinks before my eyes, curling in on herself, obviously terrified of what my mother is going to do next.

But all my mother does is turn off the scanner and sit down at the table with Christina. "You know what that means, don't you?"

Christina shrugs. My mom looks up at me. "Dad told us," I mumble.

She turns back to Christina, who is trembling. "You didn't know before today, did you?"

Christina shakes her head.

"Almost no one does," my mother says in a hollow voice. She inhales sharply. "Have you called your parents? Do they know where you are?"

Christina nods. "I called and left a message saying I was safe, but that's it. And I didn't use my own phone. We were at a gas station right after everything happened, and I—"

"Called from a pay phone?" my mother asks. "That wasn't very smart. I'm sure your parents' lines are being monitored, and it probably told the authorities exactly where you were."

"I called from a random stranger's cell phone," Christina replies with a sudden sharpness that rivals my mom's. "Because I already figured that out."

"That's only a little better."

Christina's eyes flash. "I figured it was a lot better than an Amber Alert."

My mother has already reached into the pack and retrieved Christina's phone. "How old are you?" she asks Christina as she flicks it open to confirm that it's off.

"Eighteen."

"Amber Alerts are only issued for individuals seventeen or younger. And you should probably contact your parents again and remind them that if you choose to take off for a few days, you're well within your right as an adult to do so."

Christina blinks, wilting slightly. "But I don't . . . I'm not . . ."

"She has a good relationship with her parents," I say, hating the condescending turn this conversation has taken. "She's never done anything like this before, and I'm sure her parents won't buy—"

"I can speak for myself, Tate," Christina says quietly, making my mouth snap shut. She meets my mother's gaze. "If I can convince them, will it make these agent people leave my family alone?"

"Only if your family has absolutely no idea where you've gone," my mother says in a hard voice.

"Mom, I—" I begin, but apparently I'm not wanted in this conversation, because this time it's my mom who interrupts.

"She could tell them where we are, Tate."

"I'm sitting right here," snaps Christina. "And I won't. I mean, if I really wanted to, don't you think I would have by now?"

My mother stares at her for a long minute, and it's easy to see the sizing up that's going on. Christina's scared of my mom, but she's not about to let anyone roll over her. And my mom . . . I think she's decided she likes Christina, even if she doesn't trust her yet. There's a glint of admiration in her eyes as she reaches into her bag and pulls out a black cell, one that looks like my father's, and is likely as untraceable. "Use this," she says, handing it to Christina. "Tell them you're with Tate." She pauses for a moment, her lips pressed together, and then adds, "Tell them his father was killed in an accident, and that you'll be traveling with him to attend his father's funeral upstate. Promise them you'll be home soon. We'll deal with long-term plans later."

Christina takes the phone. She stares at its smooth face, and then composes a text. I don't need to ask her why she's not calling them. I know. She might have put up a strong front just now, but she's close to the edge, and if she hears their voices, she won't be able to hold it together. I lean forward, wanting to put my arms around her, tell her I'm sorry, anything, *anything* to wipe that fragile look off her face, but Christina turns away, giving me her back.

I stand up quickly. "Where's the bathroom?"

My mom nods toward the hallway. "Second door on the right."

I force myself not to run straight there, so desperate am I to escape the tiny, terrible sound of Christina's tears hitting the screen of my mom's untraceable black phone.

I sit on the edge of the tub and count each breath, in through the nose, out through the mouth. I get to my feet and stare into the sleek, stainless-steel-framed mirror. I take off the baseball cap and examine my face, the cut over my eyebrow, the bruising on my cheek, the grief in my eyes.

My mother did not react to my father's death like I thought she would.

She's acting like I told her he went on a business trip. No tears. Not even a grimace or a whimper. Only action. Rationality.

It hurts more than I can explain. My mom's a scientist, so rationality is kind of her thing, but this is huge. And I thought they still might feel something for each other, that even though they weren't together, they shared something special. My dad would never admit it, but come on. As smart and cagey as he was, as coldly logical, the man couldn't keep himself from using her middle name as his freaking password. And my mom, I was certain she was the same. Hell, the last time I was at her house, I was snooping around and found a picture of them in her desk drawer, taken about five years ago, judging from my mom's short hairstyle at the time. It looked like someone had snapped the pic at a party, when they weren't aware of being watched. The intimacy of it, facing each other, the way his head was bowed toward her as she smiled up at him . . . the feeling of intruding upon their privacy was overwhelming, and I shoved the picture back into the drawer and shut it tight. I thought it meant something, that she kept it there. That she still loved him. I guess not.

I have no idea how long I spend in the bathroom, but when I emerge, I am instantly aware of the smell of garlic and onions, the sound of something sizzling in a pan . . . and the warm laughter of my mother. And my girlfriend.

"Did he really think that would work?" my mother asks.

Christina snorts. "Of course he did," they both say at the same time.

I guess they've patched things up. I consider standing out in the hall, eavesdropping, but then I realize how hungry I am and let the scent of food lead me back into the kitchen. Christina is standing at the stove, poking at the sizzling vegetables. There's a glass of wine sitting on the counter next to her, which is a little weird because Christina doesn't usually drink—and Mom hasn't ever offered before.

My mom pulls a jar of sauce from the cabinet. She smiles

and holds it up when she sees me. "I'm not here very often, so the food mostly comes in jars or boxes, with a few exceptions."

"At this point, I don't care. I'll eat anything," I say.

I open and close a few cabinet doors and finally find myself a glass.

"Wine?" my mom asks.

I stare at her. "Really, Mom?"

She looks down at the glass in her hand. "You and Christina have been through a lot. This might help you relax."

"No, thanks." I don't want to relax. I want to figure out what's happening—and what to do next.

Her gaze sharpens for a moment, but then her expression is smooth again. "There's well water, then."

I fill my glass at the tap and sit down at the table. "Where's the scanner?"

She dumps the sauce over the onions and garlic and takes over while Christina sits down at the table. "I put it in my bag." She points with the spoon.

"How long have you known about it?"

"I've known about the technology for years. I consulted with Fred as he figured it out, but he's the one who created the scanner . . . after we separated."

I run my tongue over my teeth, watching her carefully. I'm dying to ask her about Josephus, if she knows him, who he is, but something holds me back. Maybe it's the way her hands are too steady, her smile too easy. If she was close enough to my dad to know his secrets, how can she be so calm? I'm not sure I can trust her—but I'm not sure I can trust anyone at this point. I decide to stick to more obvious stuff. "I get why this Race guy wants the scanner. He doesn't want humanity to know they're being ruled by aliens, right?"

Christina shivers and takes a sip of wine.

My mom drains the spaghetti, her movements fluid and relaxed. "Something like that. He's probably concerned it would cause worldwide civil unrest if people suddenly knew there were aliens among us—even if more than sixty percent actually *are* aliens themselves. Everyone would assume they were human and would probably turn on anyone they suspected of being different. Imagine how ugly it could become. Innocent people would die. And of course, it's impossible to rule out that the H2 want to use the technology for their own ends. They have a history of quietly—and at times, not so quietly—eliminating those who've challenged them. The scanner might make it easier to . . . preemptively strike. Or make sure there are no humans left in power anywhere in the world."

"But why would they do that? What difference would it make? Dad said they already have so much power. What else do they want?"

"I'm trying to figure that out, Tate. Trust me."

I'm sure my expression tells her exactly how much I don't

trust her, but instead of pushing it, I take a different tack. "So did they invade all at once? How is their existence a secret?"

"They arrived four centuries ago. Most of what we have is oral history. There were a few landing or crash sites, almost all in deep water near land, which appears to have been intentional. When the H2 came ashore, they were thought to be shipwreck survivors."

"Brayton said one of the Archers pulled actual wreckage from the Irish Sea."

She leans against the counter. "One of Fred's ancestors was fishing for cockles during low tide in Morecambe Bay, and he witnessed a crash. They may have gotten off course, or they may not have accounted for the tide cycles, but the impact was devastating—there were no survivors, unlike many of the reported crashes. A day later, he found several small pieces of wreckage, the bits that hadn't been washed out to sea by the high tide. It is those H2 artifacts that your father used to make the scanner."

"What, was there an instruction manual?"

The corner of her mouth twitches upward. "Of course not. Your father experimented until he determined that this bit of technology could read the molecular structure of the skin to an insanely precise degree. When I last talked to him, even *he* wasn't sure exactly how it worked, but he'd done enough testing to be sure that was the basic mechanism for differentiating the two species. It was a surprising find—we weren't sure why the H2 would have that technology when they arrived here or what its original purpose was."

"Wait—you said 'this bit of technology.' Were there other bits? How much did he have, exactly? What kind of wreckage are we talking about?"

She shrugs. "That is something your father never revealed to anyone, not even me. I assume he has the artifacts in his lab somewhere, but you know how he protected his discoveries." A shadow of regret passes across her face. "I know he would have shared everything with you had he lived long enough. He was waiting for the right time."

For a moment, my father's death is a smothering weight that presses us into silence, but my mom shakes it off quickly. "We have no other concrete evidence of the H2 landing. Even though most H2 survivors blended into the human population, keeping their origins so secret that they were forgotten within a generation, their leadership—an organization called the Core—took a slightly different tack. They immediately began infiltrating human politics and power bases while the rest interbred with humans, most likely to help their offspring survive the microbial environment on Earth. I think the scanner reveals the result of that." She eyes Christina, whose gaze is rooted on the ruby liquid in her glass. "There is no gradation or 'hybrid,' only human or H2."

Which explains why there are more of them than there are

of us at this point. "But didn't anyone notice the *spaceships,* Mom? Seems like those would make it hard to blend in with the locals."

She shakes her head. "Since they landed in the water, all ships were lost, and though modern technology should make it possible to recover them—and believe me, we've tried—the Core must have gotten there first, because nothing has been found. And only a handful of people actually witnessed the crashes, Tate. The rest of the world had no idea, and it's not like camera phones and YouTube were around to broadcast the truth. As you can imagine, anyone who tried to warn others was eliminated by the Core. Farmers and fishermen were no match for such a sophisticated and organized group, so most of their stories faded into myth and legend. Not every family passed along the secrets, either—only a tiny minority. For the last hundred years, though, as technology slowly connected us, The Fifty were established and have worked together to ensure that we do not become extinct."

"But did Dad trust them?" I lock eyes with her. "He said I had to be careful with The Fifty."

Her fingers tap on the counter, a nervous kind of movement. "It's a diverse group, and your father didn't trust all of its members. But we have a common purpose, and that keeps us together."

"To regain control? To reveal the H2 for what they are?"

My mother returns her attention to the simmering pasta

sauce. I keep my eyes on her—I can't look at Christina right now. If it was human against alien, would it be me against my girlfriend? My family versus hers? My stomach hurts with more than hunger.

"Even if that was the strategy, it's been impossible until now. These 'aliens' look like humans," Mom says. "Those who tried to make others aware of what was really happening were branded lunatics, heretics, cultists. Without the scanner, it's *still* impossible to prove that Earth is ruled by an alien species."

"It's impossible to prove it *with* the scanner, then, if there's no corroborating evidence," I say sharply. "What would stop these Core people from discrediting someone who tried to use it that way?"

My mom nails me with this intense stare. "The scanner is built from *alien* technology, and at this point, human technology is almost surely advanced enough to determine that it is, in fact, extraterrestrial. It's the scanner itself, in addition to the information it provides, that would serve as corroborating evidence should someone decide to go public with it.

"Is that all?" I ask.

Mom frowns. "What do you mean?"

I shrug. "The way they're clamoring for it makes me wonder . . . You said they'd salvaged all their ships, except this one that Dad's ancestor found. What if there was something on board that they've been looking for all these years, something that wasn't on all the other ships they retrieved? Because shooting up a public school in the middle of the Upper West Side isn't exactly a quiet suppression—they were desperate to get the scanner."

She stares at me for a few long seconds. "You might be right. If the H2 Core didn't find it important—or threatening—Race Lavin wouldn't have come after it. Especially not the way he did." Her voice fades to a strained whisper, and for a moment, I think she's going to cry, to finally show that my dad's death is hurting her. Memories of his last moments crash over me. He had this look in his eye that said he had so many things left to say and do, so many things to teach me. It sucks the oxygen from my lungs, closes my throat. So when my mom, back to being smooth and cold, deftly changes the direction of the conversation, I let her do it. She asks Christina a lot of questions about ordinary, everyday things, and I can tell Mom's trying to put her at ease. And it seems to be working amazingly well, because Christina's cheeks are glowing and her movements have loosened up. She even smiles a few times, though her expression falters when she glances my way. I can't really blame her.

I eat mechanically, shoveling pasta into my mouth because it's easier than talking right now. I keep my eyes on my mom. If she'd only give me a sign that I could trust her, that she cared about my dad, that his wishes matter to her . . . For a moment there, I thought I saw it, but now it's gone again. Of all the people in the world, I should know where I stand with her, and that I can depend on her. My dad kept the truth from me for years, and I knew him a lot better than I know her. I'm relying on Mom now—for both my own life and Christina's—and I wish I could use her as my anchor. God knows I need one. As we finish dinner, I ask her what the next step is. She tells me she has to call a few people and she'll know more by morning, then changes the subject again. As she talks, I continue to search every blink, every smile, every movement of her face, looking for grief or regret.

Nothing.

By the time we're clearing the table, I want to punch something. And I realize how badly I miss the Christina from yesterday, because she's the one I could talk to about this. I miss the way she'd touch my face and tell me she's all right, and I'm all right, and we'll do this together. I need her to let me hold on to her right now. I need her to let me press my ear to her chest and hear her heart beat. But after everything that's happened, I doubt she'd let me, and I'm not even sure it would help the way it did when I didn't know the truth about who we are. It doesn't stop me from wanting to be close to her, though, a desire that's growing by the second.

I scrub my plate and glass and set them in the dish rack. Christina stands with her plate but quickly sits back down again, blinking. "Whoa," she says softly.

"You must be exhausted. I've got something you can change into," my mom says, and she strides down the hall.

I sit next to Christina and hesitantly brush her hair away from her face. Her skin is so warm, almost hot. "How are you?"

"Fine," she says, her eyes slightly glazed. She looks like the day has drained her out, like she has nothing left.

My mom returns, offering a pair of yoga pants and a T-shirt. Christina takes them from her and slowly shuffles toward one of the bedrooms. I'm giving her only a few minutes, and then I'm going to check on her. She looks so unsteady.

My mother's gaze follows Christina until she disappears into a bedroom. "She cares about you a lot," she says. "And she seems like a nice person. But you shouldn't have roped her into this, Tate. She shouldn't be involved."

"It happened kinda fast," I snap. "They'd already seen her with me, Mom. They would have killed her."

Because I need something to do, I get Christina's plate and glass from the table and take them to the sink. I dump the dregs of the wine into the basin.

There's a granular, white residue at the bottom of the glass.

Something zings through me, too painful to label, too big for words. I lift the glass to the light and turn around. I catch my mother's amber-brown gaze through the filmy crystal.

"What did you do?" I whisper. She's a chemist, after all. She has to know about twelve easy ways to poison someone.

My mother steps forward quickly. Her firm, cool hands are around mine, and then she's peeling my fingers away from the glass. "It's going to shatter in your hand," she says. "You don't need another injury tonight."

"You put something in her wine." It's taking everything I have not to shake her.

My mother nods, stone-faced again. "Diazepam. One capsule."

"You slipped her a Valium?" Part of me is relieved that it's not ricin or coniine, because right now, I wouldn't put it past her. But the rest of me is still pissed. "Christina's not a child, Mom. And she's not our enemy!" I realize as I say the words how deeply I believe them.

"Don't be naïve. Anyone could be our enemy now, Tate. With Race after us, with Brayton willing to kill to get the device for himself, it's just you and me at the moment, and we need to figure this out—without an extra pair of eyes and ears."

She puts her hand on my arm, but I jerk away from her. "Me and you? What is that? You left us. You left *me*. How many times have I seen you in the last four years?"

My mother shakes her head. "Your father had you on a very tight—"

"Leash?"

She flinches. "Of course not. On a schedule. Your preparation was very important to him, and we agreed it would be that way when we decided to have children. I didn't always like it, but I respected it."

"I don't want to hear this right now," I say, waving my hands in front of me. "Stop."

"I wanted to see you more often," she says, taking a cautious step toward me. "I wanted you to spend summers with me. I wanted to take you on trips, to go visit my family. He wouldn't allow it."

"And you didn't fight him, either."

"I couldn't, not really." She takes a deep breath. "I believed in what he was doing. I knew you'd have to be prepared. And obviously, I was right. So was he. And I knew he and Chicão and your other tutors, all of whom are from The Fifty, would be able to do that."

"Are you telling me that every single fucking person around me knew about all this, while I was intentionally kept in the dark?"

She holds up her hands. "It was temporary and necessary, Tate. And think about what you've been through today. Do you really think you could have survived if your father and the others hadn't trained you like they did?"

"Maybe not, but here's what else I know," I say, jabbing my finger at her face. "I couldn't have gotten through today without Christina. She saved my life three times. And I am not exaggerating, Mom. Three. Freaking. Times. So the way I see it, it's me and *her*, and if you hurt her . . ." I pull my hand back and let it fall to my side as a fist, heavy and hot, ashamed that I've been doubting Christina so much, blaming her for something she has no control over, something she didn't even know about.

"I wouldn't hurt her. That was never my intention."

"What was your intention?"

She throws up her arms. "Honestly? Mostly to make sure she sleeps soundly tonight. To help her rest. She was practically catatonic by the time I picked you up. She looked traumatized."

She's right about that part. "But you didn't ask her permission. Were you going to try to drug me, too?"

By the look on her face, I can tell that is *exactly* what she was planning. She wanted to sedate the kiddies so she could make her plans without our interference.

I nod to myself. "All right. So much for it being just *me and you*. Looks like it's really just *you*. So thanks a lot, Dr. Archer, for the rescue," I snarl. "And for drugging up my girlfriend. I hope you have an awesome time tonight figuring things out by yourself. I'll go put my jammies on. But don't worry—I don't expect you to tuck me in."

I pivot on my heel and stalk down the hall, and my mother doesn't try to stop me. I find Christina in the third room on the right, curled up on one side of the double bed, huddled beneath a comforter even though it's pretty warm in here. Her clothes from today are scattered on the floor, and I fold them and put them on the dresser. Then I kneel by her bed and carefully skim her hair away from her face. She's breathing steadily, limp as a dishrag. Dreaming good dreams, I hope, free of bullets and blood and exploding Gatorade bottles.

For a moment I consider climbing in next to her, but it doesn't feel right like this. My mom deprived Christina of a choice tonight, and I'm not about to do the same, not when we have so much to sort out. I kiss her on the forehead, turn off the lamp, and go back into the hall. The bedroom across the way is empty. Like Christina's room, this one is plain, no decorations, just a double bed, a set of drawers, a chair, and a lamp. I open the drawers and find myself a pair of sweats and a fresh T-shirt. I take a long, *long* hot shower, wishing the whole day would peel off of me and slip down the drain, just a dream, a figment of my imagination.

By the time I emerge, the hallway is dark, and there's no light coming from beneath any of the doors. I hear the faintest sound, though, and I follow it down the carpeted hallway, all the way to the last door on the left, thinking maybe I'll eavesdrop to make sure my mom's not planning to dump Christina off on some street corner tomorrow.

I put my ear to the door.

It's not a conversation I hear, but the sound *is* coming from my mom.

The sobs are muffled, like she's got her face in her pillow. They are quietly desperate. They are gut-wrenching. Unadulterated grief, bottled up until now, when she could break down in private, when she could let it out.

She's crying for my father. I hear her say his name.

I lean away from the door, once again feeling like I've intruded upon something intimate, something too painful to share. I creep back to my own room, to my own bed.

It takes me a very long time to stop shaking.

TWELVE

THE SOFT BUT INSISTENT KNOCK PULLS ME FROM A
thick, hazy sleep long before I'm ready. "Tate? Wake up,
please," my mother says through the door.

I sit up, dazed, my eyes darting from brown carpet to pan-
eled walls to generic dresser. It takes me several seconds to
remember where I am. And that my father is gone. And that I
am in a safe house somewhere in the woods of freaking Jersey,
with my mother, who apparently has a fondness for slipping
Valium into people's drinks. Awesome.

"Tate!" Her knocking gets louder.

"Yeah?"

She opens the door and pokes her head in, looking like she's
afraid I'll start shouting if she comes in. "We need to go. Soon."

I swing my legs over the side of the bed. "What's happened?"

She's already dressed, and her hair is wet, leaving dark

streaks on the shoulders of her light blue shirt. "There are agents in Princeton."

"Agents."

"*Core* agents. I monitor the local law enforcement communications. They mentioned Race."

My stomach clenches at the mention of his name. "Seems like the security around this cabin is pretty tight."

My mom gives me a pained look. Her eyes are slightly puffy, a souvenir of her grief. "It is. And its location is secret—your father is . . . was very good at that kind of thing. But if they set up roadblocks and checkpoints, we'll have a hard time making it out. We have to leave before then."

"All right," I say, rising from the bed, already headed for the dresser.

"All right." She hesitates for a moment. "Christina's up. She looks better." Then she leaves me there to stare into the drawers at clothes that once belonged to my father.

I pull on a henley shirt and some jeans, and then rummage around for a belt. I need to be able to move fast, to run if I have to, and I don't need my pants sliding down to my knees at the worst moment.

I emerge into the hall at the *best* moment, though, so I hope that's some sort of omen. Christina comes out of the bathroom, a towel pulled tight around her body and another wrapped up around her head. She jumps when she sees me, and her towel turban falls to the floor, sending damp tendrils of hair over her bare shoulders.

This is the way I would like to begin every morning. My God.

"Hi," she says.

"Hi. Sleep well?" Damn, my voice just cracked.

She smiles, and it is the most delicious thing, a sweet curl of her lips. Has she forgiven me, or is this only a temporary truce? "I did, actually. I needed it. How about you?"

I barely slept at all. Laid awake with fists clenched and muscles jacked tight, fighting back the tears. "Yeah, like the dead. How long will it take you to get ready?"

She gives me a look that tells me she's seen through my bullshit once again. "Not long."

This is the moment when I should say something cool, something funny, something that halts the slow slide into awkwardness, something that makes things better. But . . . I miss it somehow, like arriving a moment too late and watching the train pull out of the station without me. Christina's smile fades, and her fingers curl deeper into her towel, holding it firmly in place over her chest.

When we hear my mother's voice coming from the room right next to the kitchen, it's like someone has thrown us a life preserver. Both of us tune in at the same time, needing to focus on anything but the weirdness.

"I understand. Don't tell them anything," my mother says.

We stare at each other, wide eyed.

Christina bites her lip. "Do you know who she's talking to?"

"No." I hate this feeling, like I can't even trust my own mom. It makes me feel cornered. Alone and trapped. She's not letting me in because she seems to think I'm still the twelve-year-old kid she left behind four years ago. I was hoping we'd drop that shit after we had it out last night, but now I'm not so sure.

"She . . . she's not going to . . . hurt me, is she?" Christina asks, interrupting my thoughts. "Because I'm—" She winces. "Because I'm not like you?"

I touch her shoulder. "I wouldn't let her." I already have. But I'm not going to make things more complicated by telling her that. Christina flashes me a nervous look and beelines for her bedroom door, leaving me standing there, straining to understand the rest of my mom's conversation. I make out a few words here and there—I think she's talking to someone about when we'll be arriving.

I hear her getting off the phone and decide I've had enough. I pull my dad's phone from my pocket and hit SEND on George's number.

He picks up immediately. "Tate. I was just about to call."

"Hey," I say. "You . . . know about Dad, right?" He must, since he knew it would be me on this phone. I squeeze my eyes shut and sink onto the bed.

"I know," he says quietly. "I'm so sorry, Tate. I'm so sorry.

I know it was tense between you two, but your father loved you—"

"I know that," I whisper. "You don't have to tell me."

His voice is thick with grief as he says, "He was so proud of you. He didn't talk about it a lot, but it was so obvious, every time he mentioned you."

"It's my fault he's gone."

"Tate, there was no way you could have known what would happen. You can't blame yourself."

I do, though. And I think I always will. But that's just one more reason to protect the scanner. "Do you know why they came after us?"

His breath huffs into the phone. "I knew about the scanner, if that's what you're asking. I helped negotiate the meeting between your dad and Brayton. He's in custody, by the way, but we're working to get him freed."

"What? He shot at me!"

"But he's one of us. He won't be allowed to do that again, though. It was desperate and a huge violation of our rules."

"Attempted murder usually is," I snap.

"And we'll deal with him, trust me. The Fifty are calling an emergency board meeting. Most of them don't know about your father's invention, though, Tate. We're trying to decide what to tell them."

"Where's the meeting?"

"Each of The Fifty has a representative. We meet in Chicago."

"I'm with my mom. Should we try to make it there?"

"No, there are already reports of increased Core surveillance on members of The Fifty. They'll be expecting you to come here, so it's the last place you should be right now. Your mom has a good plan, Tate. I was so relieved to hear from her that—"

"She called you?"

"She did. She—wait, hang on—" There's a muffled banging in the background, and George curses. "Hey, I have to go, but I'll see you really soon, all right?"

I bow my head. "Sure." I hang up and manage to scoot into the kitchen before my mom comes out of the office with her bag over her shoulder. Knowing she talked to George drains some of the tension from my muscles.

"I've packed you and Christina some toiletries and clothes," she says to me. "Let's load the car."

My stomach growls. I never thought I'd find myself wishing for a Meal Number Five, but here we are.

She sees me put a hand over my belly and smiles at me. It strikes me as a special kind of look, fond, *motherly*. Foreign.

"I'll get you something to eat on the way," she says.

"Sounds good." I hope "on the way" means "really soon."

Christina is true to her word and gets ready quickly. She's done that all-purpose ponytail thing girls always do, and she's got on a pair of black yoga pants and a loose autumn-orange jersey with a wide neck. As strange as it sounds, I am intensely attracted to her collarbones.

"Where are we going?" I ask my mom.

"Virginia. Charlottesville. To a colleague's. They wouldn't suspect we'd run there."

"Why not?"

She glances impatiently at the time. "Can we talk on the way? The longer we stay, the more likely it is they'll be able to hem us in."

Once again, she's treating me like a kid. I clench my teeth as we follow her to the minivan. I'm kind of wishing we had something a little zippier, but then I remember it's bulletproof. There are a few tiny pockmarks on the tinted windows and black paint, but that's the only sign this thing survived a gunfight yesterday. As we get in, my mom hands me the scanner. She nods for me to put it in Christina's backpack and climbs into the driver's seat without a word. It feels like a peace offering, her letting me keep Dad's invention close—though I wonder what she was doing with it this mornng while I was sleeping.

The clouds are a steel-gray blanket today, not allowing a ray of sunlight through. It almost feels like it's still nighttime as we roll along the narrow gravel road, through the woods and back to civilization. I want to cling to the cover of the forest. I don't want to go back out there and be a target. I know that's cowardly, and that's one of the things that makes me different from my father. It burns in my chest, blistering me with my own inadequacy.

In a shockingly short time, we've reached 95 South. My

mom has mercy on me and pulls into a McDonald's and buys breakfast for all of us before getting on the highway. I inhale three Egg McMuffins and can't help but picture the look on my dad's face if he could see me now. By the time we're on the entrance ramp, I'm feeling sort of sick. And scared. My greasy fingers grip the seat. I watch every car we pass, waiting for their eyes to land on me before I remember our windows are tinted.

"You never told me how you actually got ahold of the scanner," my mom says after a while. "I'm amazed Fred would have—" Her lips press together.

I cross my arms tightly over my chest. "No, you're right. He didn't tell me much of anything until he was . . ." I rub my hand over my face. "I got into his lab and stole it. This is pretty much all my fault." I can barely push the words out because my throat is so tight.

Christina reaches from the backseat and touches my arm, a soft brush of her fingertips. But I can't look at her. If I do, I'll probably lose it. Staring at my shoes seems like the best strategy right now.

"You know what they say about hindsight," my mom says, her voice soft. "Don't be too hard on yourself."

While my mom drives south, my gaze lingers on her furrowed brow, on the circles under her eyes. She looks tired. And about to unravel. Like she hasn't quite been able to stuff her grief from last night back into its little box yet. Though I don't enjoy seeing her miserable, it's oddly comforting to know that his death got to her, that he still mattered to her.

We ride in silence down through Jersey, then into Pennsylvania. Christina pulls her iPod out of her pack and slips in her earbuds. She curls up by the window, staring out at the passing scenery. Part of me is desperate to know what she's thinking, but most of me is too chickenshit to ask for fear she'd actually tell me the truth.

We get caught in major construction traffic in Philly. The highway narrows to two lanes, and the tension in the minivan ratchets up to a painful degree. We're stuck here in the crawling traffic, boxed in on every side. Once again, I'm scanning the cars around me, from the woman applying mascara using her visor mirror to the guy screaming into his Bluetooth headset to the girl singing along to her radio to a dude I am fairly sure is trying to jack off in a way he thinks is subtle but is actually not. His unfocused eyes are on the singing girl, but the mascara woman appears to have spied his slack-jawed and glazed expression in her visor mirror and is watching him with a disgusted look on her face.

Each of them is doing their own thing. Unaware of whether they are H2 or human. Just . . . people, living life. Yesterday morning, I was like that, completely unaware that humans are not the dominant species on the planet.

My mom isn't watching the people around us. Her eyes are on the construction workers and police cars clustered at the side of the road up ahead. It's some kind of checkpoint. Tiny beads of sweat shine at Mom's temples. I look at the backpack in Christina's lap, my stomach knotting. Fear is contagious. I'm tempted to ask my mom for one of those Valium. Or maybe offer her one.

Christina takes out her earbuds. "Are you all right, Dr. Archer?"

"I'll be better once we get through this traffic jam." My mother's voice is even, but her shoulders are tense.

There's a state cop standing in front of his cruiser, watching the cars and trucks and SUVs and motorcycles roll by, occasionally waving some over or having them lower their windows so he can check ID. His brimmed hat is too low for me to see his eyes, which is enough to fill me with a jittery, sick kind of energy.

"You're fidgeting, Tate," my mother says. "Get into the back, please."

I do, happy for the moment to let her be in charge. "Dad said Race works for the government," I comment. "But when he showed up at the school, he had the NYPD with him. Like he was working with them."

My mom nods. "Race is part of the Core, and he's posted in New York. He's officially a member of the CIA, but he operates his own special unit, from what we've gathered. He had a few encounters with your father over the years."

"Did he know about the scanner? He showed up at the school so fast."

My mother shakes her head. "No, but judging by the way

he handled things, I think the Core, or Race, at least, realizes what the scanner can do and that it was built from their technology. Your father's family kept the H2 artifacts secret for centuries, but I have to wonder if the Core was on the lookout for it because they reacted so quickly. And I think perhaps Fred knew that, too, which was why he was so careful to keep it secret."

And I blew all of it wide open and got him killed. I close my eyes and rest my elbows on my knees. My mom seems to sense what's going on with me, because she says, "Tate, I wasn't talking about what happened yesterday. With one exception—George—the few people Fred told about the scanner left him feeling betrayed. Each of us had our own ideas about what should be done with the technology." She sighs, and her expression is full of pain and regret. "He felt such a sense of responsibility. If people died because of what he discovered . . . He was determined to keep that from happening."

But as it turns out, he was the first casualty.

I'm working up the nerve to ask her what *she* did that left my father feeling betrayed when Christina says, "What if those cops up ahead are looking for us specifically?"

Christ, she sounds so scared. Like she's reliving yesterday. Another rush of guilt crashes over me.

Mom stares at the cop at the checkpoint. "It's possible. But Race doesn't want other people—H2 or human—looking for it or exposing it. He's probably using every resource he has to suppress what happened at your school yesterday. If you get caught by someone other than him, he risks losing control of the scanner."

"Maybe we should go public," I suggest. "It's okay to shout 'fire' in a public theater if there's actually a fire, right?"

My mother frowns. "Not a good analogy. What Race is doing now, the Core has been doing for centuries. He wants to eliminate the threat to the status quo and retrieve their technology. We need to think carefully before we decide our course of action." She looks over her shoulder at me. "When we get to Charlottesville, I'll figure this out."

"*We'll* figure this out," I say, almost under my breath.

Her gaze lingers on mine for another second before she turns back to the wheel. "If this gets ugly, please let me do the talking."

"Fine." I have no idea what I'd say anyway.

We're about five car lengths away from the cop now. The traffic is funneling into one lane. We have to go by single file. I'm really hoping the cop doesn't pay too much attention to the pockmarks along the side of the car. Maybe he'll think we got caught in a hailstorm. Or maybe we're screwed. I pull the backpack from Christina's grasp, slide it to the floor, and nudge it under the front passenger seat.

"Here," Christina says, offering the car adapter for her iPod to my mother. My mom gives her a funny look, then takes it and plugs it in. Christina taps at the iPod, and a few seconds later, we are treated to the bouncy strains of her cherry-flavored pop music. "Seems like we need to avoid *looking* like we're fugitives." She pats my mom on the shoulder in a singularly ballsy way. "Sing along, Dr. Archer."

"Oh, I'm not Dr. Archer at the moment," says my mother, reaching into her bag. "I'm Andrea Parande, resident of Garden City." She pulls out a driver's license. My mom was obviously ready for this eventuality.

"If the officer asks, just tell him you don't have ID." Her eyebrow arches. "I think your name should be—"

"Will," I suggest. "Let's not get crazy."

"And I'll be Miranda Hopkins," Christina says as she scoots all the way across the seat. She puts her arm over my shoulders and ruffles my hair—casually brushing it down over the cut above my eyebrow. "Relax, Will. You look like you're about to detonate," she whispers. Then she sings softly in my ear, her breathy words sending chills rolling down my spine. It feels like forever since she touched me like this, though it's only been twenty-four hours, and it's a jolt to my system. The good kind.

I glance up to the front, and in spite of everything, I laugh. My mom's nodding in time with the beat and tapping her fingers on the wheel. She slides down the driver's-side window like she doesn't have a care in the world. Christina nuzzles her face into my neck, hiding her face from the cop. I bow my head and inhale her, knowing she's putting on a show but willing to take anything she'll give me right now. Also—I need it, too, to hide my face, to pray we won't get busted. I put my arm around Christina and lace my fingers with hers, anchoring her close to me while the minivan inches forward.

And then it's our turn. We roll slowly past the cop. My mother looks right at him and holds up her ID in case he wants to take a look. Christina's got her face buried in my neck. My hand is in her hair, holding her there, letting her turn my blood into a streaming mess of conflicting signals, cascading floods of endorphins and adrenaline, of cortisol and dopamine.

The cop peers at us through Mom's open window. I can see up under the brim of his hat. I can see his eyes.

They are on Christina. Then he raises his gaze from her to me and smirks. He gives me the barest of nods, then waves us past.

Holy shit.

Everything inside me lets go at once, and I tilt Christina's chin up and kiss her, hard, harder than I should, because I have no idea what else to do with this energy that's built up inside me over the last half hour. She's right there with me, like she needs it, too, like she's using me for the same reason.

But then we both pull back at the same time, because, somehow, we both know there are things that still need fixing, and this won't do it. Christina gives me an apologetic look and kisses my cheek, then scoots back across the seat. I glance up at the rearview mirror to see my mom's eyes glued to the road with a laser intensity that tells me she saw the whole thing. I wipe my lips, wishing I'd remembered she was there *before* I stuck my tongue into my girlfriend's mouth.

Mom accelerates smoothly as the lanes open up. She switches the music off and gives the adapter back to Christina, her hands trembling slightly as she returns them to the wheel. I realize for the first time that my mom probably has that Valium for a reason. That she doesn't carry it around as a weapon of convenience, to sedate her enemies at will. She carries it around because she needs it for herself, for when things get to be too much, for when she can't cope. And that makes me feel like an asshole, because I've been really hard on her, not just over the past day, but over the past four years. She holds it together so well. Well enough that I always considered her some sort of superhuman. And she is, kind of, but she's also a woman who's lost the man she loved—and who has a messed-up jerk of a son who's gotten himself in a shitload of trouble. I reach forward and squeeze her shoulder, and she puts her hand over mine and squeezes back.

I sag against the seat, lay my head on the headrest, and close my eyes. Only a few more hours to Virginia, to what I hope will be another safe place where we can sink out of sight and decide what the hell to do with this scanner, this piece of plastic and alien circuitry that everyone wants, that some are willing to kill for. Once again, part of me wants to destroy it, but my dad built it—apparently worked on it for years—and he said it was important. I'm convinced there's more to it than just telling the difference between human and H2. Not only because of what my dad told me—it's made out of a freaking alien spaceship, after all, and I really think it's something unique that the H2 don't already have, since they've apparently salvaged all the other spacecraft wreckage. The ship that crashed in Morecambe Bay might have been special somehow. I need to work this out—it feels like there's something lingering just out of my reach. But right now, my head is aching, and I can't close my fingers around the thread of logic I need. For a moment, I let myself drift. I pretend that I'm just on a road trip. It's easy enough to believe right now. That cop seemed more interested in ogling Christina than looking for fugitives, and I'm starting to feel hungry again. It's been an entire eighteen hours since someone's shot at me. It could be a normal day. I could be a normal kid with a normal life, though I'm not even sure what that feels like.

I'm so busy daydreaming that I don't even notice that my mom has accelerated until we're doing over eighty, until she says, in this deadly calm voice, "They're following us."

THIRTEEN

CHRISTINA AND I WHIP AROUND AND SQUINT OUT THE
rear window. I have no idea how my mom spotted them, but
she's right: There are three black SUVs streaking by the sparse
traffic like it's at a standstill. Mom gets onto the Wilmington
bypass, her eyes flicking to the rearview every few seconds.

"Maybe it's not them," Christina whispers, almost to herself. I don't say anything, because I can tell it's a wish more
than anything else.

My mom has to hit the brakes to keep from plowing into a
car going fifty in the passing lane. She begins to weave in and
out, trying to put some distance between us and the SUVs, but
they're closing in quickly.

"We can't call the police, can we? We can't," Christina says.
She sounds almost as desperate as I feel, and something in me
seizes up and turns hot, like a lump of molten iron, cauterizing

all the soft, bleeding parts of me, shoring me up on the inside. I don't care what I have to do; I'm going to make sure she gets out of this. My mom was right; she shouldn't even be here. But since she is, it's my job to make sure her parents get to see her again, that Livia gets her big sister back.

I look around the interior of the vehicle. "I don't suppose you have a weapon."

My mom shakes her head and gives me a sad smile. "I'm not a walking arsenal like your father was."

I'd feel so much better if he were here, if he were in charge. Just as I'm thinking my mom probably would, too, she snaps, "Seat belts."

We obey. The SUVs are coming up hard, black, and menacing, the three of them swerving aggressively between cars, and now they're within a few car lengths. One of them jerks to the right and floors it, shooting up the shoulder. It pulls abruptly back into the slow lane to avoid a shredded semi tire, cutting right in front of a Cadillac driven by a white-haired old lady. She overcorrects, and orange sparks fly off the guardrail as she bounces off of it and skids to a stop.

Whatever fear my mom had before is pushed down somewhere deep inside of her, alongside her grief and whatever else she doesn't want to share. She looks totally calm, and I'm grateful for that as one of the SUVs muscles up behind us, close enough for me to see the chiseled outline of Race Lavin's severe face. He's at the wheel, and he's staring right at our rear window like he can see straight through the tint, even though I know that's impossible. His jaw is set with determination as he moves up and nudges our bumper. Christina yelps.

My mom stomps on the brakes.

The collision throws us forward, but the seat belt catches me before my face hits the seat in front of me. My mother guns it again, picking up speed as we streak along the highway in the far left lane. Race is a few car lengths behind us now, but it doesn't seem like the collision did much to his vehicle. It must be armor-plated, too. The other two SUVs are in the middle lane, and one of them's trying to cut in front of our minivan while the other holds steady beside us.

"They're trying to box us in," I say.

The SUV next to us glides closer, crowding us. But the driver keeps having to swerve into the slow lane to get past the traffic in the center lane. Finally, though, he swings by a few cars on the right, then comes roaring toward us.

This time the impact wrenches a scream from Christina, who is thrown against the window frame.

"Fuck this," I mutter, unbuckling my seat belt. If they force us off the road, we're doomed. If this ends any other way than them giving up, we. Are. Doomed.

So I'm going to make them give up.

I reach under the seat and grab Christina's backpack. I pull out the buns, the chips, the oranges, the lighter fluid . . . and the Super Soaker. It takes me only a few seconds to form my plan. I rip the mesh bag of oranges open and pull out three, then shove the bag at Christina. "Can you help me? You up for this?"

She pales as she looks down at the oranges. "Um. Sure?"

"I need you to throw those at them."

Her laugh is *just* this side of hysterical. "What?"

"Throw them. Buy me some time."

"Tate," my mom says. "I don't know what you think you're doing, but—"

"Lecture me later, okay? But right now, let me do what Dad trained me to do."

My mom presses her lips together tightly, but doesn't argue as she clicks the button to release the front-seat control of the rear windows. "They've probably guessed we're shielded," she says, "which is the only thing that's keeping them from shooting at us now. That and the risk of harming civilians, which they'll avoid if they can. But if they sense an opportunity, they'll take it."

I pull the bag of oranges out of Christina's grasp. "Never mind. Sit tight."

"Are you crazy?" Christina says in a high voice. She snatches the oranges back and hits the button to open the moon roof.

"Be careful," my mom says. "When we get back on Ninety-five, the traffic's going to be heavier. If you can get them to give us some space, I might be able to lose them."

I start to work while Christina peers out the window. Race

is still on our ass, and the other two are jockeying for position in the center lane. I bite a hole in each orange, spitting the peel onto the floor. Then I gouge out the sticky insides as the juice runs between my fingers. I stuff the centers with the buns and chips and whatever paper I can find inside the van, which isn't easy because I keep getting thrown around as my mom swerves from lane to lane, occasionally braking, then flooring it in the next second.

I glance over to see Christina pop up through the moon roof, hurl an orange, and plunge back down into the van, only to lunge upward with another and another a second later. Her first two throws are wild, missing the SUV next to us by a few feet, but the third orange bounces off Race's windshield.

And out the rear window, I see exactly what I was hoping for.

His mouth is quirked at this odd angle. Just a hint of amusement on his harsh face.

He thinks we're harmless and stupid.

With my oranges prepared, I unscrew the cap on one of the bottles of lighter fluid and load up the water blaster. I have two bottles. Twenty-four ounces to play with.

"Move over," I tell Christina, and then I stand up on the seat, thrusting myself into the open air. The wind at my back throws me forward, pressing my stomach against the edge of the moon roof. Race slows a bit when he sees I have something in my hands. I take aim and squirt his windshield, coating it as quickly as I can before turning and nailing the SUV right next to us. It swerves a little, then turns on its windshield wipers. The driver is sneering, probably thinking what idiots we are, trying to drive them off with oranges and a water gun.

I drop down through the moon roof as the first shots are fired. Shit.

Two of the SUVs have passengers. One of them's taking aim at our tires.

My mom curses and swerves back into the middle lane, right toward that SUV, but the driver brakes and gets behind her, cutting in front of Race. Christina pops back up and throws another orange, which bounces off that SUV's windshield. The driver rolls his eyes.

Time to hurl *my* oranges.

I take the wand lighter, fire it up, and light the inside of one of the oranges. It smolders, then catches. "Christina, I need you to throw this at the SUV behind us when I give the word. And then you get back down as quick as you can." I hand it to her. She nods.

"Now!"

We shove through the roof together, gasping in the roaring wind and catching ourselves as we're pushed forward over the roof of the minivan. She hurls the orange . . . and then it's just like skeet shooting. Except, when my stream of lighter fluid hits that burning orange, it doesn't shatter.

It turns into a fireball.

And when that fireball hits the already soaked windshield

of the SUV, it explodes. The flames completely cover the front of the vehicle, the hood, the glass.

Enough to panic the driver. He jams on the brakes, and before we drop down into the minivan again, we hear the crunching-rending crash as he careens off the highway. The SUV rolls over and disappears down an embankment.

One down. Not done.

We lurch forward as Race rear-ends us again, and then to the side as the other SUV sideswipes us. My head cracks against the window before I can catch myself.

Wincing, I light another orange. "Want to try another one?"

"Definitely." Christina pulls her ponytail tight and takes the smoldering orange from my hand. "Say when."

"When!"

We jump up again, aiming at the SUV next to us. Christina cocks her arm back to throw.

The gunshot makes me jerk.

Christina drops from beside me like her legs have been cut out from under her. I catch the smoldering orange as she disappears through the moon roof and find myself staring at three perfectly round drops of blood on its orange skin. It's a completely disconnected moment, a thousand years of agony wrapped in a fraction of a second. My mom starts swerving back and forth, pulling me from my trance, and I realize she's trying to prevent them from picking me off, too. I should get back down, get to safety.

Fuck that.

Fuck that.

I hurl the orange right at the open window of the SUV beside us, the one where a gray-haired agent is once again taking aim, this time at me. While the orange is still in midair, I swing my water blaster up and let fly, right at his face. The fluid sparks off the orange, creating spiraling droplets of fire as it becomes a stream of flame that blasts across the space between us, straight through that open window. The savage pleasure I feel when the occupants of that SUV start to scream almost scares me. Almost. But right now, most of me is gone, and all the rest of me wants to do is hurt them.

I drop back into the minivan. Christina is lying sprawled across the seat, and there's blood in her hair, and I cannot bring myself to look any closer. If I do, I'm going to implode, disintegrate from the inside out, and my mom needs me, too, so I'm going to have to fall apart later.

I light the third orange and refill my water blaster with the second bottle of lighter fluid. There's only one SUV chasing us now, and it's Race. Oddly enough, there aren't any police yet, and I have to wonder if he told them to stay away so he could slaughter us in peace.

I wonder if he's regretting it now.

Except—there they are, cresting a hill about a mile or so behind us, distant flashing reds. He's called in reinforcements. "Mom."

"I see them."

On autopilot, I drive myself upward. Race is still behind us, and he's rolling down his window. Gun in his hand. I hurl the orange at his windshield and swing my water blaster up.

And I miss.

He swerves to the side just in time, and the fireball orange bounces off the side mirror before falling into the road, leaving a pathetic trail of flame behind it.

This time I'm the one who falls back into the minivan like my strings have been cut. God*damn* it.

"Don't worry about it," barks my mom. "Now put on your seat belt and make sure Christina's secured. We're taking the next exit."

I kneel on the floor mat and wrap a seat belt over Christina's torso, clicking it into place and pulling it tight. But now that I've gotten this close to her, I can't pull away. I have to know.

With trembling hands, my fingers slide down to her wrist, and I hold my breath. It comes whooshing out of me in a rush when I feel her pulse, fast but steady. I lean down as my mom veers to the right and bounces off something. I barely notice, barely register the impact. Because Christina just moaned, and she's alive, and I am not letting her go. My hands are in her hair, searching for the source of the blood soaking her blond locks. And thank God, it's not a hole—it's a deep cut. The bullet must have grazed her skull, leaving a long, deep gash. But she's bleeding. A lot. I tear a strip off the bottom of her shirt and press it to the wound.

I sit up and look around, catching sight of a road sign. We're somewhere near the Delaware-Maryland border. The cops are as far behind us as they were before, but Race is hard on our tail.

"Are you secured?" my mom yells.

I yank a seat belt around me. "Yes."

"Then hang on!"

She wrenches the wheel to the right, and we cut off a huge bus in the slow lane, which slams on its brakes. Wheels screeching and smoking, it fishtails and skids to a halt across the two right lanes. My mom slows down as Race shoots around the nose of the bus and blows by us in the passing lane. And then she stomps on the gas and rockets toward him across three lanes of traffic.

I throw myself over Christina right as we T-bone Race's SUV. I hear my mom grunt with the impact and realize the airbags must have been turned off. I don't have time to wonder if she's all right, though, because as soon as we hit, we're moving again, lurching backward and then forward. My ears ringing, my head pounding, I push myself up to see us barreling down the road, front end dented and steaming. On the grassy median strip behind us, Race's SUV is on its side, wheels still spinning.

The engine starts to whine as my mom hurtles toward the next exit. She takes the ramp at high speed and slows only slightly as she makes turn after turn on the local roads. I drag myself onto the seat, aching all over, and brace Christina as my mom takes a sharp, sudden right onto a two-lane highway. The van's frame shudders, and there's a *thunk-thunk-thunk* sound that tells me our ride is not long for this world.

Mom briskly rubs at a bump on her forehead, which, thankfully, appears to be the only injury she sustained in the crash with Race. She pulls out her phone and puts it to her ear.

"Call Bishop," she says.

After a few seconds, I hear a muffled male voice answering. "I need safe passage and haven for members of the Archer, Shirazi, and"—she glances back at Christina with narrowed eyes—"Alexander lines. Yes. Only three. Medic attendance is required. Yes, the authorities are engaged." She looks in her rear and sideview mirrors. "No, we are not currently being followed."

The person on the other end replies while I strain to hear what he's saying. Then my mother says, "We'll be there. Probably on foot. Thirty minutes." She hangs up. "Get your father's phone, please," she says to me.

I pull it from my pocket and hold it up.

"Use the GPS. Get me directions to William Penn State Forest."

I do what she asks. "Where exactly are we going?"

"Off the grid."

FOURTEEN

"STAY ON THIS ROAD FOR THE NEXT SEVEN MILES," I SAY.
Then I set the phone on the seat and carefully gather Christina
in my arms. I keep the scrap of shirt pressed to the side of her
head, but it's almost soaked through. Her hair is sticky, tangled, and painting my arms with thin crimson streaks.

"Hey," I whisper to her, holding her tight. "Wake up. Come
back."

She doesn't move, doesn't tense, doesn't twitch. A chill
goes through me. Twenty-four hours ago, I was trying to stop
my father's bleeding, trying to get him to stay with me. I feel
just as helpless now.

"She needs a doctor, Mom." I don't even try to control the
tremble in my voice. I'm not sure whether it was the impact of
the bullet or that she hit her head on the van's roof as she fell,

but she's deeply unconscious. Her pulse is steady, and she's breathing, but that's all I can say. For all I know, she's hemorrhaging and the parts that make her Christina are irreparably broken. For all I know, she's dying quietly in my arms. "Sooner than thirty minutes," I add.

"It's the best I can do."

"Can't we take her to a hospital?"

"We can, but we'll have to leave her there, and I guarantee you, the Core will find her quickly, and they will try to use her to get to us. And they won't be gentle."

I swallow hard. "So where are we going?"

"The family compound of one of The Fifty. A place where we can get some medical care for her, and some help getting where we need to go."

"Aren't we past the time for cryptic bullshit?" I snap. "Who the hell are these people?"

"I'm sorry. I wish your dad had explained all of this to you earlier."

"Me too." I know so little about my dad and this world I'm a part of, and it's making me nuts. But— "It's not like he knew any of this was going to happen." How could he have anticipated what a fuck-up I would turn out to be?

Mom sighs. "Your father believed there are still about three billion humans left."

"No, he said there were less than that. And that the number

is dropping fast." It reminds me of that screen in my dad's lab, with one number jittering up while the second shrank in a jagged progression.

My mother gives me the saddest smile. "Most of those humans don't know they're members of an endangered species, just like most H2 don't know they're aliens. And maybe it wouldn't matter to some, but the Core have been so covertly merciless over the years, so it clearly matters to them. And The Fifty are well aware of their humanity and carefully protect it. As you know, the Archers are members. My family, the Shirazis, are as well, the only members in southwest Asia. There are at least five families in China, three in India, and a scattering across Europe, Africa, and South America. There are no members of The Fifty from Australia. There are several families based here in the States, the largest and most powerful being the Alexanders, the Fishers, the McClarens, and the Bishops."

I recognize several of those last names—George's last name is Fisher, and the driver who died yesterday . . . Peter McClaren. "What about the Archers?" My dad's parents died when I was little, and he was an only child. "Do I have family I don't know about?"

My mother's amber eyes meet mine in the rearview mirror. "No. You are the last of the Archers."

It takes me a minute or two to remember to breathe. Brayton's words echo in my head: *Your bloodline has extended for centuries . . . Don't do anything to jeopardize that.* "Wait, Brayton said he was related to me," I finally stammer. Not that I'd want to claim him as my family. Quite the opposite.

She nods. "Most of our families are interrelated, but Brayton is an Alexander, not an Archer. As you can imagine, over four hundred years, many of the lines have just . . . ended. But the ones that remain—their purity has been maintained, and that has meant arranged marriages. It's one of the reasons the families stay in contact with one another."

"What?"

She keeps her eyes on the road. "I know that must sound primitive to you, but you have to understand that we are essentially an endangered species, and it's only been through careful breeding that we have survived."

"*Breeding*?" Oh my God. "So, you and Dad . . ."

"Were lucky," she answers quickly, and her smile contains a thousand memories. "When I came here to study, the Archers hosted me, and I met Fred when he was home for Christmas break that year. The attraction was instant."

Something inside me loosens. I needed to hear that, for some reason, that my parents really loved each other, that I am not the product of cold and analytical *breeding*. "So The Fifty have some sort of—what? Government, or something?"

My mom shakes her head. "Not at all. The Fifty was formally established about a hundred and fifty years ago, though many of the families had forged alliances centuries before that. Because the Core is so deeply enmeshed with governments

177

all over the world, the human families seized whatever power they could in private industry. Black Box has existed under one name or another since that time. It's a front, I guess you could call it, a way of amassing capital and resources to defend ourselves from the Core, who have, throughout the centuries, picked off a large number of us through either official or unofficial methods."

"Like what, assassinations?"

"It always looks like an accident," she says grimly. "But they've also maliciously sabotaged, prosecuted, and imprisoned anyone who threatens to reveal their secrets. At this point, though, through Black Box, we have weapons, contacts, and clout. It's been almost a stalemate for nearly fifty years, with neither side aggressing unless the other steps out of line."

"Like I did yesterday," I say in a hollow voice.

"Don't worry. I'm going to handle this. We'll be okay. But . . . when we're with the Bishops, follow my lead and tell them Christina is human."

"Why?"

She shakes her head. "It's just easier that way."

I can tell from looking at her that she's not telling me something, and it trips my wire. "Cut the bullshit and start treating me like an adult. Right. The fuck. Now."

Her eyes go wide. "Excuse me?"

I lean forward. "I'm not twelve. And I've lived ten years in the last twenty-four hours."

Her shoulders sag. "I know, Tate, so have I. I'm trying to do my best—"

"I get it! You're my mom and you want to protect me. So did Dad." My throat feels like it's being squeezed by an invisible hand. "But I'm not helpless. And I need you to understand something he never did: This girl, right here? She's important. I need to hear you acknowledge that, and to promise me you'll help me save her." My voice breaks and I grit my teeth.

"I'm doing everything I can, Tate, I—"

"But you need to let me do everything *I* can, Mom. It's the only way we're going to get through this. And if anything happens to Christina . . ." I clear my throat. "I want to know you understand that."

"Okay," she says softly. "I know you're not helpless. You were amazing just now. I'm so proud of you. It's . . . it's very difficult to willingly expose your own child to danger. So be patient with me, please," she finishes in a strained whisper.

My nostrils flare as I draw in a long breath. "I'm trying to. And I appreciate what you've told me so far. But I need to know all of it. Everything. Stop trying to protect me. I'm part of this, and I can help."

She's quiet for nearly a full minute before she says, "The Fifty have differing opinions on how to interface with the H2. Some prefer peace and negotiation, and some prefer a more aggressive strategy. Those differences mean the occasional feud. But we always help each other when it's needed."

"And now we're going to get help from the Bishops. Tell me about them."

Her knuckles are white over the steering wheel. "They have a compound in this area. Their patriarch, Rufus, knew your dad. The Bishops are originally from the same region in Britain as the Archers, and there have been close ties between the families ever since. But in general, they keep to themselves and are very suspicious of outsiders."

"You told them there were three of us. One Archer, one Shirazi—and one Alexander."

"They *need* to think Christina is human, Tate. It won't be good if they know she's H2."

"How not good?"

"Fatally not good. They've lost members of their family to the Core, and they're not a forgiving bunch. We're going to tell them she's Brayton's niece."

My heart slams against my ribs as I look down at Christina's pale face. "What's going to keep them from fact-checking?"

My mother's eyebrow arches. "When I said some of the families are feuding, that's what I was talking about. Rufus and Brayton hate each other. Rufus may maintain some communication with the other families, but the Bishops and the Alexanders are basically enemies. It's a long story for another time, but the result is that the Bishops won't know or necessarily question that she's a member of the Alexander family, because they haven't had contact with them in years. She's blond like the Alexanders, so that helps."

Christina and Brayton look *nothing* alike, but I guess we can't afford to be choosy right now. "Anything else I should know?"

"Two ears, one mouth. Listen more than you talk and let me handle the politics." She holds up her hand when she senses I'm about to interrupt. "It's too complicated to explain all the details. You're smart, and you can follow my lead."

My mouth snaps shut, and I nod.

Christina's eyelids flutter, and a low whimper comes from her throat. She opens her eyes and stares up at me for a moment, but there's nothing there, just this glazed, confused look that makes my stomach clench. Her eyes fall shut again, leaving me aching.

My mom's phone buzzes, and she holds it to her ear. "Ready." She watches the road as she listens. "Copy that." Then she repeats a set of coordinates. "We'll be there soon. Thank you."

I program the coordinates into my dad's phone. It's a point inside the state forest. We're only about a mile from there now. "You said we'd be on foot."

She turns off the two-lane highway onto a single-lane gravel road. "I'm going to ditch the car. Not that it's going to last much longer anyway. Can you carry her?"

"Yeah, but I'm worried about moving her around."

"I'm sorry, Tate. They'll be able to care for her as soon as we meet up. They're bringing their medic."

"They have their own medic?"

"They're pretty self-sufficient," she says as she pulls off the road at a spot that allows us to drive into the woods. I haven't seen a house in at least half a mile.

"And does Race know they're out here? Seems like he'll show up on their doorstep if he thinks we've run there."

"As long as there has been a grid, the Bishops have stayed off it. And your dad once told me he'd helped Rufus set up decoy compounds throughout the country. Basically, there's a lot of evidence that the Bishops are elsewhere, but little evidence that they're here."

"This Rufus guy sounds completely paranoid."

My mother shrugs. "For the moment, we should consider that a lucky break."

She parks about thirty feet off the road, behind a fallen oak tree. When she turns off the engine, it makes this choking, shuddering sound that tells me it's breathed its last. "I'm going to touch base with Angus McClaren and let him know where we are. He's the CFO at Black Box and the patriarch of the McClarens."

"And you trust him?"

She pivots in her seat and looks me in the eye. "I do. He's one of the first people I called last night. He's a good friend, a powerful member of The Fifty, and he's not a huge fan of Rufus Bishop. Think of it as insurance."

I nod, though I'm not sure what Angus McClaren—who's probably in Chicago for the emergency board meeting George mentioned—can do for us if Rufus Bishop decides to hurt Christina.

While Mom hops out of the van with her phone already to her ear, I put on the backpack, reassured by the weight of the scanner inside, and lift Christina in my arms. Her head lolls in the crook of my neck, and she moans again.

My mom is hanging up as I get out. "Left a voicemail." She puts her phone back in her pocket and takes Christina's pulse, then pulls a small flashlight out of her shoulder bag and lifts each of Christina's eyelids, shining the beam of light into them. "Pupils are equal, round, and reactive to light. It's a good sign." She puts the flashlight back in her bag, and then pauses and looks up at me. Her hand closes over my forearm. "I'm going to do my best for both of you." Her eyes meet mine. "And I'll ask for your help when I need it."

"Okay." I believe her. She could have tried to dump Christina, but instead she seems determined to save her. For me. It's the only thing that feels good in all this badness. "And I'll do whatever I can, if it means Christina gets what she needs."

She gives me a small smile. "Sometimes you remind me so much of your father." She pats my arm, takes my father's phone from my hand, then turns around and begins hiking into the woods.

I follow, holding Christina tight, picking my way along and

doing my best not to jostle her. She feels so light in my arms, like some part of her has flown away and all I'm carrying is a shell. So I murmur quietly to her as I walk, trying to lure her back to me. "Fall of my freshman year, Will talked me into going to a girls' soccer game. I didn't want to go. I knew it would mean hours of playing catch-up on my language studies, but you know Will. He can be pretty persuasive."

I lift her a little higher. Her hair tickles my neck. "I went because he claimed the striker was a total hottie, but I walked away with a mad crush on the left winger." There was something about the playful but defiant flash of her eyes, the brash, unapologetic toughness of her, that loud, vibrant laugh, those incredible legs, that gorgeous smile . . . Every second that ticked by dug my hole a little deeper.

I lean my cheek against her forehead. "Do you remember looking up into the stands? I think I held my breath for a whole minute, waiting for your eyes to land on me." I take advantage of a patch of level terrain and look down at her. "And they did, for about a nanosecond. Then you saw the guy you were actually looking for and waved at *him*. I swore right then that someday, I would be the guy. I wanted to be the guy you looked for in the stands."

God, that sounds so dumb. It's absolutely true, though. It took a few years. And it didn't go the way I wanted it to. Except . . . it went better. Because I became her friend, not a boyfriend of the month. By the time we finally went out a few months ago, I knew her well enough to know this was something to be careful with, something not to rush, something to hold close and take care of. "I don't know how I got that lucky," I mumble.

Christina shifts in my arms and sighs, and it almost brings me to my knees.

My mom finds a dirt trail, and we follow it while I continue to babble to my bleeding, unconscious girlfriend about all the moments that have added up to how I feel about her now. And I realize something as I walk along, holding her against my chest, but I can't bear to say it out loud because, right now, it hurts too much.

We cross a footbridge over a rushing stream. It's started to rain, but only a few drops reach us through the thick canopy of the trees. "Tate," my mom calls back to me.

I raise my head to see three people standing by a newish-looking pickup truck with a capped bed parked at the side of a narrow road. A stout, middle-aged, auburn-haired woman spots us and nudges the gaunt, older guy next to her. He turns around and squints at us through thick-lensed glasses. The third guy, young, maybe early twenties, rushes forward when he sees us. He has fiery red hair and is extremely pale. I mean, weirdly so. As he comes near, I see that the bridge of his nose and his cheeks are covered in tiny freckles, but he still looks like some kind of albino.

"We were starting to wonder if you'd gotten picked up by

the authorities," Freckles says. He has his hand on his waist, maybe to keep his saggy jeans perched on his skinny hips. He's got on a loose, long-sleeved, hooded jersey, which must be stifling in this steamy weather. He extends his hand as he approaches my mother. "David Bishop."

"Mitra Shirazi-Archer," my mother says, shaking his hand. "This is my son, Tate, and his friend, Christina Alexander."

David nods at me, but his eyes are already on Christina. "What happened to her?" he asks, coming toward us. The other two are walking up the trail, and their eyes are on Christina, too.

"The Core was in pursuit," my mother answers. "She was shot."

"She may have hit her head when she fell," I say.

David's eyes meet mine. They are totally bloodshot. I sincerely hope this dude isn't high. Because, as I watch him turn his attention to Christina and probe for the pulse at her neck, I am getting the distinct impression that he is the medic.

"Bring her to the truck," he says quietly.

The others introduce themselves as Esther and Timothy Bishop. With serious expressions, they escort us along the path. My mother walks close by my side as the rain begins to drip heavily through the leaves overhead. A cool drop hits the back of my neck and slides down my spine. Another hits Christina's cheek, and she twitches. I brush my lips across her forehead as we take the last few steps to the pickup.

I am instantly relieved when I see that the truck bed is

basically an ambulance bay. David climbs inside and helps me lay Christina on the stretcher in the center. I start to climb in as well, but he leans over her, crowding me out.

"You can sit up front," he says, reaching for a small penlight from a tray of supplies on the side bench.

No way. "I'd rather—"

My mother's hand on my arm is as good as a slap in the face. I promised her I'd let her handle the politics, so I slide myself off the tailgate.

"I'll take good care of her," David reassures me.

Timothy closes up the back of the truck while Esther gets in the driver's seat. "We're only about twenty minutes from the compound." He comes around to the passenger side. "We've got an X-ray machine."

"We're grateful for your help," my mother says as we scramble into the back of the extended cab. Through the filmy little window between the cab and the truck bed, I can see David examining Christina, whose arms and legs are moving beneath the straps he's used to hold her in place. She looks like she's having a nightmare.

She's waking up, and she's not going to know where she is. She's going to be scared to death.

My hand is on the door handle in the next second, but my mother puts her hand on my leg and squeezes. "We'll be there soon," she says quietly as the truck's engine roars and we lurch forward. I sit back in the seat, cross my arms over my chest, and jam my hands into my armpits to force myself to stay still. Mom nudges my shoulder with hers. The look on her face tells me she *sees* me, that she knows I'm going nuts right now. Knowing she gets it drains a little of my tension away.

Surprisingly, Esther and Timothy don't ask us any questions at all. The only sound in the cab is the squeak of the windshield wipers as we bump our way down gravel roads, then briefly onto a two-lane highway, where I see a sign that tells me we've left the state park and entered Pennsylvania. I am dying to look behind me, to see how Christina's doing, but I keep my eyes up front, memorizing the route as we wind along more unpaved single-lane roads, forcing myself not to lower my guard.

Finally, Esther turns down a long driveway that ends in a wide gravel parking lot that forms a clearing in the middle of the dense woods. At least twenty vehicles are parked in two orderly rows. There are a few compact cars, several pickups, a row of SUVs, one enormous Cadillac sedan, and three plain white delivery trucks. Two men stand at one end of the parking lot, on a paved trail that tracks through the forest behind them. They are well built and tanned, their rust-red hair cut close to their heads. I think they might be twins; they look so much alike. Esther waves her arm out the window as she drives toward them, executes a wide turn, and backs her way up to where the twins are standing.

As soon as she stops, I'm out the door, my mother right

behind me. I walk around the side of the truck. The twins, guns in holsters at their hips, are helping David roll the stretcher off the back of the truck as he holds up an IV bag connected to Christina's limp hand. I am at her side just as the wheeled legs of the stretcher extend and lock into place. The raindrops on her face look like tears, and I wipe them away as she blinks up at me. "Tate?"

I lean down close. "It's me, baby. I'm here."

"My head . . . hurts," she breathes, wincing. She's got a pressure bandage over one side of her head, and David has carefully cleaned the blood from her face and neck.

"I know," I say. "You're going to feel better soon. And you're safe."

I hope I'm right about that.

David clears his throat, and I raise my head to see him standing on the other side of the stretcher. His fingers are curled over its metal railing as he gazes down at me, bloodshot eyes floating in his paper-white, freckled face. "I'm going to take her to our clinic and do a head X-ray, then I'll stitch the laceration."

I take Christina's hand, about to tell her I'll be holding it through the whole thing, when one of the twins says, "Rufus is waiting for you in his study."

He's staring right at me.

My mom links her arm with mine, part warning, part reassurance. "Of course."

Then David pushes the stretcher through the spitting rain, onto a blacktop sidewalk, carrying Christina away. The twins lead my mom and me down the same sidewalk until we reach a fork in the path and David heads down one branch while we take the other. My heart races as I lose sight of Christina. I'd planned to be with her, to protect her. To keep her from accidentally revealing what she is. And now she's on her own. But as much as I want to sprint after her, I remind myself to follow my mom's lead.

Esther and Timothy walk silently behind us as we enter another clearing, this one at least a half mile in diameter. About a dozen cabins are situated in a neat semicircle on either side. Each has a solar panel on the roof. A few of them have large enclosed porches out front. Most of the windows are covered with black curtains. In the center of the clearing are several larger buildings. I look at each of them, sizing them up, wondering about the location of the clinic where they've taken Christina.

The twins lead us up to a three-story octagonal lodge dead in the center of the clearing. Like all the other structures in the place, solar panels ring the roof. My mom wasn't kidding when she said these people were self-sufficient—it's likely they produce more energy than they consume. We follow the twins up a set of wooden steps to an enormous shaded porch. One of them holds the door to the lodge open for us while the other strides into the cool, dark room. It's like an enormous cave. All the windows are heavily curtained, and on one side of the room sit three long wooden tables. Down a set of shallow, stone-tiled steps is a sunken open area. A massive wood-burning fireplace dominates that side of the space, tall enough for a man to walk into without ducking. Hanging above the high mantel, hewn from rough wood, is some sort of sculpture. It looks like an ancient rune. I stare at it, trying to figure out where I've seen it before.

"This way," one of the twins says, extending his arm and gesturing down a wide hallway opposite the sunken area. We follow the twins until they stop on either side of a doorway. "Go on in."

My hand tightens around the strap of the backpack as my mom and I enter. The room is a library. Three of the walls are built-in bookcases, two stories high, complete with a rolling ladder to allow access to the top shelves.

Standing at the center of the room is a man.

He looks a lot like Santa Claus.

Huge white beard, round belly, rosy cheeks, curly white hair. Bushiest eyebrows I've ever seen, like someone's glued two chinchillas to his forehead.

He puts his arms out, wiggling his thick fingers. "Mitra. I haven't seen you since the wedding, but you haven't aged a day."

My mother smiles warmly. "You're too kind, Rufus." She steps forward into his embrace.

Over her shoulder, his eyes meet mine. They're all twinkly

and jolly, but there's something else there, too, a sharp curiosity. "You look just like your father, young man."

I smile, and I do my best to make it friendly. "Thanks."

"Where is Fred?" he asks my mother as he releases her. "Is he meeting you here?"

"Fred was killed yesterday," my mother says, her voice catching.

Rufus Bishop's face drains of color. There is genuine sadness in his voice when he says, "I hadn't heard. I'm so sorry." He rubs his hand over his belly, his brow furrowed. "Oh, this is so sad. So sad. How did it happen?"

"The Core came after him, led by Race Lavin," my mother says simply. "Fred was shot when he tried to escape. But Tate got away and came to me, and that's why we're here. We were trying to get to Charlottesville, but the agents gave chase. That's when Christina was injured."

His bushy eyebrows rise. "This kind of outright attack hasn't happened in years, not since Anton Cermak." He sees the question in my expression and explains. "He got himself elected mayor of Chicago and made a threat to out the H2. He was shaking hands with Roosevelt when he was shot—they claimed it was an assassination attempt against the president, but the members of The Fifty knew better." He crosses his arms over his chest, like he's made some kind of decision. "If the Core is after you now, they must have judged the threat to be immense. You'll all be safe here. We take security very seriously."

And then his pale blue, bloodshot eyes land right on me. I have just enough time to wonder why he's not asking what we did to stir up the Core before he says, "So I know you'll understand when I ask you to turn over your possessions to be searched."

He gestures toward the backpack, and his lips lift into a cold, calculating smile.

FIFTEEN

I GIVE MY MOTHER A SIDELONG GLANCE, AND SHE NODS.
I slide out of the backpack and offer it up as the burly twins
step into the room. My mother hands one of them her bag.
Rufus takes the pack from me. He opens it, and he doesn't
even seem surprised when his eyes light on the scanner. He
takes it out and holds it up.

"This is why, isn't it?" he asks me.

I put my hands in my pockets and adopt my clueless-kid
expression. "Why what?"

He chuckles. "I must look like one hell of a dumb redneck
to you, don't I?" His words are jovial, but it's not hard to detect
the threat underneath. "Let me tell you something you might
not know, boy. I worked for Black Box before it even *was* Black

Box. I'm the one who hired your father when he graduated from college."

Now I really am a clueless kid, no pretending required.

Rufus sees my surprise, and a look of satisfaction crosses his face. "Just because we choose to live out here doesn't mean we're ignorant." He turns away from me and waves the scanner at my mom. "Now. This is why, isn't it?"

"This is why," says my mother. "This is what the Core was after."

Rufus smiles and flicks it on. Blue light courses over his beach ball of a belly. He tilts his head, then shines it over my mother, briefly turning her olive skin sapphire blue. He does the same thing to me, and then to the twins. All blue. It seems like a glorified flashlight, and I relax a little as the twins lean against the bookshelves, looking bored.

Rufus switches the scanner off, looking the opposite of bored. "I'll be damned," he says softly. "He did it, didn't he?"

I make a mental note not to underestimate this guy again.

"He did," Mom says, her tone neutral, giving little away.

Rufus shakes his head and holds up the scanner. "He'd been working on this for years." His eyes flick up to my mother's. "Yes, I was one of the few he told. But now the Core is aware of its existence, and they want their technology back."

"Yes," my mother replies. "As soon as it was in the open, they came after it."

His cheeks are turning a ruddy red. "You know what they'll do if they have this."

My mother shakes her head. "We don't know anything for sure. There could be many reasons why it's important to them."

Rufus stares at my mother for a full minute, long enough to make me want to grab her hand and make a run for it. His face has turned a mottled shade of pink by the time he says, "Do you think they're going to put it in their museum of alien heritage?" And then he starts to laugh.

It's just a chuckle at first, but it's not long before he's doubled over, clutching his belly as he guffaws. "You were always such a liberal, Mitra. All the Shirazis are. But you . . . you're still friends with some of them, aren't you?"

My stomach tightens. She is?

Rufus straightens up, and he's no longer laughing. "Fred told me that you wanted to introduce him to some of them. You're blind to their true nature."

My mother stands completely still, watching Rufus with a small smile on her face. I wonder if she's fantasizing about dropping a few dozen Valium into his hot chocolate tonight.

"I'm a scientist," she says, "and I believe in things for which I have evidence."

"I wonder if the blood on your son's shirt is evidence enough of the Core's intentions?" He points at me, and I look down at myself.

196

And immediately wish I hadn't. Once again, I am covered in the blood of someone I love.

"Obviously I understand the risks and wish to be cautious," my mother says in a steady voice. "Or else I would have surrendered the technology to the Core immediately."

"What will they do if they have it?" I ask.

Rufus gives me an appraising look. "Until now, no one could tell the difference between human and H2, but with this . . . It's a quick way for anyone to know. Imagine how that could change things."

"Or you could just tell me what you think."

His eyes narrow. "When they first arrived here, there weren't many of 'em, and mixing with the native population was essential to preventing their own extinction. But now there are more of them than there are of us."

I shake my head. "But all I keep hearing is that most H2 don't even know they are H2. This Core group doesn't want people to know the H2 actually exist, right? In other words, they *don't* want things to change."

Rufus lets out a sharp bark of laughter. "Wrong. Just because they want to keep people in the dark doesn't mean they don't want things to change. With this technology, they could breed us out of existence in a single generation. Sure, they'd do it quietly so no one would know what was happening, but make no mistake—they'd snuff us out. They believe they're superior. They think they're doing the world a favor by spreading their alien genes." He's practically grinding his teeth now, and his face is beet red.

I can't tell whether he's brilliant or paranoid to an insane degree.

"We're safe here, and we have our freedom." He jabs a thick finger at my mom. "See how much freedom the Core will give us if they scale up this technology and are able to figure out where we all are."

His words send unpleasant prickles over my skin, because I'm once again remembering standing in my father's lab, staring at that screen with the population numbers twitching up and down . . . What if my dad *already* scaled it up? What was he doing?

My mother waves her hand dismissively. "With the power and weaponry Black Box has amassed, we can—"

"Brayton Alexander's been taking government contracts for years! That's why I left!" Rufus roars, blue veins standing out on his forehead. "If he gets ahold of this thing, he'll probably sell it to them!"

My mother is unruffled by his outburst. "You know very well he only sells what he's been authorized to by the board so we know their capabilities and remain able to counter them."

"Intelligence is the opposite of what it is!" he shouts, and then seems to catch himself. He crosses his arms over his heaving chest. "Fred must've gotten tired of it. It's probably why he left Black Box. Am I right?"

Mom's lips become a firm line.

Rufus grunts. "Thought so," he says in a quieter voice. "Fred and I are alike. He hated the H2. And he knew Brayton was out for nothing but profit." He glances at me. "Brayton Alexander doesn't care about being human. He only cares about money and power."

"Fred didn't trust Brayton," my mother says, but she stops there. She doesn't tell him about what Brayton did yesterday, maybe to avoid stirring Rufus up again.

But he's ignoring her now, talking only to me. "That's because your father was smart. You did the right thing by coming here instead of running to Brayton. And by fighting to keep it from the Core. You're a brave young man," he says to me, patting his belly like it's a family pet. "And now that we have it, we can do so *much* with it." His eyes have the same cold, eager glint that Brayton's did.

Mom sees it. "Rufus," she says in a low, hesitant voice.

"*All* humans have the right to know they're an endangered species," Rufus says, giving her a glare full of warning. "And they have the right to decide what they want to do about that. This technology could give them that knowledge and power."

I almost agree with Rufus. But judging by what's happened since Race Lavin became aware of the scanner's existence, I think my father was probably wise to keep it a secret. Because if it was still a secret, he would be alive, and Christina would be whole and healthy. He'd still be working on using it as "the key to our survival," whatever that means, but now it falls to me, and I don't want to fail him.

Rufus returns the scanner to the pack, and I almost make a grab for it, but the twins are staring at me with a watchful curiosity. I wouldn't even make it to the door if I tried something right now.

"Phones, please," Rufus says, his tone changing instantly from hard-edged to jovial, making it clear this conversation is over. "We'll keep them in a safe place until you're ready to leave. No reception out here anyway."

My mother nods at me and offers up her own, so I follow suit and give him Dad's.

Rufus drops them into a pocket of the backpack. "You two must be hungry," he says, hitching a cheerful smile onto his face. He calls out to one of the twins, "Paul, go tell the lunch staff to keep the dining hall open for another thirty minutes."

"Yes, sir," he says, and then I hear his footsteps clomping down the hallway.

Rufus turns to us. "We have a guest cabin. You can rest there while the Alexander girl recovers. I'll have some extra clothes and provisions brought to you." He says all this to me, like my mother isn't even in the room.

He dismisses us, and we're escorted back into the hallway. Without our phones and the scanner, I feel incredibly vulnerable, but also powerfully confused. Rufus said my father was like him. But Rufus seems so full of hate, and my father only seemed . . . cold. Then again, he looked anything but cold when he saw Race in my school cafeteria, so maybe he did hate the H2 as much as Rufus says. But he made one thing clear: A full-on fight with the H2 wasn't what he wanted. And my mother—she has H2 friends. I'm having trouble understanding that right now, too. After what we've been through, it's hard to believe that the H2 are anything other than our enemies.

It's easy for me to forget that Christina is one of them.

But as soon as I remember, the tension fills me up like liquid steel. What if David figures it out? What if they use the scanner Rufus just confiscated? What would they do to her? Very quietly, I whisper these questions in my mom's ear in Persian, the language she taught me as a child.

She gives me an odd look, maybe because, for the past four years, I've refused to speak Persian in her presence. Then she glances around us. "*Nguran nbash*," she whispers. *Please don't worry.*

I manage to choke down a turkey sandwich in the nearly empty dining hall. My mother seems equally tense, but she's covering it pretty well. She's trying to make friends with Esther, one of the crew who drove us here, and Esther seems happy enough to oblige. She asks my mom a lot of questions about some of the other families in The Fifty, since the Bishops have been tucked away here for quite some time. Esther has a shy smile and bad teeth, and I wonder what it must have been like to live here in this compound all her life, sheltered from the real world and the benefits of modern dentistry.

She walks us out of the dining hall and down one of the sidewalks toward the row of cabins on the eastern edge of the clearing. It's stopped raining, and several people are strolling about. A group of young boys runs by with fishing poles over their shoulders and buckets in their hands, headed toward the southern edge of the clearing, near where we arrived. Some of them are shirtless and tanned, but two of them are bundled up, wearing long pants and dark, hooded ponchos. They laugh and chatter with one another, telling jokes I'm certain would offend their parents, and suddenly I miss Will so much that my throat gets tight. We had that a few days ago, the ability to see the world as a giant amusement park. Every time I was with him, he'd make me forget what awaited me at home, and the biggest thing I had to worry about was not pissing my pants from laughing so hard. I've lost that now; the events of the last day have stolen it from me. I'm not sure if I'll ever get to see Will again.

We pass a young woman with a baby carriage, but the top of it is covered by a thick, dark shade, so I don't get to see if there's an actual kid in there. She stares at me as we walk by, with this unselfconscious, slack-jawed sort of expression.

Probably because I look like I've recently ax-murdered someone.

A few guys stride past pushing stacks of boxes on hand trucks, and they're wearing shorts and T-shirts and talking about some upcoming gathering. I hear the word *H2* and start to listen more closely, but that's when the last guy in line shoulders by, wearing long pants and a long-sleeved, hooded sweatshirt.

"David?"

The guy turns his head. He's got the same red hair, the same pale skin and freckles, the same bloodshot eyes. But it's not David. This guy has deep lesions on each of his cheeks, crusty and brown with deep red centers. The pupils of his eyes have a cloudy sheen to them.

"Oh, sorry," I say, trying not to stare.

He walks by me without a word.

"Oh, that's Matthew," says Esther with a fond smile. "My brother Timothy's boy. He's shy."

"Are he and David brothers?" my mother asks.

"No, cousins," says Esther, and then she gives me a sly look. "So . . . are you and Christina married?" Her gaze lasers over to my left hand.

"I'm sixteen," I say, because . . . what the fuck?

"Engaged, then," Esther says with a knowing nod.

I'm about to say exactly what I think of that when my mother says, "Nothing official yet. We're still in negotiation with the Alexanders."

Esther folds her arms over her stout middle as her gaze

travels back to me. She's sizing me up in a way that makes certain parts of me shrivel. Jesus.

"Interesting," is all she says, and then she's busy asking my mom about Kathleen McClaren, who was apparently a pen pal of hers when they were children. I wonder how Kathleen was related to Peter McClaren, if she was his mother, maybe, or an aunt. If she's mourning for him now.

By the time we reach the guest cabin, I am ready to start climbing the walls. It's been well over an hour since I've seen Christina, and that's long enough for shit to happen. They've left us alone here, with no one to guard us, but I'm not stupid enough to believe they're not paying attention. Rufus is way too clever, and even if he trusts us, he'll still be watching.

It's what my father would have done.

I believe my mom might be thinking the same thing, the way her eyes travel slowly from corner to corner, lingering on the air vents and outlets.

"I need to know how Christina's doing," I say quietly in Russian.

She stops her scan of the room and turns to me. "*Ya znayu.*" *I know.* "And Rufus speaks more languages than you do, so don't bother."

There's a knock at the door. My mom opens it for a girl carrying a stack of folded clothes, towels, washcloths, and two toiletry bags. I can just see her wide blue eyes peeking at me over the teetering supplies.

"Hey, let me get that—" I start to say, walking forward as it topples. I catch the bags and two of the towels before they hit the floor, but the rest of it goes flying. Something soft lands on the top of my head, and I pull it off to see that I am holding a pair of granny panties.

My mom snatches the underwear away, burying it in a pile of clothes she's picked up off the floor.

This is not the kind of moment a guy wants to share with his mother.

The carrier of the clothes clutches a few remaining garments in her shaking hands. She lets out this little giggle and holds out the clothes to Mom. Standing there with her skinny arms and flat chest, the girl can't be older than twelve or thirteen. She's got the same reddish hair that most of the people in this compound seem to share, and a heart-shaped face . . . and she looks a lot like Esther.

My mother takes the clothes. "Thank you . . ."

"Theresa," the girl says.

"Thanks, Theresa," I reply. "I could definitely stand to clean up."

She giggles again and bites her lip. And now I suspect two things.

One: Esther has sent her prepubescent daughter down here to flirt with me.

Two: This girl can help me figure out where Christina is.

So I walk Theresa to the front porch of the cabin. She's

a jittery, nervous creature, and I feel bad for her, being sent over here in some twisted play for my attention. I don't know exactly why Esther would do that. Does she hope I'll ditch Christina and take her daughter away with me?

Then I gaze over the compound. This is the size of their world, a half-mile-wide clearing. Maybe escape is exactly what Esther wants for her daughter.

Theresa is wringing her hands and shifting from foot to foot. "I'll be helping with dinner tonight," she says.

"Yeah? Are you a good cook?"

She gives me a bright smile. "I make good mashed potatoes."

I put my hand on my stomach and give her a regretful look. "Normally, I could eat a gallon of those, but my stomach is feeling kind of . . ."

Her face falls. "Oh. Are you all right?"

I shrug and grimace. "I don't know if it was something I ate or what. I could really use some . . . I don't know. Antacid or something. Do you guys have a pharmacy around here?"

And then, little Theresa gives me what I want. Her eyes dart over to a two-story building at the southeastern edge of the clearing, about an eighth of a mile from the main entrance and close to the place where the boys with fishing poles disappeared into the woods. "Well . . . I guess maybe I could . . . bring you some medicine, maybe?"

I smile at her. "I'm sure that would fix me right up."

She blinks up at me with the same gooey-eyed look I've

seen on the faces of several of the freshman girls this year. "I'll be back!" she announces as she skips down the stairs and runs straight toward the building she was staring at a second ago.

I watch Theresa until she disappears through the front door of that building, then head inside to talk to my mom.

SIXTEEN

MY MOTHER GIVES ME ONE OF HER ARCHED-EYEBROW looks as I come through the door.

"Mashed potatoes tonight," I say.

"I hope your stomach feels better by then," she replies, flicking her gaze toward the old radio sitting on the end table. Probably where she suspects the surveillance device is located.

I pick up a towel and a set of clothes. "I'm going to take a shower."

I go into the bathroom, which is pretty basic, just a toilet with a pull-chain to flush, a sink, and a shower stall. I turn on the water—and then sit on the closed toilet lid and wait. My mother knocks and comes in a second later. She closes the door behind her. Probably the one place in the cabin we can talk without being overheard.

"I think I've figured out where the clinic is. If she's better, can we leave?" I ask.

My mother gives me a pitying look. "She's going to need more than an hour to recover, Tate," she says in a gentle voice.

My fists clench. "What if she wakes up and accidentally says she's H2 or something?"

"I think Christina's smarter than that."

"I need to get to her. These people are creepy. It's obvious Rufus knows his way around technology, so why do they dress and act like they're living out on the prairie somewhere?"

"Rufus is determined to keep his family safe from the world. Isolation and group conformity make it easier for him to control them."

"So basically, the Bishops aren't just a family—they're a cult." And my injured, vulnerable H2 girlfriend is at their mercy.

"Unfortunately, I think you understand them well." My mother reaches out hesitantly and touches my clenched fist, like she wants me to relax. "I swear, Tate, I'm doing my best. I'm sorry he took the scanner. We'll get it back." I watch my mother's hand on mine and feel the gentleness in the gesture, but also the strength.

I loosen my fingers and her hand falls back to her side. "I know, Mom. I believe you." Then another thing occurs to me as I think about how old-fashioned Rufus and his family are. "Hey, are any of the Bishops named 'Josephus'?"

Her brow furrows. "Not that I know of. Why?"

"Dad mentioned someone named Josephus. Right at the end. Like he was important."

She becomes very still. "Tell me exactly what he said." After I repeat my father's last words, she says, "There's no one by that name in The Fifty. Are you sure 'Josephus' is a person?"

I shake my head. "I assumed, but . . . that wasn't smart, I guess. Did he ever mention that name to you?"

"No. But your father and I hadn't talked much in the last few years," she replies, her voice small and sad.

I look away from her, giving her a chance to compose herself. I'm on my own with this mystery, and now I realize it's maybe not as straightforward as I'd hoped. I let out a long, exhausted breath. "Will the Bishops stop me if I just . . . walk down to the clinic to see Christina?"

"I think it would be better if you do exactly that instead of looking like you're sneaking around. We don't want them to think we're hiding anything."

"What would they do if they knew about her?" I ask softly.

"If I thought there was any other way to help Christina, I wouldn't have brought her here. And as soon as she's stable, we'll go." She squeezes my shoulder and leaves me alone.

I take the fastest shower ever and change into a plain white T-shirt and cargo shorts. They must buy these clothes in bulk or something. I emerge to see that Theresa's come and gone, leaving my mother with a little cup of antacid and instructions written in a childish black scrawl on a piece of notebook paper. The note ends with *I hope you like my MASHED POTATOS!!!!*

The bottoms of her exclamation points are all little hearts.

While my mother takes her turn in the shower, I step out of the cabin to get my bearings, using the sun to orient me. It's emerged from the clouds and is hanging high over the clearing, warming my face as I descend the front stairs. Most of the north side of this compound is taken up by a huge garden plot, which is probably where Theresa's getting her potatoes. I head south along the blacktop sidewalk, reaching a large set of solar panels between the cabins and the central buildings. Enough to power more than just the lights in the thirty or so buildings in this place, considering there are also panels on all the roofs. Because our cabin is the last in the row on the eastern side of the clearing, I get to walk the length of the array, and I take full advantage of it. I never know what kind of information will come in handy, but years of drilling by my dad have made constant assessment of my environment second nature.

The control system for the array is rigged up against the side of the last panel in line. It's a simple key entry. Not a lot of security there, which means their perimeter security must be fierce, and probably what's sucking up all this energy they're generating with the panels. With that noted, I jog down the sidewalk to the clinic building. Every cabin I pass, the curtains part, just a crack, enough for a pair of eyes to track my progress. With my dark hair and gray eyes, I'm easy to peg as an outsider.

It doesn't take me long to reach the clinic. From behind the building, out in the woods, I hear shouts and shrieks and splashes, the sounds of boys being boys. Through the trees, the glint of sun on water tells me there's a good-sized pond back there, separating this clearing from the winding road Esther and Timothy used to get us here.

The door to the clinic is open, and I walk right in. It doesn't have a reception area; it's basically a small entryway and a long hallway with rooms on either side. From one of them, I hear voices, so I walk slowly down the hall.

". . . looks quite fetching," David says, his voice trembling with laughter.

There's a soft, feminine groan. "You're a horrible liar," Christina says. She laughs. Then gasps. "Ow."

"Sorry," David replies sympathetically. "Too much too soon. Let me help."

I stick my head around the doorframe in time to see him lowering the head of her bed until she's lying flat. He's leaning a shade too close, and his pasty hands linger near her shoulders, her pale cheek . . . and I can *tell*. I can tell by the way his fingers twitch toward her and pull back, by the way he's looking just a little too long at the slope of her neck, at her mouth. I know that feeling so well, that barely-bottled-up, highly pressurized *want*.

This dude is hot for my girlfriend.

She doesn't look that hot right now, actually. She's got a bandage on the left side of her head, and her tangled hair is piled over the top and hanging down the right side. A small clump of it is lying on the floor—David must have had to shave some of it off to get a clear shot at the gash. Her skin is nearly as white as his, and there are purple circles beneath her eyes.

Which only makes it worse. The idea that this guy is lusting after her when she's so vulnerable nearly sets me off. I'm at the foot of her bed before I'm fully aware of moving, and David's head jerks up. I have no idea how I look to him, but his eyes get wide and he steps away from her bedside quickly. He puts his hands in his pockets and clears his throat. If I were in a different kind of mood, it would be comical.

"No skull fracture on the X-ray," he says to me. "I have no idea how she managed it, but it looks like she's escaped with only a concussion. Still, she should probably have a CT scan as soon as possible."

I look into his bloodshot eyes, the pale blue irises, only a touch of cloudiness. In them I see this earnest kind of friendliness, plus maybe the tiniest glint of anxiety. That's not what I'm looking for, though—I'm looking for knowledge. Awareness. Suspicion.

I'm looking for whether or not he knows she's H2.

"Fifteen," Christina says softly, drawing my eyes back to her. "What?"

"That's how many stitches it took," David says. "But it was a pretty neat gash, so nothing complicated. She didn't lose much hair at all." He smiles at her.

She smiles back. "I'm going to be wearing my hair down for

a while, though." She winces and closes her eyes. "And dealing with this enormous headache, I guess."

"Oh, sorry," David says. "I said I'd get something for you. Hang on."

He walks out of the room, and I sit carefully on the side of her bed. She looks toward the door, and then up at me. And when she does, I see it, the confusion, the terror, everything she's struggling to contain inside of her. "He said we were being chased by H2 agents and that I got shot. He told me you were okay but . . ." Her eyes are getting shiny and it's making my throat hurt.

"I'm completely fine. The minivan was wrecked and you were hurt, so we had to come here."

I lean forward and kiss her on the cheek, then whisper very quietly in her ear, "Your last name is Alexander. You're Brayton's niece. You are a human. Not an H2. Got it?"

I draw back a little, and I can tell by the look in her eyes that she does, in fact, get it, and that if she was scared before, that's nothing compared with what she's feeling now. "When can we leave?" she asks in a choked-off voice.

I lower my forehead to hers, barely touching, afraid to hurt her but needing the contact. "As soon as you're better."

"I don't remember getting shot." Her palm is flat against my chest, and I'm not sure if she wants the closeness or is too weak to push me away.

Reluctantly, I lean back to give her some space. "What do you remember?"

Her smile seems like hard work. "Watching you inhale three Egg McMuffins." She takes a shaky breath. "Then it's like the screen goes dark."

Most of the day has been torn out of her mind. Post-concussive amnesia. "Did you say anything to him?" I incline my head toward the door.

What I'm really asking: *Did you tell him you're H2?*

"No," she murmurs. "I don't think so."

"She only wanted to know where you were," David says from the doorway, driving my heart into my throat as I wonder how long he's been standing there. He has a little steel tray in his hand, and on it sits a small paper cup. He holds it up. "Tylenol."

"My hero," Christina breathes, slowly propping herself on an elbow.

David gives me another nervous glance, but he can't hide his smile as he walks forward with his offering. I'm having trouble hiding my smile, too, because damn. Even after having her head split open, this girl can turn on the charm.

She takes the pills and lies back on the pillow, closing her eyes. "I'm so tired," she says, reaching for my hand. Her grip is pretty weak, but I feel the silent request for me to stay by her side. So I do, and soon her hand relaxes and her breaths become even and deep.

"You guys have been through a lot," David comments, pulling a broom from a nearby closet and sweeping up discarded gauze patches and bloody blond locks of hair. "When she became fully conscious, I was worried that she'd suffered a more serious brain injury, because she wouldn't speak. Then I realized she was just really scared."

I remember hearing her laughter as I came down the hall. "How did you get her to talk to you?"

He stops sweeping and looks at her. "I told her you and your mom were nearby and would see her soon. And then, I don't know. I started talking about my day. You know, stupid stuff."

"Stupid stuff," I mumble.

"Yeah. I guess she decided no one with a life as boring as mine could be a threat to her, because she relaxed."

"Thanks for taking care of her."

"My pleasure," he says.

I bet.

"Did you go to medical school or something?" I ask.

He shakes his head. "Ah, no. I wanted to, but we're not really allowed—" His lips press together in a thin line, and he starts over. "I apprenticed under Francis. He's the chief medic here."

"Is he off today?"

His bloodshot eyes meet mine. "He's two rooms down."

"Working?"

"Dying."

"Oh. Sorry."

David shrugs. "We all knew it was coming."

I shake off the sudden chill that seems to have invaded the room. "He's been sick awhile?"

"Yeah. Skin cancer."

I think of the guy I passed earlier, the one with the weird lesions on his pale face. "That happen a lot around here?"

David keeps sweeping, but his shoulders are stiff. "It's called xeroderma pigmentosum. Basically, your skin can't fix itself after a sunburn. And yes."

I've read about this condition. It's incredibly rare. But around here . . . all the dark curtains on the windows of the cabins and the lodge. The baby carriage with the heavy covering. The people wearing hoods and long sleeves in eighty-degree weather. "And it's genetic," I add, starting to feel sick.

His laugh is dry as a desert and bitter as hell. "Yep. Autosomal recessive. How'd you guess?"

Christina shifts in her sleep, and I realize I'm clutching her hand tighter than I should.

In isolating his family to protect them from the H2, Rufus has exposed them to an enemy just as deadly. A stagnant gene pool. Xeroderma pigmentosum is the kind of thing that can spread when your second cousin is also your father, when your aunt is also your mother.

The Bishops are destroying themselves.

And I can tell from his pale skin and the way he hides from the sun that David is one of the victims.

"Why do you stay?" I ask.

"Because we're safe here." He looks back at Christina. "She's safe here, too." The longing in his voice is painful. I can see how badly he wants to touch her, how deeply this fantasy crush has sunk its teeth into him.

I wonder what he would do if he knew what she was.

I have a choice to make, right now. I can make this guy my enemy, or I can try to make him my friend. I think he's a good guy, and for Christina's sake, I nod. "You made sure of that today, and I'll never forget it."

For a second, we look at each other, and I have a strong feeling he's in the process of making the same decision about me. After a few moments, he seems to have made it. He lowers his eyes from mine and laughs quietly to himself. "No problem."

I have no idea what he's decided.

He puts the broom away in the closet and walks to the door. "When she wakes up, she can go. She might be dizzy and headachy, but there's no reason she has to stay here. Just stick close to her. The stitches can come out in a week."

This is the best news I've heard all day. Maybe we'll be able to get out of here tonight. "Thanks."

David pulls up his hood. "Yeah. I need to go tell Uncle Rufus. He'll be thrilled."

"Really? Why?"

"I guess Timothy didn't catch you before you came down here. Rufus has decided to host a gathering to celebrate your dad's memory tonight. The three of you are the guests of honor."

SEVENTEEN

RUFUS BISHOP THROWS A MIGHTY IMPRESSIVE SHINDIG.

It seems like everyone in the entire compound has been working all day to put this thing together. There are paper lanterns strung along the beams over the long tables in the main lodge, centerpieces made out of cattails and a bunch of other meadow flowers, and a lot of food that was probably roaming the woods or swimming in the nearby pond this morning. Apparently they brew their own beer here, too; there are two kegs of it set up on the upper level of the main room, and everybody has a mug in their hands.

As we walk in with my mom, Christina holds my hand tightly. When I got her back to the guest cabin a few hours ago, she basically told me to get lost, then spent two hours in the bathroom with my mom in what I can only describe as some kind of female bonding ritual. One centered on getting her hair to look normal despite the large white bandage taking up most of the left side. As much as I care about her, I really couldn't help, so I spent the time strolling around the compound. Smiling and greeting people. Watching and learning.

The security around this place is nuts, and yet I'm betting half the folks here aren't even fully aware of it. They only know to stay inside the fence, or else. The system seems as geared toward keeping them in as it is toward keeping intruders out, but it's difficult to see if you don't know what you're looking for.

Fortunately, I do. I'm fairly sure my father designed the system. I remember seeing very similar plans in his files.

About a dozen yards beyond the decrepit split-rail fence that surrounds the compound, the actual perimeter defense begins. Powered by the impressive solar array in the clearing, the tree-mounted cameras are at the level of an average man's chest, sweeping their electronic eyes back and forth in a narrow path, which tells me one thing. It's not focused on surveillance; it's an invisible fence, extending from the ground to at least twenty feet up, judging by the movement and angle of the cameras. If someone crosses its path, two things will happen. Alarms and defensive response. I took a chance and wandered along the fence a ways, until I spotted them—almost perfectly camouflaged, high-powered, fully automated rifles. The defensive response around here is pretty lethal.

The Bishops could bag a lot more than deer with this system. Yeah, I learned a lot while my mom was sequestered with

Christina in the bathroom. And what I'm learning right now is that my mom's a genius in more ways than one, because Christina looks incredibly good considering what she's been through today. Her thick, blond hair is clean and shining and covers the bandage completely. My mom even managed to get Christina a light purple dress, which fits her slender figure pretty well but is a little long for my tastes—though as I watch every male in the room turn in her direction, I'm suddenly really glad for that.

I put my hand on the small of her back, and she looks up at me. We haven't gotten a chance to talk, and she has no memory of most of what happened today, including our kiss in the van, and how we worked together to fight off Race and his men. I really don't know where I stand with her. "How are you feeling?" I ask, hoping she'll give me a hint.

"Like someone played soccer with my head as the ball," she says with a brave smile. "But I'm all right."

I lean down and kiss her temple, relieved when she doesn't pull away. "We don't have to stay long."

"Just stay close to me, okay?"

"You got it."

Rufus is sitting at the head of one of the tables, and he lifts his mug in our direction and gestures for us to join him. His curly white hair is in stringy ringlets around his head; it's pretty hot in here. It might be the roaring fire at the other end of the room, licking at the carcass of a spitted pig. I feel really sorry for the guys who drew the short straw and are having to turn the crank.

My mother, who has acquired herself a plain blue dress with a straight neckline, introduces "Christina Alexander" before giving me a pointed *be careful* look and heading over to greet Esther and a pasty guy I assume is Mr. Esther—and who may also be her brother or a first cousin. I shudder, trying not to think of exactly how much inbreeding produces so many cases of xeroderma pigmentosum.

Rufus greets Christina with a grandfatherly handshake. If I didn't already know he hates Brayton Alexander with a fiery passion, I never would have guessed by the way he's treating Brayton's "niece."

"We're so glad you came through all right, young lady," he says to her, patting her hand. "Hell of a thing."

"David is an excellent doctor," Christina replies with a winsome smile. She's wearing her charm like chain mail, and now I get why she wanted to look good tonight. It wasn't vanity. It was the need to protect herself.

Rufus nods at her, then glances over at David, who's manning one of the kegs and has been looking over here every few seconds. "He was always a smart boy. My youngest sister's son." He makes a little cross gesture over his chest, which I'm guessing means she's dead. I wonder if she had the same illness her son has, or if she was just a carrier.

The music starts all of a sudden, a piano played by a ghost-pale woman and a fiddle in the hands of a boy who looks no more than ten. A guy about my age drags a slightly older girl in a flowered dress into the middle of the floor, and they start dancing.

I feel like I've stepped into some kind of pioneer movie.

Rufus gives me a nod. "Take your girl onto the dance floor before I steal her away from you," he says almost cheerfully. Then he winks at Christina, whose fingers curl into my sleeve.

I try to read her expression. She's smiling, but even under the warm lights, she looks pallid. "I'm not sure she—"

"Are you saying you don't want to dance with me, Tate Archer?" she asks playfully. Her grip on me doesn't let up.

I snake my arm around her waist. "Well, since you're twisting my arm . . ."

She sticks her tongue out at me as we walk down the stone-tiled steps toward the dancers. It's such a familiar, adorable gesture, the kind of thing she's done to me a thousand times across a crowded cafeteria or as she's running by on the soccer field, and it fills my chest with golden happiness. I swing her onto the dance floor without a backward glance at Rufus. All I care about right now is the girl next to me.

We join the crowd in front of the fireplace. Most of the dancers are young, either our age or a few years older, and they perform like . . . well, like it's the only thing they do for fun here. They weave their way around us with agile, rapid-fire steps, smiling and laughing and . . . checking us out. Christina and I are more accustomed to the kind of scene where you just bounce up and down with your arms in the air. Or, really,

I am. She's a bit more graceful. The guys around us appear to be noticing. I see more than one girl looking pouty while her partner stares at Christina.

I circle my arm around Christina's back and stroke my fingers down her cheek. "You look beautiful."

My breath catches when she raises her head and captures me with her dark blue eyes. In them, I see the fire. Not a reflection of the flames in the fireplace, but the part of her I was so afraid I'd lost to a bullet today. The part of her that strips me down and builds me up at the same time.

Christina smiles; she seems to know the effect she has on me, and I think she enjoys it. She reaches up and brushes my hair off my forehead. "So do you," she mouths. Then she pushes away and holds on to my hands while she moves her feet in this boxy step that most of the people on the floor are doing right now. "We'll be able to show off at prom!" she says, laughing.

I do my best to keep up, but really, I'm pathetic, which is okay because it keeps her giggling. I'm not usually so off-kilter, but Christina is a powerful distraction. It's not because she's gorgeous, even though she is . . . It's because she's here, alive, conscious, and for the moment, we're safe. With all the security here, I have trouble believing Race Lavin would come crashing in. Oddly, right now, prom feels possible, like we could step from this world and end up there, like it wouldn't be that hard to leave all this behind and reenter our lives from last week.

The other dancers let us monopolize the center of the floor while they whirl wildly around the perimeter. Christina and I stay close and keep our steps light. Hers falter every once in a while. She's not confident on her feet tonight, and I keep my arms around her, ready to catch her if she falls.

But I don't even get a whole dance with her before the first guy takes his shot. He's an inch or so shorter than Christina, but about twice as wide. He taps me on the shoulder, then shakes my hand with enough bullshit macho squeeze action to make me want to pull guard like I'm in a jiu-jitsu tournament and teach him a thing or two. Instead, I smile and squeeze back. And okay, maybe I lean over him a bit to remind him what a freaking hobbit he is, but then I sidestep and introduce him to Christina.

After all, she's the reason he's here.

He invites her to dance, and I ask her, "Are you up to this?"

She tilts her head and smiles at the hobbit. "Will you take it easy on me?"

His grin is huge. "Yes, ma'am."

He grasps her hand, much more gently than he did mine, thankfully. Then I'm watching him do a waltz or a jig or whatever it is, and she's laughing and stepping on his feet and he's staring at her face with a look that reminds me uncomfortably of that dude who was jacking off in his car.

I remove myself from the dance floor but keep a close eye on Christina, wondering if I need to put an end to the hobbit's fantasy. Someone pushes a mug into my hand. "I think she can handle him," says Rufus with a rough chuckle. "Come on up here and keep me company."

I follow him up the steps toward the tables, catching a glimpse of my mother chatting amiably with a bunch of red-cheeked middle-aged women who keep turning their heads and raking me with glances that give me chills. The bad kind.

By the time I get to the table, someone else has interrupted the hobbit's fantasy, a guy with massive shoulders who looks like he could snap the kid in half. The hobbit hands Christina over and watches with a resentful glare as Shoulders whisks her away. My hand tightens over the handle of the ceramic mug. It feels like we've jumped straight from a pioneer movie to the hillbilly edition of *The Bachelorette*.

"We raise our boys to be gentlemen," Rufus says to me. "They just don't get a chance like this very often."

I look over at Rufus, at the merry but razor-edged twinkle in his eye. This is his empire, half a mile wide, almost completely self-sufficient, surrounded by an invisible but lethal fence that keeps the outside world *outside*. What kind of man makes his own kingdom like this? What drove him to do it?

"How long have you been here?" I ask.

He finishes off his mug and slaps it onto the table. His mustache is all frothy. "About eighty years ago, my grandfather decided to take our family underground. It was after the Cermak assassination, actually. After the H2 made it clear they would come after us in a blatant, public way if we stepped out of line. We've been a few different places, but here? Ah, maybe forty years. My father sent me away to college, and I worked for Black Box for a while. I came back about twenty years ago, but I stayed involved with the company until I realized how corrupt it had become."

He glances at my mug. I take a sip and am surprised at how good it tastes. I take another gulp, and then I say, "So . . . Black Box . . ."

"It's a front. A means of income for The Fifty families, as well as a source of power and influence to counterbalance the threat of the Core. But the real action is behind the scenes— our best minds, thinking two steps ahead. Or in your father's case, four steps ahead. Black Box was intended to be the way we'll protect ourselves when the Core decide to eliminate us, though some idiots believe that would never happen." He grunts. "You're mechanically inclined, like your father was."

I shrug. "Sort of."

"Don't be modest. Fred was proud of you. Last time I saw him, he told me you'd invented a liquid-transfer system for DNA assembly using some automated Lego toys of yours."

Warmth creeps up my neck. My dad told him about that? "It was just a class project." One I now hold the patent for.

He chuckles. "Just like your dad. The H2 were able to take over this planet because they were centuries ahead of us in terms of their technology. They might have lost their tech when they landed all their spaceships in the ocean, but they knew what they were doing."

"From what my mom told me, they've reclaimed most of the wreckage."

He arches an eyebrow. "Except for what the Archers found. With his discovery, your dad gave us the power to easily know enemy from friend. He gave us the ability to control our fate."

I watch the dancers as I think about that. Rufus wants to use the scanner the same way he thinks the H2 will. I'm not sure I buy the idea that the H2 would breed humans out of existence, though, because what would that change? Most H2 don't even know what they are anyway, and the human population is dropping every day. And yet, the Core is coming after the scanner like it's something they desperately need, so I agree with Rufus that they don't just want it for the sake of having it. They want it to use it.

So what did my father want to use it for? Rufus is talking like he knows exactly what my Dad was doing, but he might be bullshitting just like Brayton was. I wish he *did* know more about my dad's activities, though, because then I could ask him about Josephus. I could ask him how and why my dad had moment-to-moment population numbers for H2 and humans—including those fourteen anomalies that indicated the counts on that screen in his lab weren't mathematical estimates . . . they were real-time figures. But again, I don't trust this guy, so I'm going to keep my mouth shut.

Rufus hands his mug to a little girl, who scampers over to the keg so David can refill it. Then he stares at the dance floor.

At Christina, who is now partnered with a guy who has an Adam's apple the size of Brooklyn.

"You don't think much of Brayton Alexander," I say.

His mouth twists into a pouty, un-Santa-like sneer. "Greedy, self-serving *bastard*," he rumbles. "When he started selling inventions—including some of your father's—to the Core, I was done."

I'm really wishing my mom had told him Christina was a McClaren.

"My mom said that he only sells things approved by The Fifty, that there are other things he's not authorized to sell. You think he's not following those orders?"

"Other members of The Fifty call me paranoid, but I call them stupid and naïve." Rufus takes his refilled mug from the little girl, and thanks her for it by giving her a whiskery kiss on the cheek. "Few of them take the threat seriously. They think it's better to cooperate with the Core, that the H2 will be more likely to leave us alone if we keep their secret. Appeasement is what I call it. I wonder what they'll think if the Core gets ahold of the scanner. They'll see what the H2 are really like."

"And you know what they're really like?"

"Without a doubt." Rufus's eyes reflect the massive fire at the other end of the hall. "They slaughtered one of my ancestors, and the Bishops never forget. Then and now, the H2 are nothing but bloodthirsty aliens, and they need to get the hell off my planet."

EIGHTEEN

I STARE AT RUFUS, WONDERING IF HE REALLY MEANS what he just said. If he had his way, would he wage war with the H2? Does he actually think humans could win? He talks like he knew my father, but Dad flat out said the scanner should prevent interspecies conflict, not cause it.

My gaze darts to my mother, who is taking cautious sips from her mug. I know she brought us here because Christina needed immediate help, and going to the hospital meant handing her over to Race and his goons. But I suddenly wonder if this is much better. She was hoping we could stop over here and make a quick exit, and now we're caught. Rufus has the scanner, and his intentions seem no better than Race's or Brayton's. And if he finds out Christina is one of them—

A pair of knees bump into mine, and I'm so startled that I nearly drop my mug. Standing before me is a girl. Her rather impressive rack is inches from my face. "Want to dance?" she asks breathlessly.

Rufus's belly laugh shakes the table. I'm glad he finds this funny. "Go on, boy," he says, giving my shoulder a shove. "Be a gentleman and don't let her down."

I spend the next half hour or so being manhandled by Bishop girls of all shapes and sizes while I watch Christina going through the same thing with the boys, except they seem to be more respectful about it. I stumble my way through steps and do my best not to fall. I am being dragged around the floor by Yolanda, whose frisky fingers are trying to find their way into my waistband, when I see Christina sink to the floor. I am by her side in an instant, nearly taking Yolanda's fingers with me.

Christina's latest partner squats on the other side of her. "She just dropped, man, I'm so sorry."

Christina clutches her head in her hands and shrinks away when the guy tries to tug her to her feet.

"Give her a minute," I snap, fighting the urge to punch him. I'm not angry at him, not really; he's simply the most convenient target.

He holds his hands up. "Like I said, sorry."

A hand pats him on the shoulder, and he scuttles out of the way to make room for David, whose pale face is almost glowing in the dim firelight. "Hey, Dancing Queen," he says gently to her, "I think you overdid it."

Christina moans softly. "God, it feels like my head is splitting open," she whispers.

"Time for more Tylenol," David announces.

"Fuckin' H2, man," says the hobbit, who's standing by the fireplace a few feet away.

Christina flinches, and David, who has his hand on her arm, gives her a concerned look.

"They had no cause to shoot at a girl, but I guess we shouldn't be surprised they did. Makes me want to go on a little hunting expedition," Shoulders says as he watches David and me help Christina to her feet.

Christina rests her sweat-damp forehead on my chest, and I feel her trembling as she slides her arms around my waist. I don't know if she's scared or sick, but whatever it is, she needs me. I put my arm around her back and hold her close.

"The Dancing Queen is done for the night," I announce, and lead her up to the tables to sit down, leaving behind several disappointed-looking Bishop boys. My mom meets us at the top of the steps. "Can you get us some water?" I ask. "I don't think she should be drinking beer."

My mom nods and heads off in search of water, giving me a chance to settle Christina into a chair. The music is starting up again now that we're no longer providing the entertainment.

"You don't have to hover over me," Christina says, but she's already got her head in her hands again.

"This was too much," I say quietly. "We shouldn't have come."

"We had to come." She lowers her hands from her face. She looks like she needs to sleep for a week straight; I see now that all that flirtatious energy from before was only an elaborate disguise. "Your mom told me they would be really insulted if we didn't."

"But you—"

"She said it didn't matter." She gives me a weak smile, and she must see the anger building in my eyes because she adds, "She was nice about it, though."

David slides into the chair on the other side of Christina. He's considerably less sweaty than the other guys, and it's because he hasn't been dancing. I wonder why he didn't ask Christina when he had the chance. "Tylenol," he says, offering her a little paper med cup and a sappy smile.

"I wish you had something stronger," Christina says.

He shrugs apologetically. "This is all I can offer you." His eyes are riveted to her face. "I'm sorry you had to do this. You should be in bed."

I bet he didn't ask her to dance because he didn't think it was good for her. This guy is killing me. I can't decide whether to punch him for looking at her like that or shake his hand for trying to take care of her.

I'm reminding myself to be nice when my mom shows up with the water. She hands it to Christina and leans over, looking her right in the eye. "You'll feel better soon, won't you?"

"Yeah," mutters Christina. "Thanks." Her hand shakes as

she takes the pills and chases them with the water, and it makes me want to shove and yell and drive everyone away from her, including my mother.

But as my mom walks by me, she gives me the same look she gave to Christina, only this time I can read it better. *Don't do anything to offend them, and we'll get out of this all right.*

Even though the golden happiness in my chest has melted away, leaving only bitter residue, I nod. Then I draw Christina close and guide her head to my shoulder.

For dinner, we get seated near the head of the main table. I'm next to Rufus, and my mom is across from me. Christina sits on my other side, looking a little better after that second dose of Tylenol, though she's only picking at her food. To her left is a guy Rufus introduces as his oldest son, who looks a few years older than me. Like so many of the others, Aaron Bishop has auburn hair, but he has dark green eyes and tanned skin. Rufus beams when he looks at him, enough to tell me Aaron is next in line to the Bishop throne, such as it is.

He leans around Christina to talk to both of us. "My dad told me you guys escaped from the Core. That must have taken serious skills."

"And a lot of luck," I say, "but thanks."

He grins. "I wish I could have been there, man. I'd give my left nut for a chance at those guys. Or any H2, for that matter." Apparently Rufus has passed his hatred of all H2 to his son.

And maybe every single Bishop in this room. Suddenly I've lost any appetite I had.

Christina tenses. "Isn't that, like, most of the population?"

He looks at her like she's cute but stupid. "Exactly."

Aaron's younger brother Steven, one of Christina's many dance partners who is now sitting next to my mom, scratches at a dark, crusty patch on his pale, freckled face and laughs. "Society has gone to the dogs."

"I don't know how you guys live with it," Aaron says. "Makes me sick to think about it, being surrounded by them every day."

"We didn't know we were," I say honestly. "When did you find out?"

"We don't hide the truth from our children," says Rufus.

My mother takes a sip of beer from her mug, then sets it down. "The other families don't tell their children until they are at least sixteen. Not until they can bear the secret and the responsibility that comes with it. It makes it easier to live in the world. Imagine a young child telling his classmates that he's a human and some of them are aliens. Imagine a middle schooler gossiping to her friends about it—and think about how quickly rumors become viral these days. Those disclosures could bring harsh consequences for everyone involved. If the Core got wind of it, maybe they would act. Even against the youngest of us." She looks right at me. There's no apology there, just simple explanation. I can't bring myself to be angry at her for it, because I know what happened the minute Mr. Lamb called Race Lavin. But I have to wonder: What would it have been like to know? Would I have been friends with Will? Would I have gone out with Christina? I'd like to say I would have, but if I had been raised like Aaron, would I have been so different from him?

"Ignorance is bliss," Aaron says in this friendly, not-really-friendly voice. I'm not sure why the tone of the conversation changed so quickly, but it surely has. Aaron looks like he's dying for a fight.

My mother glares at him. "There are many kinds of ignorance. The Core have historically been our enemies, but the rest of the H2 are innocents."

His smile is greasy and I hate the way he's looking at her, like he's better than she is. "Easier to cozy up to the enemy than stand up and fight them, I guess."

"Is that what you're doing here?" Christina snaps.

I grab her hand and squeeze.

Rufus laughs out loud, though his gaze skates over Christina in a way that sends a jolt of fear through me. "Don't rile our guests, boy," he says to Aaron, but there's no anger in it at all. In fact, I think he's proud of his son.

Rufus bangs his empty mug on the table a few times, and the room gets quiet. "We're here tonight to honor a man most of you have never met," he says in a loud voice. "But I knew him, and I can tell you he was worthy of honor."

My throat is getting tight. I swallow back the grief and sit up straight, trying to look like a guy who deserves to have a father like Fred Archer, even though I spent half my time with him resenting every particle of his being, however unfair that was. I glance at my mother to see that she's shoved her feelings down deep tonight. I wish I knew what she was thinking, because it might help me figure out what's going on inside of me. Christina seems to sense the tremors beneath my surface. Her thumb strokes the back of my hand.

Rufus is standing behind my mother now. His fingers wrap over the back of her chair. "Fred was one of the last of the Archers, who were once a powerful family, who for centuries carried and guarded evidence of what really happened when aliens invaded our planet. Fred Archer was a scientist. Maybe more than the rest of us, he understood what it meant to be human."

While he talks about the early, idealistic days of Black Box, I sit there, aching. I'll never get to talk to my dad about any of this. He's not here to tell me what to do, to explain things to me, to tell me who to trust.

Rufus heaves his belly around my mom's chair and edges back toward the head of the table. "More than ever, we need men like Fred Archer, who understood the superiority of our species and the importance of defending it."

The superiority of our species . . . I look up at the heavy wooden sculpture above the mantel, and now I know where I've seen it before. My history books. It's not the most well known of the Aryan signs, but it's definitely one of them: Odin's Rune. I swallow hard and hold on to Christina.

The Bishops haven't isolated themselves because they're scared.

They've done it because they think they're better. They're not white supremacists; they're *human* supremacists.

Is this what my father believed?

I look at my mother, whose expression is stone. Her eyes are on Rufus, but I'm not sure she's really seeing him. Christina is gripping my hand so hard that she's shaking. Probably because she can see the hatred for the H2 snapping and flashing in the eyes of almost everyone in the room.

Rufus takes another step to the side and puts his meaty hand on my shoulder. "This young man is now the last of the Archers, the one responsible for his father's legacy, for carrying on his line, for maintaining the purity of his blood."

Christina becomes very still.

Which is when Rufus lifts his other hand high in the air. I twist in my seat so I can see his eyes, which glint with something cold and deadly.

He's holding the scanner.

"And he's brought us this!" He switches it on over my head, and blue light glints off my silverware and my heart rate goes stratospheric. "Fred Archer gave us the power to iden-tify whom we could trust and whom we couldn't. This is his final gift to us. When the light is blue, you're looking at a pure-blooded human!"

There's nothing I can do. No way I can stop this. It feels like my world is unraveling in slow motion as he waves it at the row of people sitting across from me—my mother, his younger son, David—and beams of blue light streak across the table as everyone starts to clap.

Then he holds it over Christina's head.

She stares at me in horror as red light courses down her face.

NINETEEN

AFTER A SECOND OF COMPLETE STILLNESS, HALF THE people at the table shoot to their feet while the rest sit there, wide-eyed, like it's taking them a little longer to process that there's an H2 among them. Aaron moves faster than the others; he grabs Christina's arm and jerks her toward him. All reflex and rage, I hit him with a throat strike that bugs his eyes and leaves him gasping. He lets her go and I pull her away, tossing her chair toward a couple of the others pushing past Aaron to get to her.

Rufus grabs me by the collar of my shirt and yanks me backward. My legs get tangled in my own chair, and I fall back hard. Christina lands on top of me as my head *thwacks* against the wood floor.

When the stars clear from my vision, my mother is standing over us.

I don't know where she got the gun, but I assume she swiped it from someone—and she's got it leveled at Rufus's head.

One of the twins is standing next to him, and his gun is pointed at my mom's face.

"How dare you?" Rufus pants, waving the scanner at me and Christina, sending blue and red light scattering in crystalline prisms around our bodies. "How dare you bring that creature here?"

Christina's breath is coming in high-pitched gasps, and she's holding on to me like she's drowning. With my ears still ringing, I hoist myself up and bring her with me, keeping my arms wrapped around her, shielding her any way I can. There's a bunch of Bishops behind us, next to us, everywhere I turn, and I know this is hopeless. I might be able to fight a few of them, but there are nearly a hundred of them and only three of us.

When my eyes refocus, the first thing I notice is David, who looks like somebody's punched him in the balls. His bloodshot eyes are glued to Christina, and I take a step to the side so we're both solidly behind my mom.

"She didn't even know she was H2 until a day ago," my mother says in a high, commanding voice. "She's not a part of this fight, but she's saved my son's life several times, at great risk to her own."

"I can't allow her to leave. Now she knows about us," Rufus hisses. "She could alert the Core to our location."

"So could we," my mother snaps. "But that won't happen. I promise you."

"But she's H2!" the hobbit shouts.

"Yeah, but *they* brought her here," says Shoulders, glaring at me.

"It's against The Fifty's bylaws to keep members of The Fifty against their will," answers a hard-faced woman standing next to Rufus. She looks like she wishes she could, though.

"But so is threatening or endangering another member of The Fifty!" someone else calls from the crowd. "And by bringing that *thing* into our secure compound, they've endangered *all* of us!"

There's a rumble of approval from the crowd. The hard-faced woman nudges Rufus. "But if Angus were to find out . . ." Her lips keep moving, but whatever she says to him is drowned out by shouts from the other Bishops.

Aaron, who's still rubbing his throat, takes a step toward me, trying to edge around my mom, but she instantly shifts her position so she can aim at his head while keeping an eye on the gun-wielding twin.

"I know you're smarter than to eliminate the last of the Archer line," she says. "Turning The Fifty into The Forty-Nine would not be a popular move for any present or future patriarch. You wouldn't be the first family to be ostracized. How long would you survive without the income and protection The Fifty provides, Rufus?"

Rufus's Santa-face is cherry red, veins popping, mouth working. "You have violated the sanctity of my home!" he roars, startling the rest of the Bishops into silence.

"We apologize for abusing your hospitality," she replies coolly. "We would not have imposed had the situation not been desperate."

"Lower your gun," barks Rufus, and I realize he's talking to the twin, who obeys immediately. "Mitra," he growls, wanting her to do the same thing.

With her weapon still leveled at Aaron's head, my mother turns to look at Rufus. I can't see her eyes, but I can see his. All his merriness has evaporated, burned away by his outrage. It looks like his dearest wish is to kill her. Painfully. It drives the breath from my lungs. I'm not sure our status as members of The Fifty counts for much at this moment. In the hushed, tense quiet, I can almost hear their wordless battle of wills, the struggle between two people who understand the world we live in far better than anyone else in this room. My mother looks so small, so insignificant beneath the shadow of his rage.

But then . . . Rufus blinks.

My mother's shoulders relax, just slightly. "You'll arrange for our safe passage out of here," she says. She still hasn't lowered the gun. "You'll provide one of your vehicles, and we'll be on our way."

"Timothy!" Rufus barks while he glares at my mother.

"Give them their things and take them to the lot. The rest of you, back off."

Unbelievable. Aaron, his brother, the twins . . . all of them take half a step back, and I can breathe again. Christina sags in my arms, the relief of the moment too much for her. I feel the same way but manage to hold both of us up.

"Kill the H2!" comes a shriek from the back. It's Theresa, who's standing on a chair, pointing right at Christina. It's a childish, pathetic gesture, but there's an immediate roar of approval throughout the room. I no longer feel any sympathy for her at all.

Especially when I look around and see the effect this one skinny, stupid girl has had. All these Bishops, raised on hatred and ignorance . . . The fuse she's lit is short—it takes only a moment for the crowd around us to ignite. Hands come from everywhere, behind me, on both sides, clutching at Christina. She screams in pain as someone gets a fistful of her hair. I lash out, all elbows and knees, driving some guy's stomach through his spine, making another's knee buckle. But it's not enough, not even close, because a few seconds later, Christina is ripped from my side.

She arches back as they lift her up, everyone trying to claim a piece of her, all of them trying to punish her for the crime of being H2. Even though at least three people have their fingers tangled in her hair, she turns her head. And sees me. She blinks, and the tears streak down her face as she stretches a trembling hand in my direction. The agony in her eyes draws a foreign, animal sound from my throat. I lunge through the bodies, fighting to get to her, my mind a solid wall of panic. I'm about to watch her torn apart. I've never felt so powerless.

Something hard hits the side of my head and sets off bombs inside my skull, bright flashes of white-hot pain. I fall to my knees, and through the ringing in my ears, I hear my mother's voice. No longer commanding, she's screaming, too. One word, over and over.

My name.

I try to get to my feet, but someone punches me back down. I'm losing. I'm losing Christina. Losing everything. I'm—

When the shot is fired, everyone goes still.

"Put her down or I'll put *him* down," my mother shouts.

A space clears around me, and I push myself to my feet, shoving away hands that may have been trying to help. I don't give a fuck. All I care about is—

Christina plows into me, sobbing, and I let out a sob of my own as I clutch her to my chest. My hands are shaking as I run them over her, trying to make sure she's all there, that no pieces of her are missing. After a few seconds, I manage to tear my eyes from her and look around. A hundred pairs of eyes are on my mother, who is standing near the wall with the muzzle of her weapon digging into Aaron Bishop's temple. I scan the floor around her, looking for who took the first shot, but then realize she must have fired it in the air.

Breathing hard, Rufus holds up his arms, shining the scanner's light over his family's pasty faces. "We'll have our time!" he shouts. "I promise you we'll have our time."

Then he turns back to us and gestures for Timothy to hand my mother her bag and Christina's pack. "These three will have their property back and safe passage out of here in exchange for *this*." He waves the scanner at me.

In his eyes, there is a challenge. He expects me to shout, to object; I can see it all there in his bloodshot glare. He's not going to kill me, because he knows there would be consequences for his family. He thinks I'm a stupid kid, though, and he's hoping I'm going to do something brash so he can put me in my place. I grit my teeth and hold on to Christina, and I do not look away, even when his lips curl into that cold, calculating smile. "Not so much like your father after all," he says.

We'll see.

My mother takes a step backward. "Tate, time to make our exit."

The journey to the parking lot feels a lot like tightrope walking on a high-tension power line. No fewer than twenty Bishop boys surround us, and it pisses me off to no end that half of them probably started the evening wishing they could get into Christina's pants, and now they want to lynch her in the square. She stumbles along bravely, but I'm guessing it's taken everything she has to survive the last few minutes. I know it's totally caveman, but after she trips over her own feet for the second time, I scoop her up in my arms and carry her. Normally, she'd never allow something like this; she'd want to hold her head high and leave under her own power, but right now, she puts her arm around my neck and clings. David, who is walking silently beside us, aims his flashlight ahead of my steps.

Timothy hands my mother her bag and a set of car keys. "Gray sedan, end of the line," he says.

My mother gives me the keys. She's holding the gun in her other hand. "Get in the car, Tate."

I open the door, and Christina practically dives in. She puts on her seat belt and then draws her knees up to her chest and lowers her forehead onto them, like she can't face the world right now. My mom joins us a second later. She hands me the gun. "Hang on to that for me."

I can't help but find this moment surreal. I thought my mom was the peaceful academic type, not keeping any weapons around, whereas my dad never went anywhere without one—but it turns out she's as badass as he was.

She pulls out of the lot and drives slowly up the gravel road. I watch out the rearview for following headlights but don't see any. We're not a mile down the road before I lean forward and tap her on the shoulder. "Pull over."

"Tate—"

"You know I have to go back and get it."

"No—"

"*Mom.*"

She pulls to the side of the road and slumps over the wheel. "I do know. He shouldn't have it."

Christina's fingers curl into the shoulder of my shirt. "What will they do if they catch you?"

I stroke my fingers down her cheek. "I'd rather not think about it. But they won't."

I actually don't know if I'm right or not. I just want to make this easier on her.

"Can I have Dad's phone?"

Mom pulls it out of her bag and stares at it. "The GPS should be working, but it seems like Rufus has some sort of jamming capability, because it isn't picking up the satellite signal." She drops it back in the bag. "You're going to get lost in the dark."

"I'll improvise, then. Can I have the keys?"

She hands them to me, and I use them to rip the fabric off the rear speakers. I break through the brittle plastic grate covering the woofer and pull it out. It looks like a little flying saucer. I yank it away from the wiring harness and then get out of the car while I pull the guts of the thing away from the magnet inside. Then I find myself a few rocks by the side of the road and use one as a chisel and the other as a hammer to knock the magnet loose.

When I return to the car, Christina is staring at me with this half-terrified, half-puzzled look, but my mom smiles. "You're making yourself a compass."

"You got it. Do you have a pen?"

My mom reaches into her bag and pulls out a ballpoint pen. I pull the little metal clip off and magnetize it by sliding the speaker magnet from one end to the other several times. "I think we're about one mile to the southeast of the compound. I can't go back along the road, because they'll be watching. I'm going through the woods from here. Shouldn't take more than forty-five minutes over this terrain."

She gives me a sharp look. "There's security."

"I know. But I think I know a way through it."

Her eyes linger on me for several seconds. I know she wants to stop me, but then I realize she's not going to. She thinks I can do this.

I use the pen to draw my map on the inside of my forearm, and I hold it up to show her. "Does that look right?"

She pulls my arm toward her and takes the pen from me. After a few seconds of scribbling, she lets me go. "Now it does."

I look at my arm and see she's added a crossroad and shifted the orientation a few degrees. "All right."

"If they catch you, tell them Angus McClaren is aware that we're here and expecting to hear from us. And tell them I'm calling him if I don't have you back by dawn. He'll instantly freeze all Bishop assets. We'll see how Rufus protects his family when he hasn't got a dollar to his name." The darkness can't hide the ferocity on her face.

I toss the speaker magnet onto the floor of the car. I don't need it now that I've magnetized the metal clip. "Good to know. One more thing?"

"What do you need?" my mom asks.

"Your Valium."

"Why?"

I arch my eyebrow. "You never know when you need someone to get a good night's sleep."

She's silent as she gives me the bottle.

Christina grabs my hand as I swing open the back door. "I'll see you soon," she whispers, then looks away and grits her teeth like she's keeping herself from saying more. I'm thankful for that right now, because if she asked me to stay with her, I'd have a hard time leaving her side.

I squeeze her hand. "You will."

The night air is sweet and cool on my skin as I kneel next to the water-filled ditch by the side of the road. The clouds have cleared, and the silver crescent moon reflects off the black puddle at my feet. An old liquor bottle is half submerged in the muck. I pull it out and manage to break off the bottom third so I have a cup with some jagged edges. I fill it with water and head into the woods. With the moonlight at my back, I plot my course using the map on my arm and the compass I've made by dropping the metal bit from the pen into my cup of water. If I stand still for a moment, the thing points due north. It keeps me oriented, and after a long, slow hike—avoiding a few painfully obvious booby traps the Bishops probably added to supplement the more sophisticated system designed by my dad—I am at the shore of the pond. From here, I can see the lights of the Bishop compound. I'm perilously close to the security perimeter. I hide my compass behind the trunk of this enormous oak with a huge, bulbous knot on its side, then squat next to the softly lapping water and wait for a few clouds to pass, allowing the moon to give me all its light.

This pond is the weakness in the perimeter. The body of water is maybe a quarter mile long and kidney shaped, and I'm on the southeastern edge, where a narrow stream branches off from the pond and winds its way into the woods. It would have taken a lot to angle the invisible fence around this long stretch of water. What the Bishops did instead: they laid the system around the edge of the pond, cutting right over the stream. There are stone markers sunk into the earth on either side of the bank that show where the boundary of the security system is, subtle unless you know to look for them. Every Bishop does—they'd know to avoid the invisible line across this part of the pond. They probably stay down at the side nearest the clearing and avoid this spot like the plague.

I take off my shoes and shirt and leave them on the shore. I pull out the bottle of Valium and examine it. Waterproof . . . ish. I shove it back into my pocket and creep down within about ten feet of the boundary, listening hard for any telltale electronic sounds that would tell me that my life is about to end. I gasp as my toes sink into frigid mud. The water is like ice here, having just bubbled up out of the earth. Fighting the chatter of my teeth, covered in goose bumps, I sink low, submerging myself in the stream. The automated rifles that protect the perimeter only scan from ground-level up, so if I'm underwater, I should make it through. I take one last opportunity to gauge my distance—miscalculation would equal a bullet to the head—and plunge beneath the water.

It gets deep quickly, popping my ears, burying me in silence. I drag myself along the muddy bottom, completely blind, relying on the map inside my head. I have to go at least ten yards past the boundary markers. It's the only way to know I'm safe. It's slow going, because I need to stay as deep as possible to avoid catching the electronic eye of the camera. It takes only seconds for my hands to become numb clubs on the ends of my arms. But I count every stroke, every yard, every second, forcing myself to maintain rapid, purposeful movement. Finally, I let myself drift upward and then swim another dozen yards a few feet below the surface. Then, with a silent prayer, I roll onto my back and break the surface, just enough to draw a long breath.

And I don't end up with a bullet in the chest, so I think I'm okay. I swim to the shore, shivering as the breeze hits my skin. Tensing to steady the tremble in my hands, I pull the Valium from my pocket again and shake it, reassured by the dry rattle of the pills inside.

Now I'm within the security perimeter, near the Bishops'

clearing. That was the easy part. The next part will be harder, but chaos has always been a specialty of mine. I pad forward in my bare feet, letting the rotting leaves and damp earth mute my footfalls. I run my hands over my wet hair and then down along my arms, brushing off drops of muddy pond water. My pants are still dripping as I reach the clinic. Its windows are dark. I edge up to the back door and give it a try. It's open.

I push the door slowly, wincing as it creaks, because I know there's at least one person in here—Francis, their chief medic who's lying ill in one of the rooms down the hall. I listen for a moment, but it's silent, so I get myself inside and close the door again. I figure there has to be a supply closet somewhere, so I start opening a few doors. Some contain boxes of medicines, all carefully labeled. It's amazing the stuff these people have—all sorts of heart medication, even what I think might be chemotherapy drugs. But I don't need anything so complicated. I find a few bottles of iodine crystals in the second closet I search. Perfect. I also find a scalpel, which I pocket.

In the third closet, I find the cleaning supplies, including a few gallons of ammonia and a roll of paper towels. I sit back on my heels and slide the jugs into the hallway.

"Welcome back," comes a voice from across the hall. I spin around to see David standing in the doorway of one of the clinic rooms, his arms crossed over his chest. Like he's been watching me for a while.

Well, *shit.*

"Thanks," I say, standing up slowly. I really don't want to hurt this guy, but I'm already planning the quickest way to tie him up with an extension cord and lock him in this closet. He's a freaking weed, so it shouldn't be too hard.

His chuckle holds absolutely no humor. "No need to look at me like that. I'm going to help you."

"Huh?"

"You came back to get the scanner, right?"

"Yeah."

He leans forward like he thinks I might be slow. "I'm going to help you do that."

"Why?"

He frowns. "I love my family, but they're going to hurt somebody, and they're going to use that thing to justify it. Because if the person isn't human, they won't . . ." He lets out a sharp breath. "You saw them tonight."

Once again, I can *tell*. By the look on his face, by the sound of his voice. He's not doing this to save some faceless person in the future. He's not doing this to save his family from themselves. And he's certainly not doing it for me.

He's doing this for Christina. For a few hours this afternoon, she made him wonder what his life would be like if he wasn't stuck on this compound. He told me he wanted to get out, and that he wasn't allowed. And today she showed up and gave him a glimpse of what's out there, and he can't shake it loose. That has to be it. Oh, that and the fact that she's ten times hotter than any girl in this compound.

Whatever. Hell, I'll take what I can get.

He looks at me with those bloodshot eyes. "You're not going to hurt them, are you?"

"I'm going to try my best not to, and if you're helping me, that's going to make it easier."

"What's with the cleaning supplies?"

I look down at the ammonia. "Diversion?"

He nods. "They're all in the lodge right now. Mostly the men. The women have taken the children home for the night."

"Good. Can you get to Rufus?"

He grimaces. "I can't snatch it for you. If they think I took it, they'll turn on me. Maybe kill me. I'll do what I can, but . . ."

I pull the bottle of Valium out of my pocket. "I don't need you to snatch it. I just need you to make sure he gets a good night's sleep."

TWENTY

I EXPLAIN MY PLAN TO DAVID AND SEND HIM OFF TO slip a Valium or five into Rufus's beer. David could so easily screw me over here, but somehow I know he won't. He gives me his hooded sweatshirt and heads off to the lodge in his T-shirt, since he's safe from the sun right now.

I dump my iodine crystals into the gallons of ammonia. I've only done this in chemistry class, never on such a large scale, but if it works, it will be exactly what I need.

Chaos.

I cap the bottles and sneak out the back of the clinic again. I have some time, because it's going to take at least half an hour to sedate the old man. I don't think Rufus will let any of the others have possession of the scanner—but he won't put it away, either. He'll have it with him. Which means I need him to stay put.

But I need everyone else to move.

With my hood up and my head low, I unroll the paper towel and position two layers of it in the stiff grass beside the sidewalk in front of the lodge. From inside, I hear men's voices. It's like this angry hornet buzz, punctuated every now and then by a shout, a curse. I'm betting they're arguing over how many H2 they can kill before dawn. Just like David said—anyone who flashes red is not going to be treated like a person. They'll be treated like an enemy.

I am in the middle of pouring the contents of my bottles over the paper towels when someone stumbles out of the front of the lodge.

It's the hobbit.

He's got his hand on his half-open fly. I think he might have gotten lost on his way to the bathrooms. He squints at me in the darkness. "Matt? That you, buddy?"

Still hunched over my paper towels, praying the dark substance I'm pouring on them isn't going to dry before I'm ready, I . . . grunt.

The hobbit leans forward. "What're you doing there?"

"Cleaning up," I say gruffly. I have no idea what the fuck Matt's voice sounds like.

"Eh, okay. All righty . . ." He contemplates his open fly like it's a wonder of modern technology. "Keep it up then." He belches, then staggers back through the front door of the lodge.

I finish emptying my ammonia bottles and toss them in the grass. Sticking close to the buildings, I skirt between the lodge and the dining hall, and then sprint across the field to the solar panel array. I almost hate to do this; it's going to affect everyone who lives here, including the women and children. But the men are going to be after me in a raw second when they figure out what I've taken, which means I need to kill the power so I can get past the security system quickly. Which means doing permanent damage to their solar array.

Using the scalpel, I pick the lock on the access panel. It's painstaking work—especially with only a razor-sharp blade as a tool—but after several minutes I manage to switch the wires and reverse the polarity on the solar panels without slicing one of my fingers off. As soon as I secure the final connection, there's this echoing snap, followed by ominous, sparking crackles as the system surges and fries itself to nothing.

One by one, the lights in the buildings go dark.

As soon as the lodge goes black, I take off running.

In my head, it's like I can see it, the sands falling through an hourglass, whittling away the time I have, the time until the substance on those paper towels dries completely, until someone jostles it just the right way. I get to the back of the lodge and flatten myself against it in time to hear clomping footsteps on the front porch, someone yelling that he's going to check the array. He's going to be very unhappy when he finds out what I've done.

I creep over to the third window from the left, and as promised, David has left it open for me. I nudge the curtains aside and watch the last few men heading out the front door of the lodge, speaking in slurred voices.

I hoist myself into the main hall. The only light in the room is supplied by the low amber flames in the fireplace. It's enough to show me Rufus Bishop hunched over in his chair, an overturned mug still clutched in his hand. I cross the room and stand over him, my heart slamming against my ribs. His other hand is resting on the table, meaty fingers curled . . .

. . . over nothing.

"I wondered if you'd come back." Aaron Bishop steps from the hallway behind me.

He's got the scanner in his hand.

"That doesn't belong to you," I say, taking a step toward him. I might have been worried about the time running out before, but now all I want is for it to speed up. What if my diversion doesn't work? All Aaron has to do is shout, and I'm caught.

But judging by the cruel twist of his lips, he wants to play a little first. "Where's the H2?"

"Safe from you."

He lets out a huff of laughter. "How could you pollute your blood like that? Or are you just fooling around?" He nods at Rufus. "He gets all high and mighty about that stuff, but I don't blame you one bit. What's it like to screw an alien?"

It's going to be fun to hurt this guy. "Give me the scanner."

He looks down at the technology in his hand. "And what are you going to do with it?"

"Keep it away from people like you."

His expression twists with disdain. "People like me? At least I *am* a person. You'd rather hand it over to a bunch of fuckin' aliens?"

I shake my head and wipe my hands on my pants, never taking my eyes off his. "My dad didn't create it to help either side kill."

He's just opened his mouth to reply when there's a series of loud cracks from the front of the lodge. It sounds a hell of a lot like gunfire. Judging by the yelps and cries to take cover coming from outside, that's exactly what the Bishops think it is.

My nitrogen triiodide trap has detonated.

Aaron whirls toward the front door with panic in his eyes. I take my chance and slam my fist into the side of his head, then yank the scanner from him and take off. I lunge through the window and go out headfirst, rolling to my feet immediately. I can already hear the thumping of shoes on hardwood behind me.

Scanner in hand, I sprint across the clearing. The guy who was sent to fix the array sees me coming and must hear Aaron yelling behind me, because he steps onto the sidewalk and adopts a low wrestling stance. From the way he's all bleary and weaving, I can tell he's about as sharp as the hobbit was.

So I don't even slow down. Two steps before I reach him,

I jump, plant my foot on his shoulder, and sail right over his drunk ass, landing on the other side and moving forward again before he can pick himself up off the ground. Behind me, Aaron's steps are staccato thumps against the asphalt. He appears to be the only one of this crew who's sober. He's also extremely fast, and he's gaining on me. My bare feet are torn and aching as they pound the blacktop. It's a relief when they hit the leaves and earth, and I hurtle into the trees blindly, trying to stay ahead of Aaron. I vault over the split-rail fence and loop around the pond because I have no idea whether the scanner is waterproof. As I draw parallel with the southeastern shore, I hear a faint cough and roar—someone's firing up a generator. Of course, these people have a backup electrical system. Which means . . .

The security system will be live again at any second.

I throw myself forward, desperate to make it through the invisible fence, all too aware of Aaron's ragged breaths behind me as he closes the distance. He's not hesitating, even though I can easily hear the high whine of the cameras on either side of us booting up. Surely he has to know the system's coming online, has to—

Crack.

I jerk and stumble, then clumsily run my hands over my chest, surprised to find it intact. A gurgling moan comes from behind me, followed by the piercing shriek of the alarm, letting all the Bishops know an intruder has passed through the invisible perimeter. I spin around, disoriented, half convinced those automated rifles are about to cut me down.

Aaron lies a few yards away. He's curled on his side, and even from here, I can see the wet black ooze over the fingers he's pressed to his chest. His eyes, glittering ebony saucers in the moonlight, are fixed on me with absolute terror. There's blood flowing freely from his mouth and nose. He's drowning from the inside out.

With the scanner hanging from my tingling fist, I take a step forward. And then I realize that if I try to help him, I'll be shot as well.

I can't do a thing for him.

"I'm sorry," I say, and I mean it. I know a fatal wound when I see one, and though I hate him, I didn't want him to die.

From just over the split-rail fence, there's an agonized cry. The drunken solar-panel fixer has seen Aaron. He shouts over his shoulder to turn off the generators, his voice broken and panicked. And then his head swings back around—and his gaze lands on me.

I stagger back under the weight of it, the heat of it, the hatred. The blame. The promise that once they turn the generators off, the Bishops are going to come after me with everything they have, and they won't care about the consequences. I whirl around and plunge into the trees, crashing through the brush. I don't slow down to get my compass or my shoes, I just sprint, hoping I'm heading in the right direction.

My entire focus is on survival, on putting as much distance as I can between me and the Bishops. I lose track of time, of distance, aware only of the whoosh of my breath and my heartbeat pounding in my ears. I can hear them behind me. The beams of their flashlights hit the trees around me. I keep going, grateful with every step that I'm still alive, that if I keep going maybe I can find my way back to my mom and Christina. Assuming I'm heading in the right direction. I am sweat-slick and panting by the time my toe catches on a root and I end up sprawled on the forest floor. The deep, earthy smell of rotting leaves fills my lungs as I push myself up. The scanner is lying a few feet away. I lie very still, listening for the sounds of the mob coming after me, but somehow, I seem to have lost them—all I hear is the hoot of an owl and the trickle of water from a nearby stream.

Slowly, aching, I get to my feet and wipe my hands on my pants, then look down at my bare, muddy, bleeding feet.

I have no idea where I am. I have no idea how long I've been circling in these woods, but I know it's been a while. I'm damn lucky I haven't fallen right into one of their primitive snares or shallow, wooden-spike-filled pits.

From far behind me, deep in the dense maze of trees, there's a shout. I spin around to see the pinpoint of a flashlight bobbing in the distance. I haven't lost them after all.

But if they're back there, that means that I need to move in the opposite direction. My feet throbbing, my brain foggy with fear and fatigue, I creep away, listening for signs that they're hemming me in. I should have been back at the road ages ago. Will my mom and Christina still be waiting for me if I make it back? How long will it take Mom to call up her friend? What would the Bishops do to me in the meantime? Those thoughts keep me moving when all my body wants to do is drop.

Finally, up ahead, I hear the faintest of sounds, one that definitely isn't coming from the forest. It's a car horn. I can't believe it—my mom is taking an incredible risk, but it's all I need to get me going in the right direction.

Between the honks, I hear enough to know the Bishops have recognized the noise as well, because one of them calls to the other, and the flashlight beams bounce more quickly as they start to run. If they catch us now, they won't be thinking about their assets in some bank in Chicago—the only thing on their minds will be avenging Aaron's death. And when I consider what they'll do to Christina, it sends a new, frenetic energy sizzling through my arms and legs.

I hurdle fallen tree trunks and stumble through brambles, holding the scanner close to my chest, bouncing off oaks and shouldering past spindly maples as I try to put some distance between me and the Bishops.

They start firing as soon as the car comes into view.

My mom, who's standing just outside the sedan, dives into the driver's seat as I leap over the muddy ditch separating the woods from the road. Christina throws open the door to the backseat and grabs me by the shoulders, using all her weight to heave me inside as a bullet *thunks* into the rear panel of the car.

"Go!" I roar, and my mom hits the gas pedal, lurching forward as I try to pull my legs all the way inside.

We're at least a mile up the road by the time I am able to get the passenger door closed, but that's not because I'm too tired or hurt to manage it—it's mostly because Christina's grip on me is iron, and I have trouble getting loose, even for a minute. As soon as the door slams, her arms are around me again, her hands in my hair, and even though she doesn't say anything, the look on her face tells me what she's been going through the last few hours.

I let her pull my head against her chest, and then I hear nothing but her heartbeat, nothing but her breath, nothing but the blood rushing through her veins. It resets me, better than any compass. I wrap my arms around her waist and don't move until we cross the border into Maryland and are well on our way to Charlottesville.

TWENTY-ONE

AS WE DRIVE, I TELL MY MOM WHAT HAPPENED AT THE compound, including how Aaron got shot by Rufus's security system. She makes a pained face. "Poor Rufus," she whispers. Then she's quiet until long after the sun rises over the horizon. I wonder if she's thinking how easily that could have been me, bleeding out on the forest floor. I know *I* am. Her shoulders finally relax as we cross the border into Virginia. We've passed a few state cops, but in our bland gray car with Pennsylvania plates, we don't draw any attention. We go through a drive-through for breakfast in Fredericksburg, and then she parks behind a trashy motel under the low-hanging branches of a pecan tree.

"I have to sleep for a while," my mom mutters. "I'm about to pass out. And we should probably lie low until it gets dark. I don't want to take any chances. Can you keep watch?"

"No problem." Sometime in the last hour or two, Christina and I have switched places, and now I'm holding her as she dozes with her head on my chest. I've cleaned my feet off with a bunch of wet wipes my mom requested at the drive-through, and it turns out that apart from one long scrape on the bottom of my left foot, they didn't sustain too much damage during my frolic in the woods. They ache to the bone, though, and I don't mind the opportunity to keep them up and stay put for a while. My brain is another story. I'm still wired.

My mom gazes over the backseat at Christina. "She wanted to come after you. Last night." She smiles. "I was wishing you'd left some of that Valium behind."

I stroke Christina's hair. "She's not good at sitting still."

"She's graduating in a few weeks, isn't she?"

"Yeah. If we ever make it back."

"College plans?" my mom asks.

"You're really asking me that after everything that's happened? Like she can just return to everyday life?"

"It's too early to say. If I have my way, this will die down soon, Tate." She rubs at her temple and closes her eyes. "Don't lose hope."

"Penn," I say, a familiar ache starting up in my chest as I look down at Christina's face, so peaceful as she sleeps. "She got into Penn." I'm happy that she'll be going to such a good school. And Philadelphia's only two hours by train. And we still have the summer. Assuming we're both alive and that I haven't been tucked away in some secret CIA cell somewhere. Assuming she still wants to be with me.

God, I'm going to miss her.

My mother nods. "It's for the best."

"What did you say?"

Her eyes meet mine. "Now that you know the truth, you need to face your responsibility."

"My responsibility."

"To make certain that the Archer line does not end with you."

There's a ball of lead forming in the pit of my stomach, cold and toxic. "We're not talking about this."

She pulls the band from her ponytail and leans her seat back. "That's fine. We don't have to talk about it right now."

Translation: *We're going to talk about it at some point.*

I slide down in the seat a little, bringing Christina deeper into the circle of my arms, and stare out the window as my mother's breathing slows, easing her into sleep. It's not like I'm ready to settle down or anything. Hell, most days, I don't think past the next few hours, let alone years into the future. Christina and I never talked much about what next year would be like, with her in college and me still stuck in high school. But the thought of losing her hurts me in ways I can't really face right now. And the thought that my mother might have some short list of human girls who would make acceptable wives? That leaves me cold. I wonder if this is why my father never liked Christina. Not because she's H2, but because he knew how hard it would make things for me.

I am the last of the Archers.

That feels like it should mean something, like it should be important. But right now, it just feels lonely.

I sit very still for a very long time, while my mother and Christina sleep, while they breathe the same air and dream separate dreams, while I try to figure out what each of them needs from me and realize there's a strong possibility I will disappoint them both.

The sun is sinking by the time my mother stirs and brings her seat upright. Christina, who has been slumbering steadily for the past several hours, murmurs something about hydrochloric acid and shifts restlessly. I hope she's not having a nightmare about chemistry class.

"You said we were going to see a colleague of yours," I say to my mom as she turns the key in the ignition and pulls out of the parking lot.

"His name is Charles Willetts. He's a professor of history at the University of Virginia."

"And he's not human."

She glances back at me. "No, he's not."

"And he knows it."

She nods.

"Is he part of the Core?" She'd go to someone powerful, and if he's not human, he must be part of the H2 elite.

"He was, at one point. But he isn't anything like Race. He won't want to keep this technology from humans. He favors the balance of power and wants to broker mutual trust between The Fifty and the Core."

"And you told him about the scanner?"

Her cheeks darken a shade.

"Did Dad know?"

Her mouth forms that tight line that tells me she's feeling so much more than she's going to say, and suddenly, I realize—"Mom, is this why you guys broke up?"

A strangled sort of noise bursts from her throat. "It was right after your father confided in a few of The Fifty about the H2 ship debris his family had been keeping secret. He'd just discovered what it could do, and what the implications might be. I'd met Charles through another colleague, and we'd recognized each other for what we are. Over the years, we'd slowly formed a friendship, and I knew he could help. And more than anything, I wanted to help Fred. Your father was so horrified by what people like Brayton and Rufus wanted to do with it, and he was so isolated. Pulling away from everyone. Angry at everyone. I begged him to meet with Charles, to hear him out, thinking that together, they could find a peaceful way to deal with the technology without destroying something that could be truly important or putting either side at a disadvantage. He refused. In fact, he was enraged with me—he said I'd betrayed him."

She quickly swipes a tear away with her sleeve. "Your father had been through so much at that point, with all sides trying to find out what he was up to and how far he'd taken it. Race Lavin seemed to suspect something, because he dragged your father in for questioning on more than one occasion, citing anonymous tips about threats to homeland security. Your father had already taken precautions and Race couldn't find anything, but it drove Fred further within himself. He didn't trust anyone. Including me. Especially me at that point. And I realized it was my fault, so I—I left. I wanted to give him some space, and it ended up being permanent. I'm sorry, Tate."

The hurt in her voice is so intense that it silences me. I totally get why my dad was mad. I would have been, too. But . . . damn. It caused both of them incredible pain. It broke up our family. Couldn't he have forgiven her? I stare out the window and watch the world go by, wishing away the ache in my throat.

Mom draws a long breath through her nose and slowly lets it out. "Charles won't hand the scanner over to Race, if that's what you're worried about. He's no longer part of their organization, but he'll know how to deal with them, and may even be able to get them to call Race off. And the Core wouldn't suspect we'd go to one of their own, which is why we're headed there instead of Chicago. I spoke with George—"

"I know. I talked to him." I look down at the sleek, black machine at my feet. "But Mom, should we really be taking the scanner to yet another person Dad didn't trust? Didn't we just escape from that kind of situation?"

"Your father wanted to protect his family. So do I. And now that he's gone, your safety is my responsibility, and I'm going to do everything I can to protect you *and* your future. If there was any ideal option, I would take it. But unlike the Bishops, Charles does not deal in hate. He only wants peace," she says with a fierce edge in her voice.

Frustration and dread hit me at once, making me shiver and sweat at the same time. My dad pulled away from Brayton, who wants to use the technology to build weapons and gain power, or maybe sell the tech back to the H2 for a profit. My dad stayed away from Rufus, who would use the technology to tell him who to kill and to reveal the H2 for what they are, sparking a possible war. He let go of my mom, who apparently wants to collaborate with the H2. And he was desperate to keep it from Race, who wants the scanner badly enough to kill whoever's in his way, even though the Core have successfully suppressed all threats in the past without the scanner's help, even though they probably have plenty of other wreckage and technology from the salvaged H2 ships. So basically, my dad wanted to keep it away from everyone, and didn't tell anyone what he thought its purpose should be. And if my mom is right, he never revealed all of his secrets, though I think he was trying to in those final moments before he died. But I don't know how to figure it out, and I have no idea who or what to believe.

So I hold on to the one thing I do believe in, and her fingers slide under the back of my shirt and rest against my skin.

"When will we be there?" I ask.

"An hour or so," my mom says. She switches on the radio and tunes it to a local news station. We listen through the weather forecast—more sunny weather on the way—and then through twenty minutes of local and national news, none of which mentions three fugitives carrying technology created from the wreckage of an alien spaceship, fortunately. As soon as it's over, my mother turns it off. "They're still keeping it quiet," she says, "which tells you how important it is. Race and his team aren't trusting anyone with this."

"Or maybe they're all in the hospital?"

She laughs. "They'd love it if you believed that."

If my father were here, he would remind me: *Pretend inferiority and encourage your enemy's arrogance.* My mom's absolutely right. "So we should assume they're still looking for us."

"Yes. We can't stay here long. Charles and I will decide what to do next. I'd like to have you back home by—" She sighs.

With Dad dead, where is my home? Once again, I'm reminded things will never be the same. Will I even get to return to that apartment in Manhattan, to my friends and to my school? Do I want to? Could I face it? That apartment is empty now, except for a grumpy, hungry cat . . . and a couple hundred deadly weapons and random gadgets, all tucked away in the cave of my dad's lab. Maybe among those gadgets are a few pieces of an alien spaceship, along with the answers to who or what Josephus is. I bet I could figure out how and why my dad was getting those real-time scans of the world population, too, and possibly even resolve that anomaly that's causing fourteen to come up as unidentified. And if I have enough time, I could hack my way into those plans that flashed when I touched the population counter's screen. I need to find out what my dad meant when he said the scanner was the key to our survival, and the answer has to be in his lab.

So come to think of it, I *would* like to go back.

My mom's phone rings. "Hi, Charles," she says, her voice filling with the warmth of an old friendship. "We're just getting into town now."

She hangs up and cruises along a few tree-lined streets leading to the campus. We head up a hill, then turn onto a narrow, one-lane street with high garden walls on either side, which then opens up to a parking lot surrounded on three sides by a two-story building. We get out, stretching our legs. Christina looks a lot steadier than she did last night, but I can tell she's worn out, still feeling the aftereffects of the concussion. She winces as she touches the bandage beneath her hair and gazes at our surroundings.

"This is the Academical Village," my mom tells us. "Charles lives and teaches here."

We go into the hushed building through the rear entrance from the parking lot and follow a maze of hallways until we reach the lobby. I look out a window to see a huge rectangular lawn surrounded by buildings fronted with wide, columned walkways. At the top of the hill is a domed building.

"That's the Rotunda," Mom explains when she sees me staring at it.

We walk through the lobby, reading signs that tell us there are lecture halls and classrooms on this level. This place smells of plaster and paint, of well-renovated and preserved history, of treasured tradition. My mom goes up to the elevator and punches a code I can only assume her friend texted her. It carries us to the second floor, which appears to contain two apartments, and one of them has a placard out front that says "Professor Charles Willetts, PhD, Department of History."

I look down at myself, barefoot, torn, smeared with dirt and blood, and straight-up reeking. I can't believe Christina was actually willing to be close to me all day, and now that I'm fully aware of my sorry state, I take a big step away from her and wonder how soon until it's socially appropriate for me to sneak away and take a hot shower.

My mom knocks, and about a second later, the door swings open, like the person inside was waiting with his hand on the knob. "Mitra," says a voice coming from the level of my waist.

I look down to see the guy, maybe midsixties, steel-gray hair, and in a motorized wheelchair. His legs are stick thin beneath black dress pants, but his upper body is stout. He reaches up to pull my mother into a hug, and she leans over to accommodate him. "Once again, I'm so sorry for your loss," he says quietly.

"Thank you." She kisses his wrinkled cheek.

My mom introduces me and Christina, and Charles's eyebrows rise to his hairline as he regards us. "You've obviously been through a great deal," he says.

"What have you heard?" I ask.

His smile fades as his gaze shifts to my mom. "Only to be on the lookout for you. Fortunately, when Race Lavin called yesterday, I was able to convince him I had no idea where you were."

"He called?" My mother takes a step toward the door, looking uncertain.

"It's all right, Mitra. I suspect he and the Core are calling any of us who are known to have had contact with any of The Fifty. It's a long list, and I'm sure I'm one of many."

I cannot explain it, not really, but I don't like this guy. Maybe it's because he's part of what broke up my parents' marriage, but there's something about him . . . I blink and try to shake it off.

The tension in Mom's shoulders has loosened. "Thank you for taking us in."

Charles is watching her with a worried expression. "Do you have the technology?"

The tension in my own body rises. "How did I know that would be the first question you'd ask?"

"Tate," my mother says in a quiet voice.

"No, his suspicion understandable and very smart." Charles ushers us into a sitting room filled with books and a collection of globes, all antique and burnished, lined up along the shelves on either side of the white-manteled fireplace. He motors his chair to a spot next to the leather couch and gestures for us to sit. I look down at its smooth, unspotted surface, hoping this guy has a good cleaning service.

My filthiness doesn't seem to be on his mind as he watches me take a seat. "Though I never met your father, I had a great deal of respect for him," he says. "His discovery will help us learn about our own heritage."

"If my dad didn't trust you, why should I?" I ignore my mom's dirty look. "I need to hear why you'd be willing to hide us from Race Lavin. Because that guy seems to have a lot of influence."

Charles rolls his eyes. "Race Lavin is an enforcer and nothing more. I'll contact the Core and have them put a leash on him as soon as we've moved the scanner to a secure location—" He holds up his hand as I start to interrupt. "Let me finish. We don't want either side to have the advantage, because we want them both at the table. That means we have to put the device out of their reach before bringing your whereabouts to the attention of The Fifty or the Core."

My mother sits across from me and Christina, who's got her arms wrapped around herself and is staring at the floor, like she hopes no one's going to notice her. Charles's eyes settle on her for a moment, possibly weighing her part in all this, and then he turns to my mother. "May I . . . may I see it?"

Mom opens her bag. My heart begins to pound. She pulls the scanner out and hands it to Charles, who takes it with a puzzled expression. "I thought it would be . . . bigger."

"Turn it on," my mother says.

He holds it away from himself and flips the switch. He watches its light pass over my mom's hands, which are folded in her lap and turn blue as the beam caresses them. Then he slants it toward Christina, and its light makes her already pink cheeks crimson.

"I wish people would stop pointing that thing at me," she snaps.

"My apologies," he mumbles as he slides the light over my arms before turning the scanner off. He didn't scan himself, but I already know full well what he is. "This is amazing. To think, this technology is actually hundreds of years old. Think of where it's been, and how it survived an intergalactic exodus . . . Think of what *we* could do with it." An odd expression flits across his face. It's almost like he's gone into a trance.

My mother leans forward, frowning. "Charles? Are you feeling all right?"

He blinks. "What? Oh, yes."

"So what exactly do you want to do with it?" I ask, not even trying to blunt the sharpness of my tone.

"Well, this technology could have been part of the H2

strategy when . . . we decided to come here. Simply put, it helps us find each other. This has implications that go far beyond this planet, young man. What if there were other survivors? What if they're out there somewhere?" He grins, his eyes alight with eagerness.

Christina sits up, her eyes a little wider. "Survivors?"

"Surely it's clear to you that the H2 who came here were refugees. Such an advanced society, with enough technology to travel through space? They could have taken over this planet. But instead they let themselves blend in. And forget." He lets out a high-pitched chuckle. "Very few even know what they are."

"Wait a minute," I say. "Are you talking about trying to find H2 out in space? And bring them *here*?"

My mother frowns, and I can tell this is something they've never discussed before, even though he's known about the technology for years.

Charles sits back, and the light in his eyes fades as his gaze travels from me to Christina to my mother. "Oh, no, I wouldn't do anything without collaborating with The Fifty. This is a chance to forge a permanent agreement. Maybe even reveal the truth of the two intelligent species on this planet, but in a planned way that won't result in societal unrest. That is the priority."

"Really? Because you looked pretty excited about finding a way to call up any H2 out there who feel like paying us a visit, as if we need more of you guys here," I snap. Out of the corner of my eye, I see Christina rock back like she's been slapped, but I'm too freaked to think about why. "Mom, I—"

"It's okay, Tate," she says. "We wouldn't do anything without consulting with The Fifty first. That's why George is on his way here. He said he'd fly out of Chicago on one of Black Box's private planes as soon as the board meeting was over. I'm waiting to receive his exact ETA, but he said he'd be here tomorrow afternoon."

Charles hands the scanner back to my mother. "I think Tate would feel better if you held on to this, Mitra," he says.

Before I can reply, Charles rolls a bit closer and looks up at me, his eyes searching mine. "Trust your mother, son. She's known me for years, and I have tremendous respect for not only her, but for The Fifty. I might have my own interests, but this situation touches the highest levels of power, and nothing will be done without consensus from all *adults* who have a stake in it. And we know you've been through so much. From what Mitra's told me, you've been resourceful and brave. But this is something you should never have been involved in."

I shoot to my feet, unable to look away from his stare. *Something you never should have been involved in* . . . As much as I hate to admit it, he's right. And the only reason I am involved? The only reason my girlfriend has been shot, and terrorized, and threatened? The reason I lost my dad?

Because I stole the scanner.

I'm not an innocent victim in this fight. I fucking *created* this fight. It's like all the air's been sucked out of the room.

Charles gives me a sympathetic smile and motors away from me. "Well, Mitra, we'd better get to work if we want to fully understand this device before The Fifty and the Core know we have it. Do you know which parts are the actual H2 technology?" He points to the side of the scanner, to the row of oddly shaped USB ports. "Do you know what those are meant for?"

Mom tilts her head. "I'm not sure. We could try to remotely access some of my old files, from when Fred and I were working on the technology together. He took it much further after I left him, but we could start there."

She stands up and walks over to his desk, an ornate, heavily carved antique with a very sleek-looking desktop computer on it. "Do you mind?" she asks him.

He rolls over to her and they begin to speak in low tones. It's like Christina and I aren't even here. I glance over at Christina. She looks like she might crumble with one word, one touch, and like everything else, I'm pretty sure it's my fault.

"I need a shower," I blurt. What I really need is to get out of this room.

Charles turns to us, the white-gray glare of the computer screen reflecting off his glasses. "The guest room is down the hall on the right. And I think my son might have left a few things behind the last time he visited." His gaze flicks toward my feet. "Maybe even a pair of loafers. Help yourself."

Christina hasn't moved. She's giving off major don't-touch-me vibes. I want to help, but I have no idea how to fix anything at this point. Also, given that I haven't slept in thirty-six hours, I have no energy to try. My arms and legs are dead weight, just meat hanging from the shell of my body. I have no more fight in me right now. I think of something General Patton once said, about how the body is never tired if the mind is not tired . . . and that's it. My mind is tired. *All* of me is tired.

So I walk down the hall in search of several hundred gallons of hot water to drown myself in, and hope that when I emerge, maybe the world will have righted itself.

TWENTY-TWO

I HAVE NO IDEA HOW LONG I'M IN THE SHOWER, BUT the water's turned cold by the time I drag myself out. The clock on the wall tells me it's nearly ten. When I finally trudge into the hall, now wearing a snazzy pair of striped boxers and a Virginia Cavaliers T-shirt, I can hear the muffled voices of my mom and Charles from the sitting room, debating about something. It sounds like they could go on for hours, so I bee-line for the guest room, thinking maybe Christina—

She's sitting on the bed. She's still wearing the dress from the Bishops' party, but the curled ends of her hair are wet, and the room is filled with the scent of soap. I guess she got herself a shower in one of the other bathrooms.

"Hey," she says.

"Hey." I sit down on the edge of the bed.

"I'm not really tired." She tucks her hair behind her ear and

283

scoots until her back is against the headboard. She pulls her knees to her chest and tugs the skirt of the dress over them so only the tips of her painted toenails are sticking out from under it.

She hasn't looked me in the eye since I walked in.

"Are you all right?" I ask.

In my head, I'm begging her. *Please be all right. Please.* Because I'm not all right, and I need her to help me. I want her to tell me we'll do this together. And that's not what's happening now, and it's making me want to smash something, or maybe to run, as fast and far as I can, until my lungs give out and I've put a few hundred miles between me and this wall of tension that's risen between us.

"I'm fine," she says, gazing at her knees. "No worries."

She's definitely not all right.

I crawl along the edge of the bed and lean back against the headboard, too, so now we're both looking across the room at this old-fashioned tapestry hanging on the wall. It's a battle scene. Dressed in a red tunic and wearing armor over his chest and shoulders, one Roman soldier stands in front, his sword raised over his opponent, who lies in the dirt with a dagger in his hand. The blue-clad enemy stares up at the Roman, defiant and determined. He may be on the ground, but he hasn't given up yet. All around them, there are men on horses, men on foot, all paired off and doing their best to kill, but these two—their world is only the size of the patch of dirt around them. Nothing matters more than getting through the battle, through the next minute.

And right now, for me, the world is the size of this bed, and there's only me and Christina here, even though it feels like she's a universe away. Nothing matters more than getting through this, whatever *this* is.

I don't know which one of us reaches for the other first, because it seems like we have the same thought at the same time. *Want. Need.* I don't know which, but her lips are on mine and her hands are on my body and everything else disconnects. My heart slams against my ribs as she straddles me, and through the thin fabric of her dress I can feel the heat pouring from her. It coils around me, cutting off my awareness of anything but her. She curls her fingers into my hair and kisses me hard-edged and desperate, cranking me so tight, it's all I can do to control myself.

But she doesn't seem to want me to. Not this time, not tonight. She takes my hand, sliding it down her hip, pressing my fingers into her skin, inching the skirt up her legs. She bows her head and her tongue is on my neck and her teeth are on my skin and it's all over. No contest. I have no idea what she wants, but I'll give her anything.

I gather the fabric of the skirt that's bunching around her knees. When my fingers finally skim the soft skin of her thigh, it's like something I've needed for a thousand years. I know she has to feel it, how much I want her, but she isn't pulling back like she always does when we reach this point.

In fact, she seems intent on pushing things even further.

Somewhere in the back of my hormone-soaked brain, that last thought sinks its fangs deep. She seems . . . intent. This is how she is with things that challenge her, that frustrate her. She tackles them head-on; she fights until she wins. And that's how this feels as she tugs my shirt up, as her fingernails scrape along my stomach and ribs. As amazing as that sensation is, it's like she's fighting me rather than something we're doing together, and I don't know—

A tear slides off her face and hits my cheek, and we both freeze. She recovers first and makes it halfway off the bed before I hook my arm around her waist.

"Don't," I say, sounding like I've run a few miles.

"Don't what?" she replies, her voice raspy.

I tighten my grip on her, because, perched on the edge of this bed, every muscle taut, she's poised for flight. And in my current condition, I have little chance of catching her. "Just . . . don't. Don't go. Don't run. Don't . . . I don't know."

I rest my forehead between her shoulder blades. This dress smells like her now, the heady almond scent of her skin, the faint honey-sweet tang of her sweat, and I breathe it in like I'm drowning. "You're about five steps ahead of me here," I say in a ragged voice. "You're going to have to circle back and pick me up."

She sags against my arm like all the fight's been punched out of her, and I pull her back against me. I'm trembling with the excess adrenaline of the last few minutes, but she's outright shaking. Her entire body shudders with the sobs that come tearing out of her. I've never seen her lose it like this. I want to figure it out, fix it however I can, but as the minutes pass and her tears show no sign of drying up, I feel powerless to do anything but wait it out.

Slowly, gently, afraid she's going to bolt if I make the wrong move, I lie down on my side and bring her with me. I curl myself around her, bowing my head over hers. "Please talk to me," I finally say.

"I heard what your mother said. I was awake."

I rack my brain, rewinding through the day and trying to figure out what the hell she's talking about, because whatever it is, it's—

"When she said it was best that I was going away for college. That we would be far apart. When she was talking about your *responsibility*," she clarifies.

Shit. "I'm not even sure what that means."

She sniffles. "It means all I've been hearing over the past two days is that whatever I am, I'm not good enough for *you*."

All these words tumble around in my head, but I can't catch hold of any of them, and even when I do, I can't put them in the right order. Not good enough for me? It's. Just. It's hilarious, actually, but I don't think laughing is going to keep her on this bed.

"Christina, you're . . . you're more than good enough," I say, and God, it sounds so stupid, I almost do start to laugh.

"You practically said it yourself about an hour ago," she whispers. "*As if we need more of you guys here.* You sounded like those Bishop people."

I scrub a hand over my face. "I'm sorry. I just don't want to be shot at anymore. But I shouldn't have said it like that. Please . . ."

She turns to me, and I only catch a glimpse of her tear-stained face before she buries it in my shoulder. "The sad thing is, I actually know that. And I feel the same way you do—do you think I want this planet to be invaded? It's—I don't know what I am," she chokes out. "I have no idea what I am."

Her sobs are quieter this time, but no less painful to listen to. She doesn't stop me when I pull her close, when I kiss the top of her head. I hold her until her sobs become little hiccuppy shudders, until she finally relaxes against me. And as I do, I think about it, what she is, what I am. Until a few days ago, I was just a guy who had hit the lottery in the girlfriend department, and she was the girl who was insane yet patient enough to want to be around me. What's different now? What's changed?

At exactly 12:47 a.m., I figure out the answer.

Nothing.

Nothing's changed at all.

"I know what you are," I whisper into her hair. "You're Christina Scolina. You're a kickass left winger. You have the most awesome laugh I've ever heard. You are so beautiful, it makes me crazy. You're my best friend. And . . . I love you."

I brace myself, because I've just said it out loud, something that feels too huge to let loose but too important not to. But Christina . . . is completely silent. With my heart pounding, I lean back and look down at her.

She's asleep.

Completely passed out. Done in by exhaustion. And a concussion. I'm surprised she had the energy to cry for as long as she did.

This time I do laugh, quietly, here in the dark. It doesn't matter if she heard me; it's still there, still real. This time, it's my turn to say to her: I'm all right, and she's all right, and we'll do this together. I'll do my part, whatever it is. I silently promise her I'll be strong enough, and I'll be smart enough. I'll fix this. I'll figure it out.

I'm still not my father, not even close. And right now, I'd give a lot to have him here. I want him to tell me what he was thinking, what exactly he wants me to do when I finally get back into his lab, how all the pieces of this puzzle fit together—Josephus, the hidden H2 artifacts, the scanner, the population counter and its anomalies, the plans that screensaver concealed. But it's not just that.

I never thought I would feel this way, but . . . I miss him. Now that he's gone, I realize what else I've lost. He loved me. He never said it, but I know he did. He showed it every time he drilled me, every time he forced me to run an extra mile or do an extra set of weights, every time he tucked those horrible protein gel packs into my bag and onto my plate. He wanted me to be strong, to stay alive, to protect my family. I want him to be here and put his hand on my shoulder one more time. This time, I wouldn't shake it off or turn away. This time, I would let him.

And though it's too late for that, I'm left with everything he's given me, and I'm not going to shake that off either. I carefully untangle myself from Christina and slide off the bed, then head down the hall. Mom and Charles are riveted by whatever's on the computer screen and don't even look up until I say, "So what's the plan?"

My mother startles, but Charles turns to me slowly, his gaze sliding from my bare feet to my boxers to my T-shirt to my hair, which is probably standing on end. "What can we do for you, Tate?"

"I asked what the plan was, Professor. So I can help you."

My mother rubs at her eyes and speaks in a weary voice. "We didn't find much in my old files. Nothing about some of the external features of the scanner, like that row of ports on the side. So we're trying to access some of the files on your father's server. It's taking a while."

I glance at Charles. "Why do you need Dad's files, exactly?"

"Because," says Charles, "on the off chance we lose control of this technology—and we're doing our best not to—we want to understand it inside and out, so that the person with the device is not the only one with the power."

"You think it can be replicated?" I'm not sure that's a good thing, but Charles looks kind of excited by the prospect.

My mother frowns at Charles before answering the question. "We won't know what's possible until we know how he put it together, and whether he used one-of-a-kind H2 artifacts or replicas. At this point, the more we know, the more leverage we have with both sides, so I'm not going to waste a minute of this time."

Leverage. That sounds good. "Why didn't you ask me to help?"

Charles lets out a choked laugh. "Your mother has a doctorate in biochemistry, and she can't figure it out, so I don't know why you—"

"No, Charles," she says to him before her gaze rests on me again. "Do you think you could figure it out? It's fairly complicated."

I roll my eyes. "Complicated? Mom, you you have no idea what I'm capable of. And Dad didn't either, which should tell you something. He taught me so well that even *he* didn't know I'd hacked his system six ways from Sunday. I may not have found everything, but I didn't know what I was looking for, either."

Charles looks intrigued. "Do you think you can get past this firewall?"

I smile. "Is it Triple DES?"

My mom turns back to the computer screen. "I . . . think

so," she mutters. "Your father's security is a lot more sophisticated than it used to be."

"Allow me." They let me at the keyboard, and I tunnel into the system using the backup universal datagram protocol port to obtain the certificate key. "I can get you in."

With the key, I access my dad's system and let my mom hunt for the files she wants using relevant search terms. After a few minutes, she points to the screen. "I think these might be helpful, but I can't open them. They're encrypted." Charles, who has been silent for the last few minutes, looks at me hopefully.

I shrug. "I can decrypt them, but it'll take a while."

"A while?" He lets his head hang, his fingers curling over the armrests of his wheelchair.

My mother puts her hand on his shoulder. "I know it's been a long night already. Do you want to go to bed and let me and Tate handle this?"

Charles raises his head. "No. Like your mother said. We can't waste a minute."

He gives me a hard look, and I stare right back. My mom's known and trusted him for years, but I have no intention of sitting back and letting him explore my Dad's stuff without me. Especially because there's the slightest bit of tension in Mom's face as she looks at him.

"Decryption will take a few hours. It'll be done by breakfast time." I access my own server and start the decryption program download. Once I've got it going, I lean back and cross my arms over my chest. "Which gives you time to fill me in on your plan."

They explain that between now and the time George arrives, we'll use the decrypted files to figure out as much about the scanner as we can. Once George gets here, he'll transport the scanner to a safe, neutral location unknown to both the Core and The Fifty. If it were anyone but George, I'd call bullshit in a second, but he was the one guy my dad seemed to trust at the end. Once the scanner is secured, Charles will act as an emissary to the Core and my mom and George will reach out to The Fifty. It won't be until both sides come to some agreement that the scanner will be retrieved.

I don't mention that I have my own plan. Those files my mom dug up don't even scratch the surface of what my dad has on his server. The bulk of his work—including the population counter and the blueprints and plans it concealed—isn't remotely accessible. There's a host of intrusion detection systems that I didn't get near while Charles was looking over my shoulder. But when I get into my dad's lab, I'm going to find *everything*. Dad left me with what I need, I'm sure of it. I just have to think like he did. He said, "When the time comes, it's Josephus . . . " And now that I've been interfacing with Dad's system, I'm more convinced than ever that "Josephus" isn't a person after all—maybe it's a password.

I can't wait until George arrives. He might know something about what my dad wanted to do with the scanner, and maybe we can go back to his lab and figure it all out while the scanner is in a secure place. We should have enough to puzzle out the basic mechanics of the scanner—or we will, once the decryption program does its thing. As a headache gnaws at the space behind my eyes, I say good night to Mom and Charles and trudge back to the guest room to take full advantage of the time between now and then.

Christina slides her arm around my waist and nuzzles into my neck as I crawl in next to her. She makes the sweetest sound, this vulnerable noise my body responds to automatically, and I draw my arms tighter around her. I breathe with her, deep and slow, and let that rhythm give me what I've needed for hours: the chance to escape for a while. Now that I've got a plan, now that I'm doing *the best I know,* as my dad would have said, I've earned this rest. I close my eyes, pretend it's Monday again, and let it carry me away.

TWENTY-THREE

THE FIRST THING I'M AWARE OF IS THE FAINT, FLUTTER-
ing tickle against my throat. I lie in the dark, absorbing the
sensation.

Christina's eyelashes.

"Are you awake?" I whisper, quietly enough so that if she's
not, I won't actually pull her from sleep.

"Yeah. I slept nearly the whole day in the car yesterday."

"How long have you been up?"

"Long enough to know that you snore."

"I do not!" Do I?

She laughs. "No, you don't. You just make this funny snuffling noise sometimes."

I rub my eyes. "Thanks for letting me know."

Her hand skims along my waist and up to my chest, over

my heart. I put my hand over hers. "I'm sorry about all of this," I say.

"I know you are. And I know you've been beating yourself up over it."

"I want to fix it. But it's . . ." I stare at the ceiling. Encrypted files? Easy. My relationship with Christina? Still trying to fumble my way through it.

Her breath skates across the hollow at the base of my neck. "It's not something for you to fix. It's something we figure out together." She kisses my jaw. "And we will." Her voice is so hushed, and in it I read how unsure she really is, and how much terrain I'm going to have to cover to win back her trust. To convince her—despite all the craziness, the differences between us, the family legacy I don't understand—that I'm still Tate, and she's still Christina, and we're friends. And a lot more than that. I want to tell her that I love her again, that I'd do anything to make sure she's safe, but I understand that, right now, words don't count for a whole lot. So I hold her tight and pray she feels it in the beat of my heart. She shifts so her head is on my chest, and I close my eyes and let it do my talking for me.

It's a quiet moment, but not a loaded quiet. A real quiet. Peaceful.

A peace that's shattered by the knock on the door. "Tate?" my mother whispers.

"We're awake," I say.

My mom pokes her head in. "We're going to leave soon. Can you guys get up?"

As the door clicks shut again, I tap my dad's phone, and the display tells me it's not yet five in the morning. At least two hours until the files will be fully decrypted. Which means something's wrong. I reach over and turn on the bedside lamp, a heavy old thing with a glass lampshade. Christina covers her eyes with her hand and moans. She peeks at me from between her fingers. "Maybe you should turn that off again. I'm sure I look terrible."

"I was thinking how much I like waking up like this."

Her cheeks get pink, and she gives me a tentative smile. "Me too."

I head over to the closet and tug a pair of khakis from a hanger, once again thankful Charles has a son and that he's almost my size. The pants are an inch or two short, but they fit okay in the waist, and the loafers are a tad snug, but I'm grateful I have something to put on my feet.

I turn around to see Christina looking down at her dress.

"Can we stop somewhere and get me some regular clothes today? I'm feeling a bit . . . Amish."

Assuming the plan is still to pick up George from the airport, we should have time to get something on the way. "I think we can manage that."

She gets up and smooths the dress, which is now hopelessly wrinkled. Her hair falls crazily over her shoulders, and except for the occasional flash of the white bandage under-neath, you'd never know she'd been shot two days ago. When she raises her head, she looks me in the eye. Warm. Real. Like things really might be okay someday. Seeing her there, smiling at me like she is, I can almost believe it.

She lets me hold her hand as we walk down the hall to the sitting room. Mom and Charles are there, and it's obvious by the circles under her eyes and the bags under his that they stayed awake talking long after I went to bed.

"Right after you went to bed, we got word from one of Clarles's contacts that Race has left New York," my mom says, staring down at the keyboard. She's changed into some of Charles's clothes, black pants and a white dress shirt that hang from her slender frame. "We notified George, who flew out of Chicago immediately. He's just landed and is on his way here."

I step forward quickly. "You think Race is coming for us?"

Charles waves his hand dismissively. "He could be going to Chicago for all we know."

"Yeah, and for all we know, you might have tipped him off when he called here," I snap.

"Tate, I need your help," Mom says, and I turn away from Charles before he has a chance to make excuses. "Can you remove any trace of these decrypted files?"

"Don't erase them, Mitra," calls Charles, rolling over to us and placing his hand on my arm. "I want to be able to—"

298

I throw him off, none too gently. "Dude. If Race comes in here, he'll not only have access to these files—my guess is he'll be able to use what's on your computer to tunnel back into my dad's server." He might not get far, but as far as I'm concerned, even a little is too much.

Charles scowls but moves away, and I notice that my mom doesn't scold me for talking to him like that. I peer at her, wondering if she still trusts her old friend as much as she did. I glace over my shoulder to see Christina watching from the hallway, looking back and forth from me to Charles. It's probably obvious how much I dislike him, but that's the least of my concerns right now. I reboot the firewall and clear the audit logs while my mother puts the scanner in Christina's backpack.

"Are we going back to New York?" Christina asks in a hushed voice as she comes farther into the room.

Mom turns to her. "You are. Once George has departed with the scanner, we'll contact both The Fifty and the Core to begin negotiations. You'll be safe." She gives me a sidelong glance. "But Tate and I will need to go to Chicago."

I finish my work on Charles's computer and head for Christina, taking her hand and squeezing it. She needs to be back with her family, but it's going to hurt like hell to let her go. She steps into me and presses her face against my neck like she feels the same way.

I'm just opening my mouth to ask Mom how exactly we're

getting Christina safely back to New York when I hear a shriek from outside, followed by high-pitched laughter.

I look at Charles, who rolls his eyes and waves it away. "Remember you're on a university campus. We get streakers on the lawn at all hours of the day and night, running up to kiss the statue on the steps of the Rotunda. Very few are actually sober when they do it."

Another scream, higher pitched. Frantic and frightened this time. Followed by silence.

Charles frowns.

My mother and I are at the front window a second later, and in the predawn darkness, I can just make out the white flesh and streaming blond hair of a girl. Naked, as Charles predicted. Next to the Rotunda steps, as Charles predicted.

Kicking and flailing while a black-clothed figure clamps a hand over her mouth and drags her into a building across the lawn.

Charles didn't predict that.

I squint and see another half dozen figures creeping across the worn grass toward our building. My heart rate skyrockets as I realize Charles didn't fool Race at all.

My mother curses under her breath. "He's already here," she says in a choked voice, whirling away from the window. She grabs my arm and shoves me toward the door. "Move!"

Charles spins his chair, gesturing at my mother. "Text George and change the rendezvous point. We have to get the scanner away from here. George can meet us at the Walmart at the outskirts of town."

While my mother uses her black stealth phone to communicate with George, Charles races down the hall and comes out a moment later with a black bag on his lap. My mother hands me Christina's backpack with the scanners inside. Charles opens the black bag and hands a gun to my mother, then pulls out one for himself.

"Do you have anything for me in there?" I ask, staring down at the dozens of ammo clips in the bag. I'm a pretty good shot with both rifles and handguns, and my mom's holding a basic semi-auto pistol, nothing fancy.

"No. And you're not staying. You're taking the scanner," my mother says as she stands next to the door and clicks the safety off.

"And you?"

She gives me a hard look. "I'm going to make sure you get out." Without waiting for my reply, she pulls the door open and pivots into the hallway, sweeping the place with a smooth, experienced eye, never lowering her weapon.

"Stairs?" she asks.

"To your right," Charles says. He offers her the bag full of ammo.

She takes it and slings it diagonally across her shoulder.

Charles clutches at my arm. "I have an elevator right here in the apartment," he says as he points down the hall that leads toward his bedroom. "They only installed it last year, special for me, so it's unlikely it would be in any blueprints Race used to plan his assault. You can take it if you leave now."

I know there's no time. I know they're coming. But— "Mom, we can all get out that way. Don't go down there. Come with us."

Her brows draw together. "I wish I could. But they're too close. If I hold their attention, they won't catch you." She touches my arm, and her jaw is clenched like she's trying hard to control her expression. "Please, just go, all right? I'll see you soon." She turns and sprints toward the stairwell without a backward glance.

I stand like my feet are encased in concrete, watching my mom head off to face a freaking SWAT team. "No." The door to the stairs slams shut behind her.

Charles pokes me in the side. "The elevator is this way."

The first shots are fired before he finishes his sentence.

"No!" I shout.

My mother is about to get herself blown away over the foot-long piece of plastic in my backpack. Just like my dad did. From behind me, I hear Christina telling me we have to go, have to run, have to get out of here. But . . . I am frozen here as the seconds pass, thinking of my father and what he would have done. Yes, he would have died to keep the scanner out of Race's hands. But would he have let my mother die? Would he have wanted me to lose both of them? I can't believe he would have.

"Tate!" Charles's voice is as sharp as a grenade blast.

I look over my shoulder, about to tell him I have to go, that I'm going to destroy the scanner or give it to Race or whatever, as long as my mother is left alive—

Charles Willetts has a handful of Christina's hair. She's hunched over his wheelchair. His gun is pressed to her temple. "I'm sorry, Tate. I know this is hard. But I need you to transport the scanner, and you can't do that if you've been captured by the Core."

"I need to get my mom," I say stupidly over the splatter-pop-crack of gunfire. "And you need to let her go."

Charles shakes his head. Christina's expression is all pain, which isn't surprising given the fact that her head was stitched up only a day ago. She's got her bottom lip between her teeth and her eyes squeezed shut, like she's sure this is her last moment on Earth. It makes me want to slam Charles's head into something very hard. He must see that, too, because he rolls back a few feet, deeper into his apartment. "Take the scanner and go, son."

"I thought you said we could trust you." And I should have trusted my gut.

Charles gives me a ghostly smile. "I'm not your enemy."

My eyes flick to the muzzle of his weapon, pressed to the side of my girlfriend's head. "You sure about that?"

He loosens his grip on her, but only slightly. "This young lady will be perfectly safe, and you'll be together again as soon as you deliver the technology to George. I just need you to focus. And you'll be faster if you're alone."

"This is stupid." I slide the backpack down my arm and hold it out. "I'll give the fucking thing to you right now, and you let me take her and leave."

He shakes his head. "George will be at the Walmart in less than half an hour, and you need to meet him there. I will *not* allow the H2 to get control of this," he growls.

My thoughts lock on to those words. "You won't allow the H2 to control it?" I think back to last night, remembering that he never scanned himself. "Who are you, Professor, and which side are you playing for?"

I take a step toward him, and his finger tightens on the trigger.

The desperate gleam in his eye locks me in place.

Right now, his allegiances barely matter. He's perfectly willing to put a bullet in Christina's skull to get his way. My hand is fisted over the strap of the backpack, and I'm fighting the urge to hurl it at him. Christina's clutching the side of this douchebag's wheelchair, and her arms are shaking.

"How do I know you can get her out of here safely?" I shout, all my cool long since evaporated. "There's a small army outside!" The gunfire hasn't stopped this entire time, and I know it's only a minute or two before they get past my mom and come up the stairs.

He inclines his head toward the door, where another

stairwell lies at the opposite end of the hallway. "I'll get her out safely. Once the scanner's concealed, I'll call my contact at the Core. They'll cooperate because we have control of something they want."

Christina opens her eyes. They are dry, filled with a cold anger that tells me Charles better not let his guard down. "I'll see you soon," she says.

I step into the apartment and Charles rolls back, making way. The barrel of his weapon is jammed so firmly against Christina's temple that it's leaving a shallow indentation. "Down that hall," he says. "The elevator opens onto a vestibule in the dorm connected to this building, and they won't be able to see it from the lawn. You can get to the parking lot from the dorm exit."

With one last look at his finger curled around the trigger, I swing the pack onto my shoulder and sprint down the hall. There's a window at the end of it that overlooks the rooftops. I hit the button for the elevator and turn to see Charles in the living room, still holding on to my girlfriend. The elevator whines and chugs—and then there's an explosion within the shaft that shakes the floor and blows a wave of dust beneath the closed doors. I stagger back until my shoulder blades hit the wall behind me. Once again, we've underestimated this enemy. "They're cutting off our exits! What now, *Professor*?" I shout.

"The window!" he calls, dragging Christina into the hallway. "Take the window!"

I fling it open and am immediately hit by the smoky, metallic scent of a firefight. Leaning out slowly, my movements punctuated by the *crack-crack* of bullets hitting glass and wood and *oh God, please not my mom,* I realize I can hear and smell the action, but can't see it. I'm above a one-story section of this complex, hidden from sight by the side of the two-story Pavilion building I've just exited. I edge my way onto the flat front part of the roof, which overlooks the lawn to my right. To my left the roof juts up in a shallow incline, and on the other side is the parking lot. I peek over and see a drainpipe. My escape route.

A man below me shouts, and I crouch low. Have they gotten my mom? Are they on their way up? Where is she? Flattening myself against the roof, I lean over, just enough to see past the columned walkway that runs along the front of the Pavilion.

And I see her, beyond jagged, broken glass hanging from empty panes. Just inside the lobby.

She's squatting with her back against one of the columns. The lights over the walkway give me an easy view of the dozen or so agents she's facing. There are two on the roofs of the buildings across the lawn, several behind nearby trees, and a bunch behind the colonnade out in front of the Rotunda. She's completely outgunned and pinned down, and all she can hope to do is hold them back for a while. Judging by the ammo-filled bag at my mom's feet, she plans to put up a pretty good fight.

With cool precision, she whips around the column and

pulls the trigger once, twice, three times, like she's operating according to a map in her head. Three agents fall from behind a tree and two columns. It's only a momentary triumph, though, because the rest of them all shoot at once, sending her to the ground beneath the ferocity of their fire.

"What the hell are you doing?" Charles snarls. I look up to see him glaring at me from the apartment window. "You are wasting her sacrifice. If she dies and you still get caught, her blood will be on your hands."

One shot makes his point for him.

My mother's cry tears me in two. I turn my head in time to see her drop, blood flowing from between the fingers she's clutching to her left arm. But after only a second, she swings the gun up with her right and keeps firing, wearing a look of pure determination.

Charles is right. I can't help her. All I can do is what she asked me to: get the scanner away from Race. I grit my teeth and push off the ground, throwing myself over the low roof and sliding down the other side. I grab the drainpipe in time to keep myself from falling, but it shudders and breaks loose in my hand. I have only a fraction of a second to decide how I'm going to go down. I thrust myself into the open air, away from the building, hurling my body at the huge red SUV below me. Its roof is nearly six feet off the ground. Better than hitting the pavement below.

I hit it hard with knees and elbows, half on the roof,

cracking the windshield. All the wind is knocked out of me, but my brain is screaming. I'm so exposed. I slide off the SUV and crouch between it and a compact car, orienting myself and trying to draw air into my lungs. Our car is across the lot. I just have to get there. Sucking in a wheezing breath, I lurch myself up and make a dash for it.

I force my legs to keep pounding the ground, force my arms to keep pumping, force the image of my mother, bleeding and hurt, from my brain. The firefight is still blazing, so she must be alive, must be fighting back. It keeps me going. The bland gray sedan is parked next to the garden fence, and I pull the keys out of the pack as I race toward it. I throw the pack on the seat and am about to get in when I hear the crunch of shoes on stone.

Mr. Lamb is standing on the tall garden fence, right in front of my car.

TWENTY-FOUR

LIT UP BY ONE OF THE OVERHEAD LIGHTS, LAMB'S WEAR-
ing a dark suit and a black tie, like he's a full-grown agent
today, a tool of the government instead of just a tool.

But even from here, I can see the brown stain on his collar.

He holds his hands out in front of him. His gun is holstered
at his side. "Tate. We can stop what's happening." He tilts his
head back toward the lawn. "It can end right now."

There's nothing but cold inside of me. I imagine this is
what Christina was feeling just now, when she was pushed too
far, beyond fear, beyond hate, beyond anything but a simple,
frigid rage. My voice is steady when I say, "Why would you try
to make this a cooperative game, Mr. Lamb? Shooting me for
the scanner is the dominant strategy here."

He chuckles, showing that gap between his teeth. "You
always were my best student. And you're a good kid. Give me

the device and we'll be able to talk this out without having to listen to a gunfight in the background."

"How did you find us?" I need to know if that wheelchair-bound asshole gave us up.

Lamb grimaces. "His recent activities aren't as covert as he thinks."

The gunfire on the lawn quiets, falling silent with one last, shallow crack. My stomach turns to ice. "Okay, you win. Hang on a second."

The overhead light is reflecting off my windshield; I can tell by the way Lamb is squinting as I duck into the car. His fingers twitch toward his holster, but he's trying to be cool here, trying to be so much more charming than he could ever pull off. I open the glove compartment and grab the car's user's manual, a heavy, thick booklet encased in black vinyl. Holding it tucked against my pant leg, I slide back out of the car.

"Maybe this will help us reach an equilibrium," I say.

His laughter is oily. "Oh, we were never equals."

I nod. "True."

He takes a step back, trying to see what I'm holding in my hand. "Don't try any of your tricks, Tate."

"Wouldn't dream of it. I know this isn't a game." Then I hurl the user's manual as hard as I can . . . about five feet to the left of Mr. Lamb. He might be tall, but even his lanky arms don't reach that far. He's totally fooled by the black rectangle sailing past him and lunges for it—backward off the stone fence. There's an angry shout as he lands on the other side.

I dive into my car and jam the key in the ignition, and then I'm barreling down the narrow lane. Lamb heaves his torso onto the wall, already holding his phone to his ear. I'm just glad he's not shooting at me.

I pull my father's phone out of Christina's pack and use the GPS to get myself directions to the nearest Walmart. Thankfully, it's so early in the morning that the streets are nearly empty, but I hear a distant siren and know the authorities are probably on their way. I hope there's an ambulance coming for my mom, and I hope she still needs it. And that's all I'll allow myself to think about now, because I need to off-load this scanner and get Christina, and then I'll do whatever else I have to do as soon as my mom is safe.

The Walmart, one of those massive supersized stores, is about fifteen minutes' drive, and its parking lot is dimly lit as I pull in. There are a few campers parked at its far edge, but apart from that, it's empty. It's five minutes to five.

I make a full circuit of the store and finally settle on a spot near a side entrance.

My father's phone buzzes with a text.

From my mother.

They left me alive. Ambulance here. Be careful.

I stare at those words, my heart beating hard. The honk of a horn jerks my head up.

A car rolls to a stop in front of mine. The driver's-side door opens, and George Fisher steps out. Relieved to see a friendly face, I get out of my car.

George gives me a sad smile. "I'm so sorry about your dad, Tate. He was my best friend." His silver hair is disheveled and he looks like he's aged years in the last few days.

"I know he trusted you," I say. "My mom does, too. But how much contact have you had with Charles Willetts? He has Christina, and I don't know what side he's on."

"I trust Charles Willetts completely," he says as he walks toward me. "Do you have the scanner?"

I pull it out of the backpack. "Are you sure you can keep it secure? A lot of people are after this thing—"

He smiles. "I can guarantee you that neither side will control this technology, Tate. It's too important."

He holds his hand out, and I pass the scanner to him. As he takes it, his fingers hit the power switch and it lights up. For a second, this bright orange light washes over George's skin, and then he quickly flips it off again, chuckling. "Oops."

I stare at the bare skin of his arm, where the scanner's beam flashed orange. "What was that?"

He backs up toward his car. "I promise you, we'll talk about all of this when I see you again, okay?"

I swallow, unable to push back the unease that's lodged in my throat. "Hey, maybe I should take it—"

The roar of an engine distracts me, and I look up in time to see a navy blue Volvo sedan come to a screeching halt less than ten feet away. My mouth drops open as Christina jumps out, her eyes flashing. She smiles grimly when she sees me. "His reflexes weren't as fast as mine."

"Is that Charles's car?" I choke out, already walking forward to touch her, to make sure she's real.

She nods. "Hand controls. Really weird. But I'm a quick study." Her expression grows solemn and she jogs the final few steps to me. "As soon as you took off, they stopped shooting and pulled back," she says, her voice muffled as she buries her face against my shoulder. "I called the ambulance for your mom right before I left."

"Thank you," I whisper, then raise my head as I hear the distant thumping of a helicopter.

George curses, and his voice sounds so guttural and odd that Christina flinches in my arms. I turn to see him getting back into his car. "Wait!" I call. "You can take us—"

He slams the door and floors it.

The black helicopter roars along the river across the highway from the Walmart, then turns, heading straight for us. It takes me a few seconds to shake the desperate wish that it's just a news crew or whatever.

The blast of a large-caliber weapon helps.

"The car won't give us any protection," I shout to Christina, grabbing her hand and dragging her toward the store.

She yanks me in the opposite direction, back toward the car. "The store's closed, Tate! Pop the trunk!"

I do as she says. There's an old tire iron nestled next to the spare, and she pulls it out, then sprints toward the store with her shoulders up around her ears.

As I follow her across the parking lot, I see George streak toward the road, little clouds of dust and gravel kicking up behind him as the bullets strike the blacktop while the helicopter pursues. He makes the sharp right turn onto the narrow thruway between the big-box stores, heading for the highway with the helicopter still behind him. Christina makes it to the side entrance of the store a second before I do. "The police will come if the alarm goes off. Whose side will they be on?"

"Race's. Unless he warns them off."

She gazes through the locked doors and into the darkened store. "Do we have a choice? Do you think George will lead him away from us?"

Before I can answer, that helicopter roars over the roof of the store and begins to turn toward us again. I know who's on it and what he's capable of, so the decision is easy. As Napoleon once said, *When the time for action comes, stop thinking and go in.*

I hold out my hand, and Christina gives me the tire iron. I ram the angled tip between the two doors and wrench it back. The alarm starts immediately, but I figure we still have at least ten minutes before the police get to us, and I think that's enough time. I pry open the second set of doors and run into the Walmart with Christina on my tail.

"I need your help," I say, pushing a cart toward her. "Go get every bottle of hydrogen peroxide they have. And every bottle of nail polish remover, too. One bottle of toilet bowl cleaner. Got it?"

She takes the cart from me. "Got it. Meet you where?"

"Sporting goods." I dart toward the hardware section, stopping to jam a plastic bin, a push broom, a few packages of dishwashing gloves, and a box of plastic baggies into my cart on the way. In the hardware section, right next to the caulking guns and how-to books, I find what I want—about a dozen cans of contact cement. They go in the cart, too.

I race toward sporting goods, wincing at the pealing scream of the alarm, listening for the sound of agents. By the time I get there, Christina's waiting, and she's already got my ingredients sorted out. She's sitting on the floor in that Amish-looking dress, methodically opening each and every bottle. "You're awesome," I breathe, pulling out a plastic bin.

"Just tell me you're going to use this to kick their asses," she says, wrenching open another bottle of nail polish remover.

"I'll do my best." I slide the plastic bin toward her. "Fill this with the hydrogen peroxide and the nail polish remover. Then I want you to stay as far from here as you can."

She pales a shade but does what I say while I pry open the cans of contact cement. When this stuff is wet, it's sticky as hell, like super-thick caramel. When it's dry, it's kind of tacky, no big deal. But when two surfaces covered in dry contact cement are pressed against each other: instant unbreakable bond.

Christina gets up and peeks into the aisle. "I would have thought the cops would be here by now."

"The last two times he chased us, he didn't have local cops with him, only his agents." I open the toilet bowl cleaner and squirt a generous amount of it into the plastic bin, which is full of fizzing clear liquid. It sizzles as I use the tire iron to stir it up, and I smile grimly as the white crystals begin to form in the solution.

"Oh my God," Christina whispers. "The helicopter is landing out front."

Since he didn't catch George, he's coming after us. "Help me fill these bags with the contact cement."

We both slide bright blue dishwashing gloves onto our hands. She holds the plastic baggies open while I pour in the caramel-like stuff, wincing at the sharp smell. "I need you to be really careful with this," I tell her. "Whatever you do—don't step in it, all right?"

She nods. Her hands are trembling, but she moves fast to help me fill the last of the bags with the gluey substance.

I give her my instructions as I start opening cans of tennis balls, raising my voice so she can hear me over the wailing alarm. "Your goal is to get this stuff all over them, okay? Throw the bags so that they burst open at their feet and this stuff gets on the bottoms of their shoes. Throw it at their faces so they have to wipe it off with their hands. Doesn't have to be a lot, but the more surfaces you hit, the more likely they'll end up with their hands glued to their faces and their feet glued to the floor. It'll be like tossing water balloons. But as soon as you hit them, get the hell out of there. Don't let them catch you."

She doesn't look convinced. "What if I miss?"

I wave a can of tennis balls at her. "Plan B." I nod toward the tennis ball machine sitting in a nearby display.

"You're going to fire tennis balls at them?"

I nod solemnly. "Now get going, and stay hidden." I can hear heavy footsteps at the front of the store.

The beeping of the alarm goes silent.

Toting an armload of contact-cement-filled bags, Christina skirts around the edge of the store, heading toward the front.

I check the chemical reaction going on in the bin. Excellent. I've got more than enough peroxyacetone to keep everyone busy. As dangerous as it is to send Christina off to throw contact cement at whoever just came through the Walmart door, it's much more dangerous to sit here next to the contents of the bin. Like I'm going to do.

While I strain to hear what's happening to Christina, I take a few more cans of the contact cement and use the push broom to spread a thin layer of it in the wide aisle right under the huge hanging bike rack. It won't take more than a few minutes to dry.

I tug the dishwashing gloves up my forearms, say a quick prayer that I end this day with all my fingers still attached, and gently place each tennis ball into the white slurry in the plastic bin.

That's when I hear the shouted curse, followed by two shots and the sliding crash of some huge shelf being emptied of its stock. I switch on the ball machine and lean out of the aisle in time to see Christina whip across an open space, still carrying a few bags of contact cement.

"There are four of them," she screams, amazing me with her ability to keep her head while she's running for her life.

I aim the ball machine toward what she's running from, pull one of the soaked, white-powder-coated tennis balls from the bin, stick it in the machine, and let fly. It sails out of the barrel of the machine with a resounding *thwock,* and I breathe a sigh of relief.

Which becomes a gasp when the thing hits a hanging sign in aisle seven and explodes with a deafening bang.

"Get down!" a guy shouts.

Now I know I have just successfully synthesized peroxyacetone, one of the most volatile contact explosives known to man.

I load the hopper with the wet balls, shove it into the open space between sporting goods and home goods, set it on corner-to-corner random oscillation, and run.

The Walmart becomes a war zone.

It would be a lot more devastating if I lit the things on fire, but each ball is already exploding with a flameless bang that sounds like cannon fire. And if I live through this, I'm thinking it's probably better not to get charged with burning Walmart to the ground on top of everything else.

I sprint through sporting goods and into home goods, hoping Christina's hunkered down somewhere, that I'll find her safe and be able to get us out of here. I nearly trip over a downed agent, who's clearly suffering a tennis-ball-related injury, probably a direct hit. One arm is wrapped protectively over his ribs while another is clutched to his head. His eyes are closed tightly and he's pale as a ghost. He doesn't even notice me there.

I slip into the hardware section, looking for any hint of blond hair or purple dress, any sign of Christina.

What I see instead is Race. Buzz cut, lean, his face angular and sharp in profile. He's crouched low, peeking around the edge of the shelving, gun in hand. Right at the end of my aisle.

He's got a thin smear of dried contact cement on his pants, but doesn't seem to have a smudge on him otherwise. With all the thunderous chaos around us, he could have shot Christina already and I'd never know.

I charge up the aisle, but at the last second, he spins around. I catch his wrist and slam it against the metal shelving. He drops his gun but kicks me in the stomach. Before I know it, I'm on my back, my head bouncing off the hard tile floor. I wrap my legs around his waist, trying to get control.

"Tate Archer," he huffs. "How nice to meet you face-to-face." He sends a quick jab to my ribs that drives the air from my lungs. He twists his hips, and that's when I realize how strong he is. He outweighs me by at least thirty pounds, and all of it's muscle. He's going to open me up and lay me out in a bare second. "You have something I need."

Sucking wind through my gritted teeth, I grab his sleeves, yank him to the side and roll him onto his back. As we struggle, my face crashes into a hanging row of caulking guns, knocking them loose. I've still got control of his sleeves and hold them tightly while I lean my weight onto his chest. "Yeah, it's fucking delightful to meet you. And the scanner's in a safe place. You won't be able to use it against The Fifty."

"We have no desire to use it against The Fifty, or any human," he says in a deep, strained voice as he tugs at his sleeves and tries to throw me off. It's not going to take him long to succeed.

"This isn't about some petty struggle between H2 and The Fifty. It's about protecting ourselves. *All of us.*"

I dig my fingers in, fighting to keep my grip on him. "Protect us from what?"

"Do you really think we came here by choice?" His face contorts as he struggles. "My ancestors were forced to leave our planet."

Charles said they were refugees. At least I know he wasn't a total liar. "Who forced them?"

For a second, Race goes completely still. He looks up at me with this piercing glare. "Pray you never find out."

He bucks his hips, nearly sending me flying, but I slam my knee into his upper thigh. He jerks to the side to protect his soft spots as he speaks again. "I need your help, Tate!" He grunts as I use all my strength to hold him down. "Your father discovered something we've needed for centuries. Something we were depending on when we arrived on this planet. It was aboard a ship that was lost, but your father must have some-how gotten hold of some of the wreckage. I have to gain access to his work." He tries to wrench himself away, but I slam him back down. "Please," he says, his expression softening. "You have no idea what's really going on. This technology is crucial to our survival."

The scanner is the key to our survival. My father's words scroll through my head, along with the memory of the popu-lation counter and those password-protected plans in his lab. I look down at Race, my thoughts spinning out of control. Could he actually help me figure this out? Would my dad want me to work with him? He told me Race was dangerous. He wanted to keep the scanner away from him. But did he know exactly what Race was after, or did he—along with the rest of The Fifty—misunderstand Race's intentions?

Race sees me wavering. "Tate. We could work together. You could help me."

At those words, something inside me goes supernova. "Your agents shot my mother," I breathe. "You killed my dad. You nearly killed my girlfriend. And you want me to help you?"

His expression hardens into resolve in a split second. He rips his sleeves from my grasp and twists to the side, catching one of my feet between his legs. Maybe he thinks he can break my ankle, or maybe he's just trying to escape, but it gives me the leverage I need. I hook my heel under his thigh and throw my full weight into my shoulders, somersaulting over his back and bringing my legs up. It catches him by total surprise, and he gasps as I roll him over.

I waste no time pulling him against me, wrapping my legs around his torso from behind, coiling my arm around his throat. He wheezes. He bats at me with his arms, even landing a few good punches to the side of my head. His legs thrash, knocking cartons and boxes from the shelves and scattering them through the aisles. He's fucking strong, but it doesn't matter, because I've got a lock on him that he will *never* escape from.

If this were a tournament, he'd be slapping the mat.

But it's not a tournament.

So I squeeze.

I grind my teeth to nothing as I watch his face turn purple. It's not enough. Will never be enough.

I don't know how long I hold on to him after he stops struggling. I have no idea. All I know is that I snap back into myself when I hear Christina scream.

TWENTY-FIVE

I RELEASE MY ANACONDA GRIP ON RACE AND SHOOT to my feet. His head lolls, his eyes half closed. He's out cold and will be for a while. The store is eerily quiet—the hopper must be empty of tennis balls.

The sharp crack of gunfire breaks the silence. Christina screams again.

"Sporting goods!" I shout, breaking into a run. Race and I aren't done, but we won't be on equal footing until I figure out what exactly my dad was working on—and make sure the people I care about are safe.

As I sprint, I hear Christina's footsteps running up the long, wide aisle toward the area under the bike rack. I step into the aisle just as Lamb collars her. She yelps as he jerks her back and presses his gun to her head. "You little bitch," he hisses into her ear, spittle flying.

Then his eyes meet mine. "I think we can both agree I tried to be nice," he says, panting. He takes a few steps forward.

I put my hands up, showing him I'm unarmed. Then I take a step back.

"No more games, Tate." He takes another step forward.

"No more games," I agree.

"I want the device. Hand it over and I won't blow her brains all over the bike helmets." His finger's on the trigger. There's a vein standing out on his forehead. And I see why he's so mad.

He's freaking covered in contact cement. I don't know how she did it, but he's got it smeared on his pants. On his chest. On his face. Crusty and drying. He must be suffocating from the stench.

Christina looks down at her feet, and then up at me. She nods, just slightly. I hope that means she doesn't have any on the bottoms of her shoes—and that he does.

I take another step back.

Lamb takes a lurching step forward, shoving Christina along in front of him. Her shoes make soft, tacky noises as she steps in the dried contact cement, but she keeps moving forward. But when Lamb tries to raise his feet to take another step, they don't move, even though the rest of him does. His body pitches forward because his shoes have bonded to the floor, and he instinctively tries to use his gun hand to catch himself while Christina fights to stay upright.

But it's covered in dried contact cement, so as soon as his

hand—and his gun—hit the dried contact cement on the floor, both are instantly bonded, hopelessly stuck to the tile. He tries to pull his feet from his shoes, but then his knee touches the floor and gets stuck, too. He roars with frustration as he loses his grip on Christina, whose gloved hands are glued to the floor. As soon as he lets her go, she wrenches herself up, leaving the gloves behind, and stumbles toward me. I catch her arm and drag her off of the sticky patch of tile. I hold her there for a second, staring at her beautiful face, making sure she's alive, here, real.

"I'm all right," she says, breathing hard. "I'd hug you, but I'm afraid I'd never come unstuck." She's got contact cement smeared on the chest and skirt of her dress. "You said there were four of them. I got Race, and there's another one down in home goods. Did you get the fourth?"

She nods, a little smile on her face. "Wait until you see him."

"You're amazing," I say, tucking a strand of hair behind her ear.

Lamb is glued to the floor. The other two agents are out of commission. Race is unconscious for the moment. "Come on." I nod at the exit. "I need to—"

Lamb is using his one unglued hand to lift his cell phone to his ear.

Goddamn, it's like I'm right back on that tournament mat with Cow-Eyes, too arrogant to see what's about to happen.

My hand shoots out and grabs a bat from a nearby bin. I slam it down on the metal joint holding the overhead bike rack in place. With all the strength I can summon, I bring the bat down again and again, until the joint groans and snaps.

A few dozen bikes crash down on Mr. Lamb. His elbow buckles and his face hits the tile. The scream that comes from his mouth sends a shiver straight through me. It's filled with both rage and terror, because now half his face is stuck to the floor.

"Race told me not to kill you," he says. "But I will. I swear I will."

Through the pile of bikes, I can see one of his eyes, and it's filled with hatred and the promise of revenge. I stare back at him, refusing to look away.

Until Christina takes my hand. Hers is cold, but her grip is strong. It's enough to bring me back. "I think we need to get out of here," she says.

"Definitely."

With my arm around her shoulders, we walk briskly out of the store, right past the fourth agent, who's sitting on the floor with his head in his hands. I shove Christina behind me and prepare to fight, but then I realize—his hands are actually glued to his face. He's making these desperate snuffling noises and trying to pull his fingers away, and is so occupied with his struggle that he doesn't even acknowledge us as we walk by.

Christina takes a two-minute detour to swipe a pair of sweats and a shirt from the girls' clothing section, and she changes quickly while I listen for more sirens and watch for Race to reappear. As we walk out of the store, the sun is rising over the parking lot, an orange ball on the horizon. I pull my dad's phone out of my pocket and call my mom's number. "Please pick up," I whisper.

"Tate," she says when she answers, her voice tired. "I wouldn't let them operate until I heard from you."

I bow my head and squeeze my eyes shut. "How are you?"

"I'll survive. Did you get the scanner to George?"

"Yeah. And . . ." I look back at the store as I hear the muffled explosion . . . probably the rest of the peroxyacetone I synthesized. "I may have destroyed the Walmart, Mom. We did some serious damage."

"I'll take care of it, whatever it is."

"Okay. Will I see you soon? We have some things to talk about."

She laughs. It sounds like two corn husks rubbing together. "Can you make it to the hospital? I'll see you when I'm out of surgery." She hangs up.

Christina gets up on her tiptoes and kisses my cheek. I turn and press my forehead to hers, then open the passenger door for her. I drive slowly out of the parking lot, wondering what the Walmart employees are going to think when they arrive to open the store.

I turn onto the access road between the stores.

George's car is a few dozen yards away, its front end crumpled against a tree.

"Oh, God," Christina gasps.

I pull up behind the car and jump out, running to the driver's side. The whole rear of the car is perforated with the deep holes of large-caliber bullets. I fling open the driver's-side door.

George is slumped over the steering wheel. I press my fingers to his neck.

No pulse.

Trying to swallow down the huge lump in my throat, I walk around the back of the car again and open the passenger door. George's arm is extended onto the passenger seat, like he's reaching for something. His blood-flecked skin reminds me of the moment it flashed orange under the scanner's light. I wanted to ask him about it. He promised he would explain. And now that won't happen. I can salvage only one thing now: the technology he died for, that my father died for, that so many have fought for.

I lean over and look under the seat, in the backseat, under George's legs in the front seat. In the trunk. In the glove compartment. And then I stand up and look back at Christina as the world crashes down around my ears.

"The scanner is gone."

ACKNOWLEDGMENTS

I'd like to thank my co-author, Walter Jury, the team at Penguin, and especially my wonderful editor, Stacey Barney, for pushing this story exactly where it needed to go. I'm grateful to the team at New Leaf Literary for supporting me throughout this project, most notably Joanna Volpe and my agent, Kathleen Ortiz, for being there and managing everything, including me. I'm forever indebted to my family and friends, who have listened to me and inspired me. Thank you to Sonia Dos Santos for her input on the nuances of Brazilian Portuguese profanity in a sporting context, and to Cathryn and Shizhou Yang for the Chinese sarcasm. And finally, I'd like to thank Dr. Edward Mottel for his expertise in explosive chemical reactions and his suggestions for how to realistically create mayhem. Any chemistry-related mistakes (and the one deliberate inaccuracy) in this book are my fault and mine alone.   —S. E. Fine